Blood Lust

BLOOD LUST

ZOE WINTERS

THE PRETERNATURALS BOOK ONE

 BOOKS

Blood Lust
© 2010 by Zoe Winters

This book is a work of fiction. Names, characters, places, and incidents are
products of the author's imagination or are used fictitiously. Any
resemblance to actual events or locales or persons, living or dead, is
entirely coincidental.

Printed in the United States of America

ISBN-13 978-0-981-94360-2
ISBN-10 0-981-94360-8

Wholesale orders can be placed through Ingram.

Published by IncuBooks

Contact: incubooks@gmail.com

For my 8th grade literature teacher, Mrs. Johnson, who encouraged me to write. Of course, at the time she told me about her friend who wrote romance novels, and I think I made a face about that because those weren't "real books". Now I'm writing romance. Hey, cut me some slack. I was a kid!

Acknowledgments

Any awesomeness found in this book is probably in one way or another due to the contributions of the following people (for one or more parts of the book):

Mary Higgins: For the idea for Theriantype.com (I had the name, but the actual site wouldn't exist without her.) And also for beta reading.

Lindsay Carruth: For brainstorming and help with fonts.

Jon VanZile, R.J. Keller, Natasha Fondren (aka Spy Scribbler), Chaz Thompson, Susan, Emma, Cara Wallace, Edie Ramer, Toni, and Cathy Randolph for beta reading.

Developmental and line editing: Kathleen.

Random Comma Police: Jackie Barbosa.

Moriah Jovan: For helping with questions regarding formatting.

Shane and Mel: Shane wanted to be thanked for posing for the cover art (which is totally untrue) but he gave me a swivel chair. Mel handed out promo postcards at conventions and listened to my constant Amazon sales rank updates. (Actually a lot of people have suffered through that one.)

My parents: For the whole: "You can be whatever you want to be" thing.

The readers (That's you!) for wanting more.

My cover artist, Robin Ludwig, for the amazing design and her jokes about wizards.

And to my husband, who likes my fiction even though he won't fully admit he's reading romance.

If I left anyone out, it wasn't intentional. I could fill up a book with those who have supported me along the way and continue to do so.

As always, every effort has been made to cleanly edit the text. If any errors jump out and bite you, please let me know at zoewintersbooks@gmail.com so the issue can be corrected in a future edition. Thank you!

Part One:

KEPT

Chapter One

The old-fashioned bell jingled over the doorway, and a gust of chill wind swept through Lawson's Bookshoppe. It was July. Greta shivered, knowing who it was even as her eyes remained focused on the counter she was cleaning. She took a deep breath and let it out slowly.

"Anthony. We're closing up early."

"We? You look quite alone. Where's your little redheaded friend? What's her name? Charlotte?" The vampire licked his lips.

"You know very well what her name is."

She was beginning to regret sending Charlee home early. The other clerk may have been only human, but Anthony Burgess often struck when people were alone and vulnerable. He always seemed amused when Charlee stood up to him, not knowing he could relieve her of her blood in seconds.

Greta focused on the counter as the Formica gave under the pressure of her hand. She met his eyes and tucked a strand of short, dark hair behind her ear, grateful her kind couldn't be enthralled.

He wore the standard vampire uniform of basic black, his blond hair pulled back in a low ponytail. A long leather coat flowed out behind him as he strode toward her. All he needed now was menacing background music. Something dark and brooding.

Anthony removed a paperback from the rack beside the checkout without looking at the title and placed it on the counter. His crystal blue eyes glowed and locked with Greta's dark brown as he inhaled deeply, not bothering to mask his enjoyment of her scent.

"When are you going to stop teasing me and let me have a taste?" He stared pointedly at her neck. "Coming up on twenty-eight aren't you? Special year. Moon's nearly full."

Her hand shook as she passed the scanner over the book's bar code. Therians, known to the mortals as Weres, celebrated their birthday not on the anniversary of their birth, but on the full moon closest to it. Twenty-eight wasn't a number to inspire ooohs and aaahs among the human set, but for a shapeshifter, the twenty-eighth birthday was bigger than the human twenty-one. It was a good drinking age for vamps, anyway.

She took his money, made the change, and slipped the book into the opaque green shopping bag. Her eyes widened when she glimpsed the title. "You just bought a book on menstruation, Anthony. Were you aware?"

He shrugged and smiled, revealing the barest hint of fang. "I like blood." He scooped the bag up, gave her one last meaningful look, then drifted out of the store.

Greta locked the door behind him and leaned against the cool wood. She could do with fewer bloodsucking patrons; they'd increased in number since the last full moon. With her birth moon coming up, she might as well have a neon *all you can eat* sign posted in the window.

It was thirty minutes before she gathered the nerve to venture outside. Most of the lights in the parking lot had burned out, and no one had bothered replacing them.

With only one human employee and few after dark human patrons, it was deemed an unnecessary expense. The residents of Cary Town might not realize what was out there, but they were shy of the dark all the same.

Greta's boots clicked loudly on the asphalt, making stealth a physical impossibility. She might as well shout to the vamps from a megaphone. *Fresh meat, right here. Come and get it boys.*

If Anthony or any of his ilk were lurking, they didn't take the bait. Nothing black-clad or fanged emerged from the shadows. Anthony had gone home, or hunting, or whatever it was he did at night. For all she knew, he hung out at the all-night grocery store scaring stock boys.

When she got home, her orange tabby sat perched on the stoop, waiting to be let in.

"Hello, Mink." She bent to scratch the kitty behind her ears and went inside, stopping in the hallway where the answering machine light blinked.

"This is your mother. I need to see you. Be discreet." Click. Jaden was more abrupt than usual. *Be discreet.* Translation: *be in fur.* Something was going down at the Lawson estate. She glanced at the hall clock, 9:45, plenty of time for a shower.

It wasn't until Greta shut off the water that she remembered she hadn't done laundry. *Shit. No towels.* She closed her eyes and focused as images flowed over her mind. *Milk, mice, open fields, birds, blades of grass, hunting, moon.* Her senses heightened as she allowed the memories to bring forth the change. The room shrank and swirled around her. Her spirit jolted from her body, hovered for a moment, then was pulled back into her new compact form.

She stretched all the way down to the pads of her paws, then shook herself and licked her black fur down flat. There was going to be a hairball situation if she didn't do laundry soon. She hopped onto the pedestal sink, admiring herself in the mirror. She loved fur. It was so slimming.

While She preened, Mink sauntered into the room and hissed. Greta hissed back. The house cat liked the therian fine in her human form but became agitated whenever she shifted. Tough. It was Greta's apartment. When Mink could turn into a human and get a job, then she'd have a vote. Greta's poufy black tail curled under Mink's chin as she drifted past the tabby.

Simon's silver Lexus stood parked like a sentinel in her mother's driveway. It wasn't unusual for the tribe leader to be at the Lawson home, but seeing the car after the odd phone message made the hairs on the back of Greta's neck stand up.

She slipped through the plastic flap in the kitchen door and kept to the corners, slinking under the dilapidated furniture. Her nose twitched, and she began to salivate as she caught the scent of a mouse. She forced herself to ignore it and edged closer to the family room where Simon and her mother spoke in the hushed tones usually reserved for church and funerals.

"We don't have to do this. Those are the old ways; surely we're beyond that now."

Simon allowed his hand to trail over Jaden's ass. "You knew this was coming. Greta was marked for sacrifice the moment she came into the world in her fur. I told you not to get attached."

On hearing her name, Greta scooted further under the chair. Therians were born in human form and died in their fur, not the other way around. Everybody knew that.

She'd read legends about therians born in their fur and having extra powers, but she'd always thought they were just stories. Surely she would have noticed if she'd developed more power suddenly.

Was this the emergency the message on the machine had hinted at? She was to be a sacrifice on her birth moon? She shuddered and tried to rein in her emotions so Simon wouldn't sense her presence.

Her mother's voice rose, taking on a more desperate tone. "I thought you'd change your mind. I thought if you loved me, you wouldn't take her. I should have followed my instincts and sent her far from here when she was still a baby."

Simon laughed. "The border patrol would never have let you cross. They're loyal to me. We have one shot and I won't have you ruining it for the tribe, not like her mother tried to."

She didn't have time to process the revelation that her mother wasn't her mother because Simon's cell phone started pounding out a sappy eighties ballad. How he listened to that shit and maintained an interest in the opposite sex remained one of the tribe's greatest mysteries.

"I have to take this," Simon said, retreating to the far end of the room.

Greta followed Jaden to the kitchen and waited while the older woman scribbled something on a slip of paper, rolled it up, and stuck it in Greta's mouth.

"Did you get all that?"

"Mrraar," she said around the paper.

"Go to this place. It's the only person in the city who can keep you safe."

Simon's voice grew louder as he approached the kitchen. Before he could see her, Greta leaped off the table and scurried out the cat door.

Humans had been busy the past several decades tearing down walls that trapped people in their homelands.

The preternaturals, meanwhile, had been engaged in building them up. Normally it didn't bother her so much; but now she could palpably feel the invisible cage that kept her locked inside the walls of the city, making her world feel claustrophobic, where before it had been a cocoon of perceived safety.

There was one person she was close to who wasn't a member of the tribe. She ran three miles, scratched on Charlee's door, and nearly jumped out of her fur when the dog barked. A redheaded woman mumbled a few warnings to the dog and flipped on the porch light.

Greta tried to look unassuming and adorable. "Mrarrr."

"Awwww, aren't you the cutest!"

Score.

Charlee bent to scoop Greta up and shooed the dog out of the house. "Go play, Sammy."

The Irish setter ignored her, choosing instead to lick Greta as he normally did, not noticing she was a cat now. Charlee's brows drew up in confusion. She swatted him on his haunches until he ran off down the dirt road, tail wagging.

"Stupid dog. Doesn't know he's supposed to hate cats. That could be good news for you, sugar plum."

Once inside, Greta sprang from her friend's arms and bolted for the bathroom. She was thankful for the flimsy door as she slammed it shut with the full weight of her feline body. She hopped up on the counter and pressed the push button lock with her paw, then dropped gracefully to the floor.

Charlee jiggled the knob on the other side. "Well, I'll be damned. Honey, how'd you lock yourself in?"

In. Out. In. Out. Think of something calming. Waves lapping the shore, rolling green meadows. Moments later

Greta was curled naked on the floor. She spit the roll of paper out of her mouth.

Printed in Jaden's cramped script, was an address in Cary Town. And a name. Dayne Wickham.

For a second, Greta couldn't breathe and thought she might shift back. It had to be a mistake. Jaden couldn't mean for her to go to him. Dayne Wickham was notorious. He wasn't just a magic user. He was a sorcerer. People still talked about the night he'd massacred more than half the tribe.

There was a soft knock on the door. "I don't know how you managed to lock yourself in there, kitty, but I've got tools and I'm going to get you out. Okay?"

Greta wrapped a bathrobe around herself and opened the door. Charlee fell back, her eyes wide, tools spread around her in a fan. She must have found a sale. Or else she was dating a contractor.

"So, yeah, I'm a cat and I need to borrow some clothes." She hoped she wouldn't have to do the whole transformation all over just to prove it. Surely, *cat goes in, human comes out* was enough evidence. Especially with no windows or other exits in the bathroom.

Charlee gawked up at her. "What are you?"

"A therian."

"A whatian?"

Greta sighed and used the term she hated. "Werecat."

"You can turn into a cat? Seriously? How? Have you always done it? Did you get bitten by another werecat? Do you have other superpowers?"

"Charlee . . . " she said with as much patience as she could muster.

By this time Charlee had managed to stand and was prowling around her, looking as if there might be an instruction manual printed somewhere on Greta's body.

"Clothes," Greta said, trying to bring her friend back to the issue at hand.

"Sure. Clothes. No problem, but show me the werecat thing." Charlee moved to the bedroom, Greta trailing behind her.

"Listen, I can't imagine how I would feel if the tables were turned, but I don't have time for show-and-tell right now. You'll be safer the less you know. They'll use a spell to track me, so I need to be somewhere with strong wards. I just need some clothes to last me a few days."

"Spells are real too? So then . . . witches . . . and . . . "

"Charlee!"

"Oh, right. Sure. Borrow whatever you want; I'll pack you a bag."

Greta pulled on a pair of jeans and T-shirt from the floor. Her face scrunched in distaste at the outfits her friend was throwing into the bag. Charlee believed in dressing sexy like it was a religion. It was a little more than Greta personally wanted to show off, but it was better than nudity.

"Are you sure this is all I can do to help? I could go on the lam with you."

Greta hid a smile. She wished she could take her up on her offer, and for a moment a fantasy of Thelma and Louise-ing it through Cary Town caught her imagination. But Charlee wasn't prepared to deal with what was out there, and Greta couldn't protect her.

She watched as her friend tossed some makeup and a couple of trashy romance novels into the bag. Only Charlee would think running for your life was the time to read romance and wear lipstick.

Greta decided she should have told her friend about her double life long ago. If not for the ridiculous loyalty she'd felt for the tribe that now intended to strap her down to a stone altar, she probably would have.

Chapter Two

Dayne Wickham sat hunched over his computer. His posture showed his age even as his face and physique refused to. He brushed a clump of dark hair out of his eyes and stared at the twitchy screen in front of him. Technology was a beautiful thing. He'd found a most reliable supplier of were-blood on the Internet.

Theriantype.com had a cross-referencing index matching the correct were-blood type to specific rituals. It was almost enough to make a sorcerer pack all his musty old books into storage and move everything to the computer. Almost.

He'd met Alistair Cranze on a magic user's message board. The wizard had recommended the site, and for the past year Dayne hadn't had any trouble. He couldn't remember how he'd managed to get by before. Werecat was considered the most magical of all were-blood types. And for this working, even more so.

The mythology claiming a witch's familiar to be a cat was rooted somewhat in fact. Werecats without a tribe had sought witches, wizards, and occasionally a sorcerer or two. They'd traded blood for shelter for centuries.

Things were different now. These days, Weres in desperate situations and in need of cash donated anonymously to one of the blood banks, and various magic users just ordered what they needed from occult shopkeepers or online. It was much cleaner this way.

Weres could be more trouble than they were worth. Most magic users had learned that the hard way, as there seemed to be a certain level of idiotic stubbornness that came with the territory of wielding magic.

Dayne rolled his mouse over the *send* button and clicked, then leaned back in his chair, interlacing his fingers behind his head. He smiled as the animated GIF wand waved, and purple digital glitter sprinkled over his computer desktop, indicating his order was being processed. The site was on the cheesy side, but a reliable company was a reliable company, cutesy bells and whistles notwithstanding.

That was one thing about the white lighters. You could trust them. They lived their entire lives according to a mission of goodness and honesty. It made Dayne want to hurl, but with few exceptions, they wouldn't betray you.

He'd just shut down the computer when a rap sounded on the front door. No one knocked on his door anymore. Primarily because he was known as the city's darkest evil and everyone was too scared to try to overthrow him. The postman had long ago learned the wisdom of quietly leaving packages by the door. Dayne didn't know what the fuss had been about. The man's hair had regrown in a mere matter of months.

"Just a moment, please." Whoever was calling after midnight could only be bringing trouble with them.

For a while, after what was later called *the tribal massacre*, the lone hero had darkened his door, convinced Dayne was up to something nefarious and had to be taken down. Or another Cary Town villain decided to rise to infamy and needed Dayne out of the way to do it.

He'd eventually managed the right formula on the wards, and most steered clear, deciding it wasn't worth it. It had been quiet for the past decade. Either the wards were working or he'd been deemed irrelevant. Either way was fine by him.

The wards dropped as Dayne opened the door to reveal a diminutive black cat with bright golden eyes sitting primly on the middle of his front stoop. She blinked up at him full of rehearsed pet store innocence, her tail wrapped around her tiny paws.

"Mrarrr."

"You must be kidding me. I don't take in strays." He slammed the door. Did the werecat think he couldn't sense the magic crackling around her? Was she that naive? Perhaps a junior wizard still under apprenticeship would have been fooled, but not someone with his level of experience.

He drained the last dregs of coffee from the mug in the microwave. There was a second knock.

"Oh, for God's sake." He was going to zap the little miscreant halfway across town and let the preternatural border patrol sort out the pieces.

Dayne opened the door this time with a spell ready on his lips, but stopped short. She was breathtaking, not that this was uncommon in a Were. They tended to have a certain magnetism. She had short, dark hair, and she was leggy. A personal weakness of his.

Black leather pants encased her legs as if they'd been stitched onto her. It seemed only magic could have gotten those pants on and would be required to get them off again. A red silky top plunged to reveal ample but not overpowering cleavage. The werecat had a large duffel bag slung over one shoulder and balanced against her hip as if she'd planned to move in.

He held up a hand before *little Dayne* could cause him to do something colossally stupid. "The wardrobe change doesn't alter my position, princess."

"I thought you'd be old," she said, wrinkling her nose.

He gave her points for not stammering that opening line. "What leads you to believe I'm not?"

"I need help."

Well, she got right down to it, didn't she? Such a Red Riding Hood. It was intoxicating. In a different mood, with a different species, he might have let her into his lair.

"Not interested. Try the Salvation Army."

The brunette wedged one high-heeled boot inside the door. "Please. I'll be killed. The tribe plans to sacrifice me."

Desperate, frightened eyes.

"And somehow I can't work up any feeling on that topic. Good-bye now."

"Wait! You can use my blood."

Dayne arched a brow. Not quite as naive as she appeared.

"I get my were-blood online. I have no use for you." In truth, he could think of many uses for her, none of which required the promise of her potent magical blood.

The phone rang, preventing *little Dayne* from taking over. "If you'll excuse me."

Appearance-wise, Dayne was nothing like she'd expected. She'd expected an old man with long robes and a beard, dark beady eyes, and a sinister thin mouth. A beak-like nose and long age-gnarled fingers would finish the look. Dayne was none of these things. For one thing, he was wearing blue jeans and a T-shirt.

For another, he was hot, debonair even. Except for the evil. Despite the danger he exuded, Greta turned the doorknob and slipped into the cottage. It wasn't bravery or stupidity that drove her, but desperation.

"Don't do this to me, Mick. You know I need this blood." Dayne stood at the other end of the room making a pot of coffee, his back to her. A cordless phone was pressed between his ear and shoulder.

Greta dropped the duffel bag on the floor without a sound and tuned her amplified hearing in to listen to his phone call. The other man's voice trembled over the phone.

"I . . . I . . . understand that sir, but we have a f-firm policy of only delivering to those who follow our code of ethics and it's been b-brought to my attention that you . . . don't."

"I'm very unhappy about this. It was Alistair wasn't it? That little shit was my bestest best friend until he found out I wasn't out saving the world every night."

"Please, Sir, I'm just doing what my boss told me. He said to tell you it's a conflict of interests to continue delivering your shipments."

"I see. Well, don't think I won't be reporting you to the Board of Magical Merchants for discrimination. There are laws against this sort of thing."

Greta heard Mick's sigh of relief over the phone. Someone like Dayne Wickham reporting him to a board of magical anything was minor, the equivalent of an angry shopper threatening never to return.

Dayne stabbed his finger against the button to end the call, then flung the phone across the room. Greta froze. His back was still to her when he spoke.

"I thought I told you to leave. Or was my dismissal not clear enough? Perhaps it would help if I spelled it out with catnip." He turned to face her. "Or I could carve the message."

His glance shifted to a gleaming silver ritual knife balanced precariously on the edge of the desk. Silver wouldn't kill her necessarily, but it burned like hell and was much harder to heal.

Dayne blazed across the floor and grabbed Greta by the wrist, hauling her back to the entryway. "Have you any idea the danger you put yourself in when you trespass on a sorcerer's property? Shall I enlighten you?"

Greta wrenched herself free of his grip. "You don't have a supplier now. I'll give you the blood you need if you'll let me stay until after the full moon. I won't cause any trouble."

She wasn't sure why she was still asking to stay. He'd just made a not-so-subtle hint about using her skin as a carving block. Hiding in a hollowed-out tree for the next several nights was sounding like a more sane option than remaining with the unhinged sorcerer.

He crossed his arms over his chest, his stance wide, and to the human eye, relaxed. But Greta could smell the tendrils of controlled anger coming off him. She'd always been able to smell emotion, but the scent seemed sharper now.

"They send one of you, all pretty and in distress, and I'm supposed to fall all over myself trying to protect you? Let's get one thing clear. I'm the bad guy. I don't rescue fair maidens."

She flushed at the *pretty* part, glossing right over the *bad guy* part.

He muttered something in Latin with his arm outstretched, and for a moment Greta thought she was about to die. Instead, the cordless phone floated from behind him to his waiting hand. His eyes remained trained on her as he punched the numbers into the phone.

"Clarissa, I'm sorry to wake you, love, but I was wondering if you might be persuaded to set aside a pint of werecat blood for me. I need it by the full moon."

"Mr. Wickham, um hi," a sleepy voice on the other end answered. "No, it's okay. You're our best customer. We actually don't have any therian cat blood in stock. We can get some, but it'll take six weeks; our supplier's backed up. You could try a local therian."

"Meow," Greta said, still in human form.

"I see. Well, thank you anyway." Dayne clicked off the phone and glared at Greta, as if she'd somehow personally gummed up the works.

"So, then I can stay?"

"I'll have to erect stronger wards. Please keep in mind, you are here for my convenience due to inventory troubles. I'm not your knight in shining armor. I don't care about your personal problems. And if you wander from the protection of this house, I will not be lured into the trap to save you. I don't get involved with Weres."

"Therians," Greta said, returning his glare.

"If I were you, I would remember that although I would like to do my ritual this full moon, there are infinite full moons available to me. You might not be so lucky. I'll be in my study gathering supplies for the wards."

His footsteps receded down the hallway, and Greta made a face. She spun in a slow circle taking in her surroundings.

She'd expected a medieval-looking castle equipped with a full dungeon, or some austere mansion. His home was neither. It was . . . cozy, though larger than the average cottage. The fireplace crackled with dying embers that had recently warmed something in a small iron cauldron.

The main room was lined with dark oak bookshelves and rows upon rows of books. The walls were stone but emitted a sense of warmth, the direct opposite of Dayne.

Maybe it was a timeshare.

Greta suppressed a giggle as she tried to imagine Dayne Wickham, the hapless victim of a timeshare scheme. It would explain his sour demeanor.

Two windows on either side of the fireplace were open with long, lightweight crimson drapes hanging in front of them. A storm was brewing. As the wind howled outside, the curtains were sucked into the screen, then puffed back out as if the wall were breathing. She was still staring at the windows, mesmerized by the sensation of the house breathing, when Dayne returned.

"Come with me. I'll need some of your blood, since you seem to be in a donating mood."

Her eyes drifted back to the knife on the table.

"If I were going to harm you, I would have already done so. I grow very quickly bored with the practice of building trust in others only to crush it at the last possible moment. Unlike some species."

Greta flinched at the look he gave her. But when he turned, she followed. The dwelling went deeper than it appeared from the outside, and it occurred to her that the floor was sloping downward as they worked their way to an underground part of the house.

The hairs on the back of her arm stood at attention as the passageway narrowed until it was only big enough for two people. Then it began to spiral more steeply down, and the smooth slope became stairs. It was such a gradual transition, she wasn't sure if it was the architecture itself, or magic.

At the bottom of the stairs was a large stone room with shelves of books lining the walls, as well as potions, pots, wands, and grisly items in cloudy jars. Cobwebs had grown over much of the area.

There were a couple of unlit torches on the wall, though the room's illumination came from a dome light in the ceiling. A steel cage stood in the back, its purpose most likely not on the up-and-up. Greta shivered. So much for Dayne not having a dungeon.

Chapter Three

He had to admit, she was a good little actress. Almost as good as Jaden had been. The werecat stood at the bottom of the stairs barely inside the cavernous room where Dayne performed his more complicated rituals. Her arms were wrapped tightly around her, a protective barrier against him, no doubt.

He didn't want to be paranoid, but he wondered if the tribe had been responsible for his were-blood supply being cut off. The timing was too coincidental for his liking. There had been rumblings that the tribe leader was getting more powerful these days. Could Simon know Dayne planned to act against him on the next full moon?

It had been thirty years since his last encounter with Cary Town's werecat tribe. Dayne had nearly died thinking he was saving Jaden's life, only to be led into a trap. If he hadn't fortified himself with so much magic, he would've been killed.

He'd gotten lucky. Shapeshifters, though made of magic, didn't know how to wield it. He'd taken out most of the tribe and managed to escape, sustaining several injuries, including a few to his pride.

Now they were sending this little number to lure him away. Didn't they have any new material? His eyes drifted to the cage in the back corner. One never knew when one might need such a contraption.

He ran his hand idly over the bit of stubble growing on his chin as he contemplated the cage. He
should lock her up until the ritual, use her blood, then
throw her out.

If anything, such an act would send a message to the
tribe that Dayne Wickham was not to be fucked with. He
was suddenly glad he was acting against Simon now,
rather than later. He'd put it off far too long.

For whatever inane reason, Jaden loved Simon. It had
taken years for Dayne's love for her to diminish to the
point that he could dispatch her lover without guilt.

He considered taking the Were's blood now and
getting rid of her. Except, even he wouldn't stoop to that
level of dishonor. It had nothing to do with anything the
tribe might plan to do to the girl.

"Are you cold?" he asked. *Dammit.*

She shook her head.

Eventually, a pouty-lipped woman, like this one, was
going to get him killed. Prudence would dictate he wait for
another full moon, but the effects of the spell wouldn't be
nearly so strong at any other time. Simon was ready to
end this now, and Dayne might not get another chance.

"Sit." He motioned to a painted white circle in the
middle of the floor.

She bit her bottom lip and slowly moved into the
center of the circle.

"Are you having second thoughts about being here?"

She nodded.

"Good."

Dayne crossed to the far wall and selected a large and
well-worn book from the uppermost shelf. He took a small
needle from the desk drawer nearest the bookcase and
opened the book to the correct page.

He pricked her finger, ignoring her indignant cry, and
squeezed several drops of blood into the center of the

circle. When he released her hand to say the incantation, she sucked on her finger. It took every ounce of willpower for his eyes not to linger on her pretty little mouth.

He focused more intently on chanting.

When he closed the book, the werecat stood and placed her hands on her hips. "I didn't want to come to you for help. You were my only choice. You're the strongest magic user in the city, and we dislike the same people. I don't know what your problem is, but I don't want to die. My moth . . . Jaden gave me your address. I was in cat form so I couldn't exactly ask questions but . . ."

Before she could finish the sentence, she was lying on her back, Dayne's hand wrapped around her throat. He stopped squeezing when he registered the look in her eyes. She'd clearly forgotten she was stronger than he was. Something he could use.

"Who did you say sent you?" He poured menace into his voice, intent on keeping her on edge and pressing his advantage.

"Jaden . . . I . . . Please . . . " Greta's fingernails dug into his arms in panic.

He released her. "Forgive me. I have trust issues."

"Yeah, no shit." Greta shot back to her feet, the slight crouch of her body showed she was ready for him. She rubbed her throat.

"Did I hurt you?"

"You scared me. I almost shifted."

"Is that a bad thing?"

"I can't fight worth a damn in my fur." She crossed her arms defensively over her chest.

"I'm sorry."

Her face flushed in anger. "Are you? Because the way it looks to me, we both have a problem and we both have a solution. You need blood; I have blood. I need protection; you have protection. This doesn't seem all that complicated to me. Does it seem complicated to you?"

Dayne crossed his arms over his chest. "I have ground rules, Were."

"Fine. I have a ground rule, too."

One brow rose. "Oh? Do tell."

While it was indeed true that she could kick his ass without blinking if he suddenly developed laryngitis, he would wager he could chant faster than she could drop kick him. Not every spell required books and herbs, candles or circles, or any of the million and one accoutrements the magical set swore by.

"Don't call me Were. If you're really that old, you know that's offensive. Whatever your therian issue is, put it aside. I'm not whoever did you wrong. I would prefer to be called by my name if that wouldn't be too much trouble."

He cocked his head to the side and studied her. She alternated so quickly between timid and smart-mouthed, he thought he might be dealing with a multiple personality. It wouldn't be the first time in his long existence. Dayne's mouth curved in a genuinely amused smile before he caught himself and returned to his former cold expression.

"Very well, and your name?"

"Greta."

"Is that your only rule, Greta?"

She nodded, the wind going out of her sails as she returned to being the frightened kitty. He wondered if she was aware of these highly irregular mood swings.

"My rules are as follows: You will not leave this house until after the full moon. If your tribe truly plans to sacrifice you, the wards will keep you safe as long as you remain inside. If you leave, you will not be allowed back in. Since I can't keep an eye on you 24/7, when I can't watch you you'll be locked in the guest room. For my own personal safety, of course."

She stood perfectly still for a moment, the tension radiating off her body as she clenched and unclenched her hands at her sides.

"I won't let you lock me up." She said it calmly, her tone completely even, but she turned and ran up the stairs. Moments later, the front door slammed.

He shook his head and sighed. The spell hadn't lied. He had. He hadn't needed her blood to strengthen the wards. The wards were fine as they were, barring his bad habit of voluntarily opening the door without looking through the peephole first. He'd needed her blood for a truth spell.

The light that had glowed around her immediately after he'd finished the incantation should have left no doubt to her honest need. Though again, he wasn't running a charity service. So why he should feel the need to help random Weres in distress like some sort of magical halfway house, he couldn't be sure.

He'd felt the fear pouring off her and conceded no one was that good an actress. He'd watched her eyes flash between brown and yellow as she'd tried to stop from shifting. Still, he wouldn't put it past Jaden to be using her.

Dayne shrugged. It was no longer his problem. Let someone else handle it. He wasn't going to become a hero; they didn't normally survive long.

He climbed the stairs and found Greta's abandoned bag beside the front door. Sorting through it, he found makeup, clothes, and a few tacky books with shirtless men and women with heaving breasts.

He crossed back to the computer, loaded the web browser, and typed, "sacrifice," "therian" into the search box. Several sites popped up, most about werecats. This breed liked their sacrifice.

Dayne clicked the link that looked most helpful. The screen filled with morbid drawings of beautiful women, sometimes men, chained down to stone slabs, blood being drained from them into a type of moat around the altar as the others shifted into their animal form.

The images showcased a type of twisted sadism that most reserved for those not of their kind. Further down the page were photographs. One in particular caught his attention.

The woman's hair was longer than Greta's, but the same shiny dark brown. Otherwise, she resembled her enough that Dayne could almost see Greta on the slab instead. He scrolled the mouse over the arrow to leave the page.

A warmth prickled over his senses. The kitty was still in the house. He should have been angry, but after the photos what he felt was relief that she was still safely ensconced in his well-warded fortress. Somewhere. Cats were experts at hiding. If not for his ability to sense magic, he might never have known.

And now she was terrified of him. Had he worked the evil persona so strongly that he'd become so? He wasn't all fluffy goodness and light, but he hadn't thought he'd sunk to mustache-twirling levels of evil.

He focused on the bookcase, causing one of the books to fly off the shelf into his hand. He flipped to the appropriate passage and whispered the incantation necessary to lock all the doors and windows, then he allowed the book to fly back to its place.

He needed to get out and socialize more. Even ten years ago, Dayne never would have made a speech like the one he'd made in the basement about locking her up. It sounded like it had come out of *Evil for Dummies*. A less insane sorcerer would lock up the books he didn't want her in, not lock her up. Or perhaps a sorcerer *would* lock her up.

He started down the hallway, his footfalls light and measured.

"Here, kitty kitty."

Chapter Four

Greta huddled under Dayne's bed, her fur pressed flat against the wall. She'd barely maintained her form in the basement. Now she was too keyed up to shift back and climb out the window. Footsteps thudded and stopped with heavy finality just outside the door.

Please don't find me. Please don't find me. Her heart beat erratically in her tiny chest, in tempo to her silent pleas. She wondered if a cat could hyperventilate. If it had been Simon outside the door, he would have heard her panting and it would have been all over.

She tried to stay focused on the plan. Of course, Dayne would return to his room. That was the point.

He'd finally go to sleep and she could slip out and eat something, then keep out of sight until after the full moon.

After all, what kind of idiot hides in the bedroom of the bad guy? It was probably a bad question given her current circumstances, but it had seemed halfway brilliant at the time she'd thought of it.

She couldn't be sure why she'd slammed the door earlier without first going through it, except that Dayne was her only hope.

Without magic to cloak her, she was at the mercy of the tribe. And no one else in Cary Town was strong enough to counteract the magic of the few witches in the tribe's employ. If Jaden thought Dayne was her only chance, then he was.

The bed dipped above her and the bed springs creaked as Dayne laid back and sighed. "You can come out now. I'm not going to hurt you."

Yeah right. She remained hidden, though she was sure he could use magic to bring her out. She couldn't be that difficult to levitate at house cat weight.

"Greta . . . "

The bed creaked again as his weight lifted, then his eyes were level with hers. He held out a hand. She hissed.

"I'm not having a conversation like this," he said, his voice sounding so reasonable she almost trusted him. "You have to come out eventually."

She wished she could ask him to back away so she could come out on her own, but her cat-shaped mouth wouldn't form human words, and it seemed unlikely he was fluent in the subtle nuance of the meow. When she finally edged out, he picked her up.

She reacted.

"Ow!" Dayne howled, dropped her, and cradled his bleeding arm. "Fuck!"

Greta scrambled onto the bed and burrowed underneath the pillow, her little black face poking out at him. Her eyes widened at the long, bright bloody trails she'd left. Didn't Dayne know anything about cats? It wasn't like she could shut that instinct off.

She inched out from under the pillow, arched her back, and hissed. She expected to see anger in his eyes, instead she saw . . . guilt? She settled on top of the feather pillow and wrapped her tail around her as he disappeared into the bathroom.

When he returned, his arm was bandaged. She could smell the hydrogen peroxide he'd used to disinfect the cuts as if he'd been wounded on a battlefield instead of getting a few cat scratches. Men could be such babies.

"I don't like blood," he said.

"Mrarr?" Greta cocked her head to the side. He'd taken *her* blood not an hour ago. He didn't seem to have a problem then.

"My own blood. I have no trouble with the blood of others."

Those calmly spoken words should have had her fleeing back under the bed to the safety she'd just left, but she remained frozen in place. She would have felt better if she could shift back to a form she could fight in. But she couldn't, not with him there.

"If I sit next to you, are you going to claw me again?"

She shook her head, and Dayne settled beside her.

"I apologize for my earlier behavior. I was nearly killed because of Jaden many years ago. So I have a hard time trusting Weres. Especially Weres from your tribe."

Greta growled.

"Therians," he corrected. "However, at this point I don't believe you're lying to me. Ordinarily I wouldn't get involved, but you're right. I need your blood. This is how it used to be done. None of this ordering blood off the Internet nonsense. Magic shouldn't be so sanitary. It has no right to be."

He'd started absently stroking Greta's fur, a soothing rhythmic motion from the tips of her ears to the end of her tail. It was causing an inappropriate response, and before she could stop herself, she'd shifted.

Fur changed to soft flesh under his hand. Greta rolled onto her side, her legs curled into her, trying to cover her nudity. Warmth flared in Dayne's stomach at the action. It was a strange and oddly endearing quirk for a Were. Usually they flaunted whatever they had to flaunt, in their skin or in their fur.

"Could you go get me some clothes out of my bag? Please?"

"Of course."

As he made his way down the hall, a visual came unbidden of those beautiful legs on his shoulders, and Greta moaning and writhing beneath him. He had to shake himself physically to loosen the thoughts from his mind.

If she'd been a dog, no pun intended, he might not have had such a problem. His resolve with her would be melted way before the moon reached fullness. And if history was choosing to repeat itself, by the time he needed her blood he'd contract a full-blown case of stupid. Dayne retrieved a pair of faded blue jeans and a flimsy T-shirt that barely qualified as clothing.

He returned and tossed them to her, then looked away. He heard her catch the garments and bit the inside of his cheek as he listened to the fabric slide over her skin.

"Okay," she said.

He turned. Clothing did nothing to help the situation. The jeans hugged the curves of her hips too enticingly, and the shirt was cropped to reveal a small expanse of golden stomach. Without a bra, her nipples protruded through the thin pink material.

For a moment, neither of them spoke.

"The gardens are warded as well," Dayne said, searching for anything to say so he could stop looking at her nipples. His eyes darted up to catch hers as she nodded. Her cheeks were flushed. Who knew a werecat could blush? Jaden had been shameless.

"Will you be sleeping in the guest room?"

"Are you going to lock me up?" Her eyebrows rose in challenge as the pink faded from her cheeks.

"I shouldn't have said that. I'm not used to being around people. I'm sorry."

This was an understatement and a testament to how much the tiny creature unnerved him. Once he'd had time to think, he'd realized how extreme his threat to lock her up had been. All the dangerous books required extensive magical knowledge to decipher. It wasn't as if she could cast a curse on him or destroy any of the wards he'd built.

"We're going to have to try to trust each other." He watched her lips draw into a tight line at the hypocritical comment, but she nodded again.

He wondered if she felt the room charge as he did. He wanted to shove the jeans past her hips and bend her over the bathroom counter. He wanted her in his bed.

"I'm hungry," Greta said, interrupting his fantasy.

His hand, of its own accord, reached out and brushed a strand of hair off her face as she passed him. She flinched.

"Sorry," he said.

"You've said that a lot today."

He didn't know why he'd touched her. He had no right. There were no strong wizards or good witches she could go to in the city. She must have been very desperate and afraid to come to him, and he hadn't done anything to put that fear to rest.

He followed her down the narrow hallway. A picture on the wall of his uncle Arthur reflected oddly in the domed hallway lighting. The photograph showed Arthur with a disapproving look on his stern features. The camera had never captured him without that look, not once in his 443 years of life. Nevertheless, Dayne felt the old man stood in judgment of him now beyond the grave, seeing how far Dayne's humanity had slipped in recent decades.

Greta moved ahead of him with an animal grace, each step precise. It was difficult to understand how normal humans couldn't sense what she was. Dayne could feel the magic pulsing off her, just as intoxicating as the last time he'd felt it thirty years before with Jaden.

It called to him, begged him to take a taste of that raw natural power, that elusive something trained magic users just didn't have. A sorcerer, witch, or wizard just knew how to manipulate the magic around them; shape-shifters were made of magic.

He kept to the corners of the room, doing an old trick he'd learned in his apprenticeship days to make himself fade into the background. It wasn't full invisibility, more like unobtrusiveness. He wasn't sure of its effectiveness on a shapeshifter, but at least it would keep his presence from spooking her further.

He had to restrain himself as Greta took the milk from the fridge and drank it straight from the carton. At first, the restraint was because she was no doubt spreading germs all over the container. Then it became about something else as he felt himself grow hard.

A few drops of the creamy white liquid dribbled around the sides of the carton and down her chin and long neck. She arched back, and some of the milk dripped down to dampen her shirt.

She moved on to a steak Dayne had planned to grill for dinner the next day. He couldn't bring himself to protest as he watched her carefully unwrap the meat and make a show of eating it. A woman eating raw meat wasn't generally a turn-on. It was the kind of thing seen in a traveling freak show, but somehow the werecat managed to make an act that emphasized bloody death into the most erotic teasing.

When she finished, she dumped the empty meat tray in the garbage and stretched her arms languidly over her head. She paused by the door on her way out of the kitchen.

"Goodnight, Dayne," she practically purred.

He shed the useless glamour. "Nice kitties don't tease."

"I never said I was a nice kitty. Nice sorcerers don't stalk."

"There are no nice sorcerers."

He frowned as the confidence slipped off her face like a mask. She turned and scurried off to the guest room without a backward glance, the spell she'd woven, broken.

He didn't know what kind of game she was playing, but he was disappointed to be the winner.

Chapter Five

Over the days that followed, a routine and tentative truce formed. Dayne stopped threatening Greta and tried to stop suspecting her of trying to destroy him. Mostly he suspected Jaden. He'd once allowed Jaden's musical laughter and shapely ass to cause him to lose sight of everything he'd learned as a sorcerer, something he was in danger of doing again now with Greta.

Jaden had been beneficial in her way. The slaughter in the tribe's sacred space had ensured the reputation he now enjoyed. It was a reputation he'd cultivated and cared for like a garden full of delicate seedlings. The consolation prize for losing the girl.

Overall, it had significantly reduced the hassle in his life. Now everything was "Yes, Mr. Wickham," "No, Mr. Wickham," "Please don't kill me, Mr. Wickham." That suited him fine.

Whatever Jaden's plan now, Greta at least believed she needed to be saved. And he needed blood. What was it they said about a gift horse?

He'd made a trip to the grocery store, stocking enough to feed an army. Weres had quite the metabolism. She could pack it away, but where she put it all, he had no idea.

It wasn't just raw meat and milk she liked. She ate cooked meat and vegetables, if baked potatoes counted as a vegetable.

He was certain the nutritional value of the average baked potato was so low they should have their own food group called "nutritionally deficient starches."

He could watch her eat raw meat with no trouble, but when she dug into a baked potato loaded with butter and sour cream, he got squeamish. She'd requested an unnatural amount of chocolate, popcorn, and ice cream, along with every werewolf film ever made. She'd insisted that if she was going to be stuck in the house, she needed entertainment.

When Dayne questioned her, she'd said, "Hey, I don't blame them for portraying the wolves that way. All the bad press is their fault." Then she'd started on another tub of popcorn.

The next day he'd caught her in the basement rolling some of his herbs in rolling paper and smoking them. Then he realized it was catnip.

He'd wanted to be angry. He had a few spells he needed that for and the good stuff was expensive, but she'd rolled around on the stone floor giggling like a maniac. They'd had the briefest of moments when he was sure he could have gotten her into bed with no trouble, but he'd let the moment pass.

That had been a mistake, Dayne thought now as he lounged in a wingback chair in the den. He did most of his guilty pleasure reading here, though there were books all over the house crammed onto every bookcase and stacked on most available surfaces.

There were spell books, of course, but also books on science and history, as well as several books on gardening. He had an impressive garden encased in a stone wall. Climbing vines and roses created a magical effect over trellises, gates, and the garden wall itself. He'd spent many hours the past few days watching Greta in her cat form running around the garden chasing things.

Then he'd grown hard as he'd watched her shift and sunbathe nude, still cursing the missed catnip opportunity. She must not have realized he had a window with a view. It was easy to lose track of the possible peepholes when the garden felt so remote from everything else. It had been designed that way, though he couldn't have foretold the current benefit he was getting from it.

The first time she'd sunbathed, he'd thought she was teasing him as she had with the milk and meat, but her manner was different. Unaffected. She was graceful and sultry as before, but there was an innocence that had been missing from her earlier purposeful seduction, and one he had a hard time admitting turned him on even more than the show she'd put on to entice him. He still hadn't managed to determine what that had been about. Greta wasn't a seductress; it wasn't her style.

Something was off, he just couldn't figure out what.

He got up to check the window again. He was a dirty old man for peeping at her, though he couldn't very well warn Greta of the window now. It would only embarrass her and create an uneasiness he didn't want to see in her again.

Satisfied with the rationalization and disappointed to find no naked Greta outside, he went back to his chair and horror novel. Three pages into chapter thirteen, he looked up startled to see her standing in the doorway with an odd glint in her eyes.

He could hear her purring from his chair. She leaned with one arm over her head to support herself, her body so relaxed and loose it looked like liquid in suspended animation. Her eyes were dilated, her lips parted.

Damn. Dayne knew this. Her lips were parted so she could breathe in the pheromones on the air around her. She was in heat. She'd found him by scent and she wasn't going to be refused. Suddenly her erratic mood swings made sense.

She slunk into the room, and it was then he noticed she was wearing one of his T-shirts and nothing else. The shirt grazed the tops of her thighs. Her nipples formed points in the fabric, making her arousal evident, in the event he'd missed it before.

She stalked him, and he couldn't move. For the first time since they'd met, he was her prey.

He'd been insane if he'd thought she was dangerous to him before, back when danger was a cute theory. She let out a soft, breathy sigh, and the book slipped from his hands to the floor. She bent beside the chair to pick it up, her ass raised delectably in the air. He sucked in a breath. Sweet mother of God, she wasn't wearing panties.

He ran a hand over her bare ass. Greta shivered and turned toward him, straightening with the grace of a preternatural dancer. He felt pinned to the chair by a force stronger than those he usually wielded as she arched back and peeled the shirt from her body, tossing it to the floor.

"Touch me." Her voice was throaty. Whoever or whatever this was, it wasn't her.

"I think it's a bad idea." Why the hell was he growing a conscience now?

"I have to sleep with someone now," she said. "If you don't do it, I'll have to find someone who will." She made her way back toward the door, her exit as much a seduction as her entrance.

Like hell, she was. "You aren't going anywhere. You promised your blood to me, and I will collect."

She didn't seem bothered that he'd reduced her to nothing more than a magical blood donor. She stood in front of him, gloriously naked and pulsing with desire, her body vibrating with the purrs he knew were more from painful need than contentedness.

"Please," she said, rubbing her breasts against him. The action was so feline she might as well have been in her fur.

Dayne gripped her by the shoulders. "How much of you is still in there? Because I promise if you regret this afterward and think you're running off, I will lock you in the cage downstairs. I'm not having your heat cycle screw this up."

She was unfazed by the threat, too lost in elevated hormones. "Don't you want me?" She pouted prettily and then turned in his arms, her ass grinding against his erection. "Mmmmm I see that you do." She glanced over her shoulder. "Well?"

His hands slid around to her front, running smoothly over her belly and up to her exposed breasts.

"Are you coherent enough to talk to me?" He was in the process of losing his own powers of coherence.

"Don't wanna talk. Wanna fuck."

He gripped her by the shoulders again and shook her. "How long does this last, and how often does it happen?"

"Depends."

"On what?"

"Exposure to eligible mates." She moaned. "Don't stop touching."

"You can't possibly live like this." He found it hard to believe Weres were running amuck having heat cycles and getting anything done in the real world.

"I take a pill. They're in my apartment." She sped the pace of her grinding.

"Like birth control?" If she didn't stop that, he wasn't going to be able to continue the conversation. Not verbally anyway.

"Sort of. Stops the cycle. Mutes it so I can function. Please fuck me now. Talk after."

"I'll go get your prescription."

"Too late, won't help once it's started. Have to get them after."

Against his better judgment, Dayne picked her up and carried her to his bedroom. What was he going to do? Have her rolling around all over him until the full moon? He was supposed to be evil. He was well within his rights at this point. With all he'd heard about the tortures of heat without fulfillment, he was providing a service.

When they reached the bedroom, he set her firmly on her feet and brushed a strand of hair from her face. She leaned into his touch. He jerked his hand away, remembering the same gesture from a few days before. This wasn't her.

"Please." Greta's breath came out in labored pants.

"Oh fuck it, I'm the bad guy."

He pushed her until the backs of her legs hit the bed. Her knees bent, and she laid back, spreading her legs wide for his perusal, her earlier shyness gone. He leaned down to kiss her.

"Please," she whimpered.

The kitty didn't want foreplay. Dayne shrugged and shucked his clothes. He tossed them blindly to the corner and took in the feast in front of him. Her fingernails transformed into sharp, razored points.

"Scoot back up on the bed."

"Please."

"Scoot back up on the bed or I'll leave you here to handle this yourself." He knew she couldn't.

She obeyed him; she probably would have walked through fire at this point. If he were more sadistic, he might have tested that theory. Instead, he went to the adjacent room, came back with rope, and tied her wrists to the bars.

"For my protection from those nasty claws of yours," he said, pointing to the healing marks on his forearm. There was no betrayal in her eyes, only raw lust as she spread her legs wider. Tears streamed down her face.

"Please, Dayne."

Superpowers or no, she could do nothing but submit when the heat took over.

He looked down at her writhing in heat. She was so fucking beautiful. Her pheromones were heavy on the air, in his nose, in his throat. In his head. Everything was her in that moment.

Her skin was silken as his bare flesh slid against hers. He wanted to take it slow, not just rut like two mindless animals, but she wouldn't let him. Her legs wrapped around him in a vice, using her considerable therian strength to pull him to her, rubbing her body against his.

Dayne gave up his plans to be noble and slid inside her. In that moment he felt one thing. Possession. This belonged to him. He felt it in the same primal way he felt magic when he'd followed the proper formulas. Whatever she thought this was, she was going to be in his bed for a good long time if he had anything to say about it.

A symphony of emotion played over her face as her more restrained counterpart fought for control. Fear, confusion, desperation, need, and finally surrender, as that part of her lost. She lurched off the bed as her orgasm took her, and he joined her.

When it was over, Greta's face telegraphed equal parts shame and fear. She turned away, staring at the wallpaper as if trying to imprint the pattern on her memory.

Dayne untied her, and she wrapped herself in the bedspread.

"God, what you must think," she finally said. She'd been making an effort to keep her crying quiet, but it flowed out of her voice when she spoke.

"I'm thinking, for a quickie, that was amazing. And that I'm probably done with my own species. To hell with playing it safe."

He smiled at her when she turned back to him and kissed the dampness from her face.

"It's worse than a vampire's need for blood," she said.

Another odd quirk. Most Weres reveled in their sexual power and slept with anything they could get their hands on. It was the one reason he'd trusted Jaden. When she'd come to his bed when she wasn't in heat, he'd believed her feeling for him was genuine. Now he knew what it had really been about. Control.

Her face was tense, no doubt waiting for him to say something cruel.

"Are you okay now?" He sat on the bed beside her, for his part unconcerned with his nudity, as he stroked her back through the bedspread.

"Yes. I'm sorry about that."

"Believe me, there is nothing for you to be sorry about. I'm evil, remember? Your petty heat cycle doesn't intimidate me."

She laughed a little. "It won't happen again if you can get my pills." Greta frowned then, lines appearing in the middle of her forehead. "I'm sure my apartment is being watched."

"I can get in undetected. Will you be okay if I leave you?"

"Yes, go."

The fridge door stood open as Greta debated the benefits of leftover spaghetti versus peanut butter and jelly. She finally decided on chicken nuggets from the freezer.

Over the past few days she'd slowly come to trust she was safe here. The longer she was exposed to the sorcerer's magical signature, the more she knew the world was shown a very different Dayne Wickham than the reality. Now her unease and fear were back.

"Stupid, Greta," she said aloud. After the display in the kitchen, she should have known the heat cycle was close. It had been too long since she'd let it go that far without the drugs that suppressed it.

He returned as she finished the nuggets, carrying her pills and something else.

"Mrarr."

"Mink!"

"You are perverse," he said.

It was only her paranoia that made Greta think he was referencing their previous joining.

He pointed at the cat. "I spent fifteen minutes trying to talk to her and get her to shift because I was convinced a therian wouldn't have a pet of the same species they changed into. I've never heard of such a thing. Then I realized I didn't feel any magic coming off her, just the residue in your apartment, so I brought her along."

Mink was rubbing her cheek against Greta's hand and purring.

"I forgot all about her because of everything," Greta said. "She could have starved."

"Not likely. She chewed her way through the cat food bag. She could have lived off it for a month. Here." He handed her the prescription bottle.

"Thank you." She popped the pill, washing it down with milk, and sank back into the chair.

Dayne sat across from her, his eyes serious. "I want us to talk."

Chapter Six

"I think we should talk about the ritual."

Greta let out a breath she didn't know she'd been holding. She'd expected condemnation, perhaps a scarlet letter magically emblazoned across her body.

Fortunately, Dayne wasn't the Puritan she seemed to be. He'd handled the heat fiasco with a surprising amount of grace, and now he just wanted to get back to the business at hand. She straightened in her chair.

She hadn't asked for details about the ritual. He could be planning to destroy the world and she'd probably let him use her blood if it would save her hide. Maybe she was a coward, but she wanted to live. She preferred not to know the gory details in case it presented her with a moral dilemma.

"What about it?" She ran a finger through the remaining honey mustard sauce on the plate and licked it clean. His eyes darkened with lust and she put her hands in her lap.

What was wrong with her? She'd just taken a pill. Could she not do anything without making it look like an invitation? She bit her lip, as her eyes roved over his body. Dayne was fully clothed, wearing jeans and a T-shirt featuring an obscure grunge band from the nineties.

No matter what he was wearing, she couldn't stop seeing the sharply defined muscles she knew were hidden underneath. The memory of their earlier coupling ran wild through her mind, becoming clearer each time she replayed it. And she'd replayed it about fifteen times now. Her cheeks flushed, and she looked away.

"Why do you think they want you? Why does it have to be you and not someone else?"

"Oh, that ritual. It's because I was born a kitten. But I didn't know it until the other day when I overheard plans for the sacrifice. I mean, how would I know? Not like I'd remember."

"Explain."

"Therians are born in human form and die in animal form. Legends got that backward, or at least about the dying part. We don't go back to human form when we die. We go into animal form trying to survive. It's the way we heal.

"It's rare to be able to shift before age five or six. Even then, it's more normal to start shifting around eight. For centuries, my people have believed our powers come from the gods. So when the gods bless someone as a proper sacrifice, meaning they allow them to be born in their fur, they must be sacrificed on the first full moon of their twenty-eighth year when their power is strongest. But I always thought it was a myth."

"I see."

Greta tried to keep the hurt off her face that he wasn't outraged on her behalf, or sweeping her into his arms. The heat was screwing with her emotions. "Is that all you needed to know?"

"For now."

She got up and rinsed her plate in the sink. "I'm going to bed then."

The sex hadn't meant anything. It was the stupid heat. She couldn't expect him to be in love with her, and it wasn't like she was in love with him either. She needed to get a grip.

It was after midnight, and Dayne was propped against the headboard of his bed making notations for the ritual. It made sense now why the drawings and photographs had been in human form. They sought a full reversal of the natural order. It was poetic in its way, if not morbid in its poetry. If she'd been born in cat form, her blood would be more potent than most.

The kind of power released from blood like that on such a ritually significant date . . . He could see why therians believed it caused the gods to bless them. That much overflow with the right ritual, her essence was bound to be absorbed.

Whether they were aware of it or not, they weren't so much keeping in the good graces of the gods as they were stealing her power. If he'd wanted to live up to his reputation, he should be bottling her blood and selling it on the black market.

From a practical standpoint, it meant he'd need less blood than he would from a normal therian on just any full moon. Without that crucial knowledge, he could have had a magical boo-boo of pyrotechnic proportions.

His personal grimoire sat propped open on his lap. He was penciling in the amount of blood he'd need, when he heard an unearthly howl. Moments later, a bundle of black fur shot across his floor and into the bed. She'd burrowed halfway under the covers before he could get to her.

"Greta, calm down."

Her fur stood on end, and she was digging her claws into his 800 thread count sheets, digging clear into the mattress. She looked past him, seeing something that wasn't there. Then a pitiful, crying meow tore through her throat. His chest tightened, and a rush of compassion overwhelmed him for the frightened animal.

"Greta, look at me. You had a nightmare. There's nothing here."

The part of her that could understand human speech had obviously receded, drawn back into the cat-shaped shell. Dayne gently stroked down her back, speaking soothing nonsense.

Gradually, the tiny talons receded back into her paws and her fur laid flat. His fingers smoothed over her until a rumbling purr started. This time he watched as she transformed back to her human form.

Their eyes met as he continued his ministrations over her silken skin. She rolled over onto her back, stretching her arms over her head as his fingers played over her breasts. He watched her reaction, half expecting her to pull away or recover her earlier modesty.

She let out a soft sigh; her eyes glazed over. He replaced his hand with his mouth, licking and teasing over the nipple of one breast as his hand moved farther south to pet her sex.

"Dayne," she panted.

He released her breast to give her his full attention. "Yes?"

"I don't know if we should."

A finger dipped inside her, and she bucked off the bed. A purr emanated from her chest as she whimpered and pushed against his hand, urging his finger deeper. He withdrew it.

"Well, if you don't think we should . . . "

He smiled down at her and watched the angry spark flare in her eyes, then die away as she caught his grin and realized he didn't intend to kick her out of his bed.

He chuckled and moved down her body to swipe his tongue over the flesh where his hand had been. She moaned and dug her hands into the sheets. He wondered between her cat side and her human side if there would be any sheets left by the time he was finished with her.

Greta was in Dayne's bed, wrapped in his arms for the second time that night. She wished she could stop the contented purring. The pills had stalled the immediate need of the heat, but the adrenaline from her fear had caused her to weaken when his hands were on her.

His fingers stroked through her hair and trailed down her back as she arched into his touch. Like most cats, she was never able to get enough.

"Do you want to tell me about the nightmare?"

She stiffened. She'd forgotten the dream. She hadn't been human enough to retain the memories. Already in her cat form and in such a primal panic, all sense of humanity had left her. She wasn't usually so disconnected from her human thoughts, even in her fur.

If she'd remembered the details of what had gotten her so scared in the first place, she wouldn't have run into Dayne's room. She shuddered as the dream came rushing back in its full Technicolor ugliness.

"I just dreamed about the sacrifice. They took me and were draining my blood out. I was dying. That's all." She couldn't tell him she'd dreamed he'd stood there and let it happen, that he'd been in on it from the beginning.

She'd run to him thinking he would protect her, but the tribe had sent her to him to ensure she'd be at the ritual. In the dream, Dayne was the one who made the cuts down her skin and smiled as the blood ran out.

She hadn't smelled any evil on him, not once she'd gotten past the persona he was trying to live up to. But then sorcerers could mask their scent with magic. Jaden had taught her that. She pulled out of his arms.

"I think I'm going back to my room," she said, unable to make eye contact. She couldn't let him see her fear.

"Are you sure? Maybe you should sleep here, in case you dream again."

She was already edging toward the door when she looked up at him.

Dayne's eyes narrowed. "You're right; perhaps you should sleep in your own room. You're only here a few more days."

It wasn't as if she'd said she wanted a relationship. She hadn't even implied it. The first time she'd been in heat, and the second he'd initiated. He had some ego. Or was his comment because he knew she'd be dead? Greta crossed back to her room and crawled in under the covers with Mink. This time she slept with her door locked.

Dayne sighed. It wasn't necessary to overreact like that. Her wanting to sleep across the hall didn't mean she was using him.

The truth spell he'd cast wasn't for short-term use. He could have done that without her blood. He'd instead wanted something longer lasting, an insurance policy to protect his interests in the event that he got too soft-hearted toward her and started doing all his thinking with *little Dayne.*

Her aura had turned dark when he'd asked her about the dream. She was holding something back. He could make her tell him, but then he was back to being classed as a monster. He didn't like the way it made him feel when he was the source of her fear.

He liked even less that he cared so much what this particular therian thought, period. It would be best if she slept in her own room. If he didn't get attached, neither Greta nor Jaden could lure him into another trap.

Chapter Seven

Greta perched on a kitchen barstool with a plate of bacon and scrambled eggs covered in maple syrup. Her long, tanned legs were crossed, flip-flops dangling off her feet. Mink stood on the counter eating off the side of her plate.

"That's disgusting," Dayne said. She wasn't sure if he was referring to her habit of eating maple syrup on her eggs, or sharing food with the cat. Mink hopped off the counter and fled to the other side of the room.

He poured a glass of juice and took a packet of instant muffin mix from the cabinet. Greta tensed as he brushed past her to retrieve a bowl, muffin tin, milk, and a measuring cup. He took a chocolate cookie out of the cookie jar and chomped on it as he worked. A stubborn crumb stayed on the corner of his mouth, and she wanted to lick it off.

She was slowly losing her mind. He was dangerous. Probably. He was part of the ritual. Maybe. She wasn't sure anymore. In the daylight it didn't seem possible he'd do that to her. Two nights before she'd dreamed purple clowns were chasing her down an alley made of Swiss cheese. Some dreams were just dreams.

"Is something wrong?" He preheated the oven and was engaged in pouring the batter into the muffin tin.

"Why are you doing that?"

"Doing what?"

She gestured to the batter. "Can't you just zap them?"

"Only an amateur magic user uses a spell for such a petty thing." He sounded like he was reciting from a text-book.

Greta spun on the bar stool, first one way, then the other. Something she hadn't done since she was a kid at Simon's house. It was getting close to the full moon and she was still hungry. But Dayne made her skin itch, and the kitchen was suddenly too hot and confining.

Her eyes cut to the doorway to see Mink slipping out of the room. In a minute, the cat would be back, whining to be let out. Greta left her plate on the counter and, without a word, followed after her.

Dayne took the blueberry muffins from the oven and dropped the tray. *Dammit.* Was he developing some type of mental retardation? She'd deflected his question about what was wrong by asking why he didn't use magic to make muffins. She had a point there.

And since when did he start eating instant blueberry muffins and chocolate cookies? Her poor eating habits were beginning to rub off on him. He never should have sprung for the cookie jar. All those simple carbs.

He was going to have to resort to magic to stay in shape if he kept eating like this. Only two more days, then she was on her own and he was back to the regimented diet. He plucked one of the muffins from the tray and ate it anyway, then went to look for her. Whatever was causing her anxiety needed to be resolved, at least reduced. Otherwise, it could affect the ritual.

He found her in the garden.

"Greta?"

She shrieked and covered herself with one of his bright fluffy beach towels. Dayne looked away, his hand over his eyes.

"Sorry," he muttered.

"Give me a second. Okay. I'm decent."

She hadn't been kidding about a second. She could put clothing on as fast as most people could take it off. He wondered if she was holding out on him about her magical abilities.

As to her decency, that was a matter of perspective. "You avoided my question earlier in the kitchen."

"Oh?" She sat on the ground and picked a daisy, tearing the petals off one by one. Her eyes followed each petal as it fell onto her shorts, and the warm breeze carried it away.

"I asked you if something was wrong."

She looked up at him, her eyes guileless. "Wrong? No. Why would something be wrong?"

Dayne felt his face darken at the same time Greta's aura did. "You're lying."

She shrugged and picked another daisy. He felt the tension roll over her as her eyes flashed to gold and then back to brown so fast it could have been a trick of the light.

He sat on the grass a few feet away and uprooted a daisy, starting on the same mindless ritual Greta was focused on. When she looked up at him, her shoulders relaxed.

He sighed. "What are you afraid of? You know they can't get to you, not even in the garden. You've been safe here the entire time, and the clock is running out. You're useless to them after tomorrow night."

He reached out and settled a hand on her knee. "Are you afraid of me?"

Her wide eyes rose to his. "No."

"Is it because of the way I behaved when you first got here? Or anything we've done since then?"

"No. I'm not afraid of you."

He watched as her eyes drifted to his hand, then away, then back again, but she didn't ask him to remove it. He laid his other hand against her cheek.

"You really are safe with me."

She rubbed her cheek against his palm and scooted to close the distance between them. Her mouth latched onto his. He returned the kiss; his hand settled on the back of her neck holding her firmly in place while his tongue explored.

In the next moment, she'd scrambled off him.

"Greta, what?" He touched a finger to his lips.

"I don't need to be starting something up with someone who may or may not be evil."

"Who said we were starting anything up?"

Her face flushed. "I'm sorry, I forgot."

"Forgot what?" He didn't know what she was apologizing for until he saw the signs of the heat.

"I was supposed to take it after breakfast. And then you came in and distracted me."

"It's all right. I understand this. I don't think badly of you. Let me help you."

She held a warning finger out to him as she struggled to her feet. "You stay the hell away from me."

He edged nearer. "You *are* afraid of me."

She didn't trust herself to speak. She needed him now. Her body sought his. After the first day, he'd been nothing but kind to her. Never raising his voice, never grabbing or threatening her. He'd gone shopping for her; he'd done everything right. Dreams were often a jumbled mixture of all the things people experience, desire, and fear. It made sense Dayne would get jumbled in too.

She had no illusions he wanted to keep her around, and she didn't want to sleep with him again if it was going to be just another meaningless ritual biology had set up as a physical act with no feeling. If she was going to be physical with someone, she wanted the feelings that came with it. She wanted him to care.

"I'm not afraid of you."

He cocked his head to the side looking past her, and she wondered what had caused the confused expression to come to his face.

"You're conflicted," he said after a moment.

"I'm not conflicted. I just want control of my own damn body." Her voice quivered more than she liked. She darted behind a row of hedges and passed through the gate before detouring to her room. She shut and locked the door.

Moments later, there was a quiet knock.

Her need flowed through her. It thrashed about like a live wire demanding satisfaction. The arousal was so strong it was becoming painful. A rumbling purr started in her chest, trying to soothe it away. She needed him inside her now.

"Greta, let me help you. You can't make it until tomorrow," he said reasonably from the other side of the door.

She sat on the edge of the bed, her nails digging into the sheets, rending long tears in them. Dayne didn't seem conflicted at all. She was glad at least one of them wasn't suffering from that problem.

"I don't want to frighten you. I don't want to open the door with magic. But I'm not sure I can stay out here and listen to you howl like that."

She hadn't realized she'd been making vocalizations. Sounds that could be either pleasure or pain. At this point, even she couldn't decipher the tangled web of sensations running through her. She left the bed without conscious thought and crawled to the door. Her finger-nails dug into the wood as she pressed her ear to the flat panel listening to him while he spoke soft words of reas-surance. She panted as she breathed in his scent.

She ripped the clothes from her body. The room was becoming too hot. She couldn't think. A horrible sound tore from her throat.

"I'm coming through the door if you don't open it."

She wanted him to. Anything so she wouldn't have to make the choice to throw herself at him. Let him be the one on a conquest, not her.

"Greta."

She couldn't form a thought that would translate itself into a sentence. The only words that wanted to work their way through her brain were, "Please fuck me now." She knew he was more than willing to oblige. All she had to do was move a few inches, and unlock the door. One tiny little turn.

Her hand reached out, and she pulled it away, biting her bottom lip.

"I'm counting down, and then I'm opening the door. Ten . . . nine . . . eight . . . seven . . . six . . . five . . . "

She unlocked the door.

" . . . four . . . three . . . two . . . "

She opened the door.

Dayne's clothes had already been stripped off. She wanted to say he'd been presumptuous, but large words like *presumptuous* couldn't be processed in her near feral state. She pounced on him and wrapped her legs around his waist.

He walked them backward to the bed. "I'm never buying Egyptian cotton sheets again."

"Please," she breathed. They both knew she wasn't asking for sheets.

Chapter Eight

Greta's eyes shot open. Her heart palpitated wildly, thrumming through her chest. Blood pounded in her ears. Dayne's arm was slung over her hip, hugging her naked body loosely against him. Why hadn't she shifted? She'd had the dream again, this time more vivid than before. Yet, despite her fear, she'd held onto her human form.

She wanted to stay wrapped in his warmth forever, but she forced herself to move. He was the face of her death; there were no doubts now. Getting the same dream twice wasn't something she could ignore. It was prophetic.

Dayne was the one holding the ritual knife that spilled her blood. She twisted and shimmied out from under him. His arm fell with a sharp oomph much louder than it should have been. Was her hearing getting better?

He rolled to his other side with a grunt, and Greta eased out of the bed. She grabbed her duffel bag from the corner, and made her way to the kitchen for her pills.

She didn't need crazy lust while trying to survive. It had already inconvenienced her twice. Now her heart hurt to leave the man she kept finding herself in bed with. Stupid heat cycle. Her body and heart were convinced he was the guy for her, but her brain knew better.

She felt a pang of regret at breaking her agreement, then her brain kicked back in as she remembered his plan had been to get her blood at the full moon. And to kill her doing it. No, she didn't feel bad leaving. Besides, she'd slept with him. To men of Dayne's reputation that was probably considered payment in full.

She wondered how he'd struck the deal with her tribe. Jaden wouldn't send her to a sorcerer if she cared about her. *Duh, Greta.* And the story he'd concocted about Jaden betraying him? Way to shine the light away. Gullible. It wasn't a lesson she'd be forgetting anytime soon. Assuming she survived her birth moon.

She crept to the kitchen, wincing when the hardwood floor creaked beneath her feet. She stopped and held her breath as she waited to see if it would wake him. The house remained silent with only the ticking of the clock over the fireplace mantle breaking the stillness.

"Mrarrr."

She jumped as Mink padded in, weaving her body between Greta's legs. "Shhh! Do you want him to wake up and come in here?"

"Mrarrr?"

Greta smiled sadly down at the orange tabby. She'd have to leave Mink behind. Covert ops were clearly lost on the talkative cat.

She rummaged in the fridge until she found a slice of ham and dropped it on the floor, hoping it would shut the cat up. She poured herself a glass of water, gulped down a pill, then slipped the bottle into her pocket and took one last look around.

Tears teased the corners of her eyes. She wished Dayne hadn't turned out to be evil. She could have imagined living here with him in his quiet cottage in the woods. It felt comfortable, like home.

"Where do you think you're going?"

Her hand had been on the knob. So close. "Nowhere. Outside for some air."

"The garden is protected; the front stoop is not. You know it's not safe out there."

She turned toward him, and her mouth went dry. He was dressed in navy silk lounging pants and no shirt. He had the kind of body college students sketched in art classes everywhere. So warm and beautiful. And he and Greta fit together perfectly, in the carnal way. She wanted to run into his arms. Her knowledge of his betrayal wasn't enough for a body that still trusted him.

"It's not safe in here either," she said after a beat.

Dayne incanted something in Latin, and Greta felt the magic swirl up as the deadbolt turned. She pressed herself against the door as if somehow it would bend to her will and unlock. This was normally when she shifted. The edges of wildness intruded on her senses, but even stronger was her own will pressing back, for once choosing not to change.

"Please," she whispered as he moved closer. "You don't have to kill me. Whatever you need my blood for, you can have it. You know that."

His brows drew together. "What are you talking about?"

She wondered which would be faster, her enhanced strength, or his magic.

He embraced her, then pulled back to look into her eyes. "I'm not going to hurt you. What exactly is going on in that head of yours?"

"Stop lying to me!" She shoved him with all her strength, and he went flying back, confirming her theory that he was only human with a few fancy language upgrades.

He opened his mouth to even the odds, and she flew at him, punching and clawing. With one last burst of energy, Greta slammed his head against the wall. Dayne crumbled to the floor, and the door lock fell open, withdrawing its simple magic now that the spell caster was unconscious.

She ran into the night, her eyes adjusted, and she fought the urge to shift. No fur. No paws. The trees were coming toward her too fast. She'd never run like this on two legs before, but her reflexes came to her rescue, causing her to zigzag through the woods without even a branch snagging her top.

When she'd put a few miles between herself and Dayne, she slowed her pace. Time to strategize. Think. The tribe wouldn't be looking for her; they'd just expect Dayne had her, keeping her *safe* until it was time for the sacrifice.

She wasn't sure how long he'd stay unconscious. She might be able to make it past the border and take shelter with a wizard. Unlike sorcerers, wizards could be trusted. Too bad there weren't any in Cary Town.

Before, she wouldn't have considered involving a human; it was too risky. But she'd run out of options. At the main road, she hailed a taxi.

"633 Oak Circle."

The driver gave her an appreciative once-over. Greta smiled, glad she'd remembered her pill. Though the heat would have to be pretty bad for this guy to inspire her lust. He had a scruffy beard and was wearing flannel, for God's sake. Mother Nature could only take one so far.

"Here we are," he said unnecessarily when they pulled up to Charlee's house.

"Thanks. Could you wait while I go get some money?"

"You tryin' to stiff me, sweetheart?" His voice held a touch of menace and some darker, violent part of Greta itched to do damage. Instead, she took a breath to steady herself.

"Just. Wait."

"Fine, but if you aren't out in five minutes, I'm comin' after you."

Greta's eyes glowed golden, and she hissed. She didn't have time for this crap.

His hands shot up in surrender. "Take all the time you need, baby."

Greta knocked for a full two minutes before a bleary-eyed Charlee opened the door, her red curly hair askew.

"What's wrong?"

"I need money for the cab first."

Charlee went and got her purse. When the taxi rolled away, she asked again.

"I need you to smuggle me out of the city."

Confusion marred her friend's face. "Huh? Just drive away."

"I can't. I know this is going to sound weird, but you were on board with the cat thing and the sorcerer thing."

"Didn't that work out?" Charlee tied the belt around her bathrobe and led Greta inside.

"It was just a way to keep me in a holding cell, so no one in the tribe against this could warn me or help me escape."

"So tell me again why you can't just drive out of the city."

"You know the toll booths on all the major exit roads?"

Charlee nodded.

"Preternatural border guards."

"Why not just take the back roads? There aren't any tolls there."

"There are wards to keep therians from crossing. The toll roads exist because there are exemptions. And some species can pass at will, like vampires. Therians have to have permission to leave and when they do, they go through the toll roads and present paperwork."

"Why therians?"

Greta sighed. "I can appreciate your curiosity, but I don't have time to get into therian politics right now."

Ten minutes later she was in the trunk, blankets wrapped tightly around her, with an opening in the top to breathe through. The blankets served to dampen her magical signature. With any luck, the guards wouldn't sense it.

Charlee's gray Honda Civic rolled to a stop.

The tollbooth guy's voice rumbled just outside, asking to see ID. Greta tried to remain calm. It could be a routine check. Though she had no idea why the preternatural border patrol would do something so obviously sinister if they weren't sure they had someone trying to cross the border. If it was a false alarm they'd have to call in a vampire to do a memory wipe, and vamps hated being bothered during their prime hunting hours.

"Charlotte Devlin?" The guard asked.

"Y . . . yes?"

"If you wouldn't mind, we'd like you to open the trunk."

Shit. Greta began frantically clawing through the layers of fabric.

"You aren't authorized to search this vehicle." Love her heart, Charlee thought she was still operating in a human world with democratic rules.

"You won't remember your rights being ignored in the morning," he said. "Now open the trunk before this has to get ugly."

Greta heard the key turn in the lock, and the trunk was flung open. She was poised, ready to jump. Her claws dug into the guard's cheek as she leaped off him. He yelped and cursed into his walkie-talkie for backup.

She was panting as she ran, desperate to put as much distance between herself and whoever the guard was calling, unsure which road might lead her to some temporary haven of safety. Finally, she spotted an open window. Someone without air conditioning had left their window open a few inches, only a screen protecting them from burglars. She wondered how such people didn't end up in ditches and on the six o'clock news.

Greta ripped the screen with her claws and hopped inside. She crept into a bedroom to search through the closet, careful not to wake the middle-aged woman snoring loudly in the bed. Greta's nose wrinkled in distaste at the clothes she had to choose from. The woman was twice her size and had a large collection of dresses with big flowers printed on them. The colors were bright and spanned the entire spectrum of the rainbow. She sighed and put one on.

Sticking to the shadows, she crept outside and paused in an alley behind a dumpster to catch her breath. A gloved hand covered her mouth. She struggled, but it was one of the tribe, someone stronger than her.

"Don't scream," Simon whispered. Her eyes widened as they caught something bright and silvery reflected in the streetlight. A hypodermic needle was poised over the vein in her throat. Then the world went away.

Chapter Nine

Dayne **woke to a pounding** he was sure was coming from the inside of his skull until he opened his eyes and realized it was the door. His fingertips skimmed over the bump Greta had left. Jesus Christ, she'd gone insane on him. He couldn't figure out why she'd thought he planned to kill her. Surely, the last activity they'd been engaged in together wouldn't lead her to that conclusion.

He crossed the room in three strides and threw the door open. His expression changed from hope to anger. "You're taking your life in your own hands by being here. You're lucky I didn't kill you that night."

The ward on the door dissolved, and Jaden glided past him into the house. She was dressed for a night on the town in a long backless black gown with a slit up one side, and strappy black heels that in another time and place would have made his mouth water in anticipation.

"You never could have killed me."

Dayne wrapped his hand around her throat. "Care to make a wager?"

Jaden pushed him off her with ease and rolled her eyes. "As fun as this is, I'm not here to rekindle our old affair. Greta got captured."

This is so unbelievably transparent. My IQ might have dropped several points the first time you rolled in playing the temptress, but I've grown as a person since then."

Jaden smirked. "I'm sure."

"I think she's perfectly safe. And if she isn't, what do I care?"

"What, indeed." She shrugged and stretched out on the couch. "It's your call. But she'll be sacrificed as soon as the sun sets."

Dayne was momentarily stunned by the sunlight streaming through the windows. He shook his head and pointed at the door.

"Leave."

"I know you care for her. Help me."

He was annoyed by how well she could still read him. "Why would you give her my address in the first place?"

Jaden looked at the ground, the confident facade falling around her feet. "Because I knew you could keep her safe."

"You didn't think sending her here might endanger her?"

"It's not in your nature to harm an innocent. You know you never felt that way about me."

One side of Dayne's mouth inched up in a grin. "Because you weren't, in fact, an innocent."

"True enough." Jaden withdrew a thin lady's cigarette out of a red leather pouch and placed it between her lips. Her eyes remained on his as she lit the tip and inhaled the nicotine.

Playing the seductress had become her full-time role, Dayne mused. She didn't seem aware she was doing it. Or if she was, she was barking up the wrong tree. She'd folded her legs underneath her, and now she unfolded them, crossing them primly to allow one thigh to peek out of the dress.

Goddammit. He was going to let Jaden lead him into a trap again. This time he was killing her. The shapeshifter was far too dangerous to be left alive.

"Very well," he said, finally. "I'm sure Greta shed some fur around the house." He'd need it for the spell to find her. "And Jaden, if this is a double-cross like the last time, you die. Don't expect old sentiments to keep you safe. If you're fucking with me this is your last chance to leave quietly."

Jaden was already looking for cat fur.

"Wakey. Wakey."

Greta opened her eyes to see Simon grinning down at her. She was in a steel cage, with barely enough room to turn around. Her wrists were tied in front of her with coarse rope.

She looked down to find herself dressed in a flowing white gown, right out of a Cleopatra movie. She would have felt somewhat ridiculous if it weren't for the mind-numbing fear.

Even with her new level of control, she should have shifted by now. But she knew she'd never shift again. Greta mourned the loss of the grass and the hunt and the stars that used to blur overhead as she ran. She felt sluggish as the drugs flowed through her veins, dampening everything. Her keen sense of smell, vision, hearing, her ability to scent emotions. It was all gone. She felt . . . human.

She'd spent a great deal of time passing for human, spending more time with them than her own tribe. Trying to blend. She no longer wanted to blend; she just wanted her powers back. A tear slid down her cheek.

"Oh, don't cry. You won't be pretty for the sacrifice. No one wants running mascara in a sacrifice. Least of all, me."

"The gods won't honor this."

Simon laughed, less a villain laugh and more a *that's the funniest joke I've heard in ages* laugh. "You're adorably naive, Greta. There are no gods."

"Then, why?"

"I want Dayne dead. I've been studying magic for ages. Your power will allow me to defeat him. Then I can run this town with no threat of challenge."

"Except for the wolves." They were notoriously hard to keep in line.

He waved a hand in dismissal, "The wolves will be dealt with."

"And the vampires," she said, not sure why she was still arguing with him.

"The vampires and I share the same agenda."

A sick feeling lodged in her stomach. "I thought Dayne was involved with the ritual."

Again Simon laughed. "I think he played that rep of his a little too well. You couldn't even trust your own senses. I sent you the dreams."

She knew Simon and Jaden had tried to be subtle about their love affair while Greta was growing up. But they hadn't been subtle enough. She'd grown up thinking of him as her step dad.

If Jaden had once slept with Dayne to lure him into a trap set by Simon and the tribe, she could see where he might never let that drop. Even if it had been his idea. She'd been born soon enough after; she'd become the new plan. She didn't have to ask if Simon had killed her real mother.

"If you do this, it'll make you insane. We can't wield magic like they can. What's the point of having power if you lose your mind?" Greta said.

"Maybe. Maybe I'm already there. Slowly draining the blood out of my daughter doesn't sound like rational behavior to me, does it you?"

She looked stricken. "You can't be my father." An image of Darth Vader burst into her head. At any other time, it would have been funny.

"I'd submit to a DNA test, but I'm sure you can appreciate the time crunch I'm on. Jaden couldn't reproduce, and I wanted an heir. I figured it was tit for tat as these things go anyway. I wanted a boy, but you more than made up for it."

"I don't believe you."

"No? Then how would I know the circumstances of your birth?"

"I'll tell the rest of the tribe what you're doing. They won't participate in this stupid vendetta against Dayne."

Simon sighed and shook his head in fatherly disapproval. "You should feel privileged to give your life to make the tribe strong. Now be a good kitty, and open up."

He reached through the bars to shove a gag into her mouth, snapping the leather straps closed behind her head. He stepped back to admire his handiwork.

"Now only we know our secret." Simon held an index finger up to his lips and smiled.

"Mmhmhmpphr." Greta's scream was muffled behind the gag. She struggled against the ropes.

"It's time."

Simon picked up the handle attached to the base and rolled the cage to the door. The wheels squeaked under her. One was uneven, and she lost her equilibrium as he increased the pace. She knew he felt the moon rising.

Greta no longer could. Suddenly, losing the feel of the moon was all she could think about. The way her skin always felt warm when the moon rose, as if it were sunlight.

The fluorescent lights blinked on and off as the cage bumped down the nondescript hallways until finally they reached a door with a red exit sign over it. The sign flickered with a little electric buzz, and Greta realized it was Simon. Power already rolled off him, competing with the electricity for dominance.

Behind the warehouse was an open field surrounded by trees. In the middle of the clearing a large ritual circle had been formed with wooden logs. The small tribe stood reverently outside the circle, wearing identical long black cloaks. Beneath the cloaks, Greta knew they were all naked. This was what they wore when they shifted together.

The tribe was just twelve members strong now. In the glory days, it had been well over thirty. Jaden wasn't among them.

A crude concrete slab stood in the center of the circle. It had been built for the occasion with large steel chains bolted into it. Simon rolled the cage to just outside the circle and produced a key from his pocket.

Another therian appeared out of the darkness to help. As if Greta could fight one of them with only human strength. How could humans stand to be so weak?

She struggled against them as they half dragged, half carried her to the stone slab, so much like the one in her dream. Except, she'd dreamed of the wrong executioner. She tried screaming again. Simon was a lost cause, but maybe the other therian.

His name was Benjamin. She'd grown up with him; they'd played together. He wouldn't do this to her. Surely, he had to see this was wrong. The gods didn't deserve worship if they wanted this. Her eyes pleaded with Benjamin, but he looked away as he took a knife from his pocket and cut the ropes off her wrists.

They hauled her onto the stone slab, and the wind rushed out of her as the last possibility of escape was ripped away with the locking of the chains. It was so loud it was as if her preternatural senses had come flooding back in a rush of self-preservation. But then the sudden sense clarity faded back to the dull, drugged feeling, and another tear rolled down her cheek.

Benjamin stood stiffly to the side, still averting his eyes from her. If what was left of the tribe banded together, they could take Simon out. But none of them was brave enough to face down their bully. No one was stepping forward to save her.

Four therians came up around the outside edges of the circle, each holding a flaming torch to light the wood that formed the ritual space.

Greta's world narrowed, alone inside the circle of flames with Simon. The members of the tribe shifted and horrifying howls, like cats in heat, lifted up into the night. She could see their glowing eyes through the flames as they prowled around the edges of the circle, keeping up those horrible half-growls, half-meows.

Simon stood at the foot of the slab, holding the golden ritual knife up to the sky. The knife had been used in full moon rituals her whole life. Consecrated, sacred, and blessed, about to be desecrated by the unholy spilling of her blood for a power-crazed Were.

"Bless this sacrifice and increase my territory," Simon said, with the knife raised in a mockery of sanctity.

He made long shallow cuts in her flesh. She wasn't sure what had been in the syringe, but whatever it was numbed the pain. How long would it take? How long before she felt her life slip away like in the dream? All at once, the howling stopped as one by one the therians worked to reclaim their human forms.

Naked men and women struggled and scuffled outside the circle of flames like grotesque shadow puppets. Greta watched the bodies drop, and then one solitary therian stood still in fur, golden cat eyes staring through the flames, before backing up and taking a running leap over the wall of fire. Her claws dug into Simon's back as she growled.

It took a second for Greta to realize it was Jaden. Simon grabbed her and tossed her out of the circle. The next shape that came barreling through the fire was human.

Chapter Ten

The two combatants rolled on the ground, grappling like high school wrestlers. Either Greta was having hallucinations of what she wished would happen in her last moments, or Dayne had done something to enhance his strength. The two men rolled toward the flames, then away again. Simon caught fire, and they rolled together to dampen it.

Suddenly, Dayne flew back. Simon's hand was held out in front of him, and green energy crackled from his fingertips. He wiped a bloody nose with his other hand.

Dayne's lip was cut, but he chuckled. "Learned a few tricks since our last meeting?"

"Coming to save the girl, Dayne? You really are pathetic. You should trade up for some shiny armor. I could give you mine if you'd like. It's just collecting rust at my house."

"I'm here for my blood. That's all."

Simon shrugged. "Well, there's plenty of it."

He gestured toward Greta. She'd become listless, no longer struggling, as the blood flowed out of her into the moat around the altar. She was using all her energy and focus just to remain conscious and aware. The voices around her sounded like they were under water.

"Well? Aren't you going to take it?" Simon asked.

"You know it doesn't work that way. Another ritual is already in place."

"I'm going to have to ask you to leave my circle," Simon said. "If you stay, you might get some of the power, and then I won't have an unfair advantage later when I come to kill you."

Dayne threw a handful of herbs at Simon and raised his arms. He shouted an incantation that caused a band of light to wrap around the tribe leader, effectively binding him.

"You can't save her," Simon said. "She can't shift forms to heal. By the time the drugs are out of her system it'll be too late."

Dayne raised his arms again and looked up, shouting an invocation. The sky opened, and rain poured down. Greta closed her eyes against the downpour and shivered, her teeth clattering.

"Great plan there, hero. She can die of a chill and blood loss," Simon taunted from the bubble that trapped him. His inability to move didn't extend to his lips.

"I should have used more sage," Dayne mumbled as Simon kept babbling. "It's safe now," he said when the fire had died.

Simon struggled within the band of light. "Who are you talking to?"

Anthony entered the circle, an unmistakable leer on his face as he looked hungrily at Greta. He wore his basic black, but his blond hair flowed loose. His face was caked with blood.

"Looks like I get a taste after all."

It looked like he'd had plenty of tastes already.

Simon laughed. "Oh, this is a great plan. Vampires are entirely untrustworthy. He'll take too much."

"Shut the hell up!" Dayne said. He turned to Anthony. "Do it."

Dayne went to one side of the altar and threaded his fingers through Greta's. "He's not going to hurt you. I could have whipped up a potion to counteract the drugs, but there wasn't time. It's clumsy, but he can siphon the poison out of your bloodstream."

Anthony knelt on the other side of Greta and gripped her chin, turning her head to the side. His breathing deepened, obviously aroused by the sight of her half-naked and bleeding. He licked a long trail up the side of her neck, and she shivered.

Dayne's grip tightened on her hand. "Just get on with it."

The vampire chuckled and sank his fangs into Greta's throat. She gritted her teeth, expecting pain, but what she felt instead was intense and unexpected pleasure. He took gentle tugs, and some delirious part of her thought maybe she should have taken him up on his offer before tonight.

"Okay, that's enough," she said as the strength in her voice returned. She struggled, but he growled and continued to drink. The drugs didn't seem to affect his strength as they had hers.

Dayne grabbed him by the scruff of the neck and pulled him off her. Anthony was laughing, driven half-mad from the power of her blood. He gave a howl of pure pleasure that could have rivaled that of any therian and ran off into the woods to hunt.

She felt the change come over her as the moon warmed her skin. The chains clanked against the stone altar, and her paws easily slipped out of them. She could feel her body mending itself, healing the damage she couldn't have taken for much longer in her human form.

"What do you want to do with him?" Dayne gestured to Simon.

Greta shifted back and quickly slipped the white gown over her head. The cuts on her body were already healed. She'd been strong enough to shift and strong enough to heal, but Simon had successfully drained some of her power into him. She felt revulsion at the kindred feeling flowing between them as they shared not only blood now, but power.

"We can't let him live," Dayne said. His eyes were intense, imploring her to understand.

"No, we can't. Help me." She dug into Simon's pocket for the key and unlocked the chains bolted to the altar. The two of them worked quickly to restrain the tribe's fallen leader.

Greta bent to retrieve the ritual knife. Her human eyes locked with Jaden's cat eyes. Jaden looked from Simon to Greta, then back to Simon. Then she turned and ran off into the woods following the path Anthony had taken.

"I'll do it," Dayne said, holding out his hand for the knife.

Greta's hand shook, and she gripped it more firmly. "No. It has to be me."

Simon couldn't continue living, and she wouldn't let him die a quick death with her power coiled inside him. It wasn't fair for him to take that to his grave. She bit her lip as she pressed the blade into his flesh. She took no joy in the act. There was nothing to be gained from orphaning herself but closure.

Simon screamed, thrashed, and begged, much less stoic even than she'd been. Greta forced herself to look away. She was tempted to snap his neck and end it, but she pressed on, unwilling to let him take any small victory to the afterlife.

It was still raining when the life slipped from her father. Dayne draped his coat over her shoulders and took her back to the cottage.

She looked so lost. She kept insisting he do the ritual. He should have told her no, but he knew she sought atonement for the blood she'd spilled. Or perhaps she still thought he planned something villainous and wanted to complete her induction into evil.

He didn't have the heart to tell her he didn't need her blood anymore with Simon dead. He took it anyway, draining about a tablespoon's worth into a small, clear vial. He opened a book, chanted, and felt the magic flare up and disperse.

He performed a spell to help the flowers in the garden grow better. With her blood, it was going to be quite the botanical extravaganza. She'd like it at least. He was deeply grateful for magical languages. It was the only thing preserving an ounce of his reputation.

The first thing Greta said after the magic faded was, "What about Charlee? She tried to help me cross the border."

"She's fine. Anthony wiped her memory last night."

They stood staring at each other, and then she flung herself at him, raining kisses over his neck, forcing her tongue into his mouth. Her hands wandered down his back and over his ass. Her eyes glittered with need.

"Damn, woman, how many days does this go on?"

"Couple of weeks sometimes. Was in a cage. No pills."

She reluctantly pushed herself away from him. Dayne could see the cogs turning furiously in her brain as she realized she didn't have to stay with him; he wasn't her only option. She turned to leave.

"You're not going anywhere." Dayne felt the possessiveness curl around him as he grabbed her hand and moved it back to his backside where she'd been kneading his flesh and practically dry humping him moments before. "Let's go upstairs."

"You really don't have to do this."

"Let's go upstairs," he repeated. He wasn't sure what could be going through Greta's mind to make her think sleeping with her was a chore. He knew how she felt about the cycle, and he was sorry she hadn't taken her pill in time. He should have thought of it before they'd started the ritual.

Gift horse.

He scooped her up and carried her up the winding staircase. "Your room or mine?"

"Yours," she murmured against his neck.

Dayne took her upstairs and made love to her.

Greta woke to birds chirping outside the window and a distinct desire to shift and go chase after them. She felt sore from the previous night's fight and . . . other events.

Her pills were on the nightstand with a bottle of water. She swallowed one down.

Dayne's back was to her, and he was curled in a ball like a large, old, and well-preserved squirrel. She wanted to curl her body around his and go back to sleep; let him wake her later. But she couldn't. She was sure she'd been a nice diversion, but he'd only agreed to let her stay until after the full moon, and she wasn't about to show her naiveté by hoping for more. She was twenty-eight, not eighteen. It wasn't as if he'd professed undying love.

The sorcerer's hand closed over her wrist. "Good kitties don't run away," his sleep-filled voice rumbled.

Greta gave him a questioning look.

"Stay."

"I thought you said just until after the moon?"

Practically every sexual encounter they'd had had amounted to pity sex. She couldn't handle further pity or possible rejection. She'd become stupidly attached to him.

"You might need me to keep you safe," he hedged.

Greta bristled and jerked her arm away. "I can take care of myself. I don't need your goodwill. Thanks anyway."

Dayne chuckled and let his hand come to rest lightly on her thigh. "Yes, I saw that in action last night when you were tied down to an altar like the star of a B movie, complete with heaving breasts."

"I was not heaving. And anyway, you just came to rescue me because you needed my blood. What was the spell for anyway?" She hoped it wasn't for something world-ending.

"Oh, please. It was a huge hassle rescuing you. If I just needed blood, I could have taken one of the morbidly rubbernecking gawkers standing on the sidelines in the woods. Please stay."

"I don't need a man."

He scooted up behind her and trailed kisses over the back of her neck. "Didn't say you did. But I'm a very old man, and I now know the joys of having a pet around the house. Though in hindsight, seeing how well you listen, I should have gotten a dog."

Greta smacked him on the arm. Dayne pulled her back and flipped them so he was straddling her. He planted a long, slow kiss on her lips. "Now, stay. You took your pill, right?"

"Yes?"

"Good. I'd like to make love again without you think-ing I'm doing it out of some twisted mercy. If you want me without the heat interfering, that is."

His hands started to stroke over her flesh and she relaxed and allowed her legs to fall open. A contented purr began to rumble through her chest. This was how Greta became kept.

Part Two:
CLAIMED

Chapter One

Earlier that night.

Anthony Burgess crouched outside a circle of flames wondering if anything was worth this much drama. An ally had asked a favor. Could Anthony be persuaded to drink and siphon drugs from the woman he loved? Sure. He wasn't doing anything else exciting that night. Why not?

Between himself and Dayne, they'd killed most of the remaining werecat tribe. Dayne had used magic while Anthony had snapped necks, as well as sampled a few for himself. He listened as the sorcerer chanted and the sky opened to let rain pour down, dampening the flames and making his passage to the center of the circle safe.

"It's safe now," Dayne said.

Anthony rolled his eyes. He wanted to say, *No shit*, but the retort died a quick death on his lips as he took in the dark-haired beauty chained to the stone slab. A feral grin lit his face when he recognized the captive as Greta from the bookstore.

He ignored the bickering between Dayne and the man who'd taken her for sacrifice. The life was slipping from Dayne's true love as Anthony looked on.

She was dressed in a long, white gown, though she wasn't a virgin, and they were at least a thousand miles from the nearest convenient volcano. Thin cuts marred her otherwise perfect tan flesh, and he could feel the power pulsing out of her. He'd wanted her blood for a long time now.

"Looks like I get a taste after all," he said with a leer.

"Oh, this is a *great* plan. Vampires are entirely untrustworthy. He'll take too much."

Anthony turned and raised a brow at the villain of the piece. Dayne had trapped him in a band of energy, but he wouldn't shut the hell up.

"Shut the hell up," Dayne said. Then to Anthony, "Do it."

As if he had to be invited. Nothing could keep him from the therian's potent blood flowing out under the full moon.

Dayne went to one side of the altar and held Greta's hand, whispering words of reassurance that the big bad wolf wouldn't kill her. Anthony could hear bits of dialogue but ignored it, too lost reveling in his own good fortune.

It had been a long time since he'd drunk from a shapeshifter. They couldn't be enthralled. They were strong. They were fast. And they weren't normally very free with their bodily fluids outside their own species. It was a rare pleasure to drink from one, and this one was more intoxicating than most.

He knelt beside her, turning her head to expose her neck. It took every ounce of control not to start lapping at the cuts covering her body, but he wanted to bite, and he couldn't siphon the drugs if he just licked her like an out-of-control puppy. He had to remember this was a favor for a friend, not a buffet. His eyes scanned up to her uncut throat.

There. A clean canvas.

He inhaled deeply and trailed his tongue over the spot he intended to bite, savoring the salty tang of her skin. The scent and taste of fear, desperation. She was on the cusp of accepting her fate, yet a thread of hope ran through her. The mixture of emotions would make her blood all the richer.

"Just get on with it," Dayne said.

Suddenly, the sorcerer didn't seem so excited about the plan. Anthony chuckled and sank his fangs into the feast provided for him.

The flavor exploded over his tongue like dark chocolate with the tiniest tinge of raspberry. But the power of the blood was stronger than the taste. He gripped the back of her neck and drank more deeply, feeling himself pulled into her web of power and unwilling to let go.

"Okay, that's enough," she said, her strength returning as the drugs left her body. He growled as she fought him, refusing to let go of her neck until Dayne intervened and ripped him off her.

Anthony laughed, energized and wild from the combination of therian blood and the drugs addling his brain. He pivoted and ran through the woods while adrenaline pumped on overload through his veins. His mind was unfocused, swirling in a dark, euphoric fog.

He hadn't felt this way since he'd experimented as a newly-turned vampire with drunks and illicit drug users. Whatever had been injected into Greta's system, combined with the otherness of drinking from a therian, had intensified his appetite. And now there was only one person he wanted to go to, to slake the thirst.

Charlotte Devlin. The little redheaded firecracker who worked in the bookstore alongside Greta. She always had a sassy retort for him.

He'd spent long nights fantasizing about drinking from her, his pants growing tight as he thought of her sass turning to desperate begging. Yet, until now, he'd resisted. Even when he'd wiped her memory the night before, he'd resisted.

She'd managed to get a little too up close and personal with the world of magic, and the preternatural border patrol had called him in to wipe her memory. He'd been tempted to drink then, but he was saving her for a special occasion. Well, the night had just been upgraded.

The haze made it hard to remember the million-and-one reasons he didn't need to be doing this.

The small, gray split-level house stood in a clearing next to the woods. He hid himself in the shadows of the trees and watched as she sat on the porch swing, barefoot and in her pajamas, her fingers tangling absently in the fur of an Irish Setter.

The dog sensed him and growled.

"What is it, Sammy? You smell a rabbit?"

The wind ruffled her hair sending her scent to Anthony's sensitive nose. He inhaled deeply and smiled. The dog tugged free of Charlotte and darted straight for him, growling and barking the whole way. He'd be a good guard dog if tonight's predator had been human.

Anthony growled back, his eyes glowing, fangs extended. The dog whimpered and ran off. The vampire turned his attention back to his quarry. She felt the chill in the air and had heard the dog whimper.

He tuned into her thoughts. This one was smart. She knew something was out there, and unlike most humans, she didn't rationalize it away. Maybe he'd let her live.

Her hand was on the knob, seconds from going inside when he made his move. He covered her mouth before she could scream, and moved her inside, away from witnesses. He wanted to take his time with this one. If he could just get hold of his senses and think for a minute.

"Shhhhhh," he said.

The drugs had made him clumsy, causing him to knock over an end table next to the sofa. A lamp went crashing to the floor, and he released her for a second to get his bearings. She took a step away from him. Her feet crunched over the glass, and the scent of her blood permeated the air. If it were possible it smelled more heavenly than Greta's, and this one was only human.

Her eyes were frozen in a mask of terror, his order to be quiet unnecessary. She couldn't have gotten her vocal cords to come to her aid if she'd wanted to. She was too stunned by what stood before her. He peeked into her mind, and saw what she saw: his long blonde hair a disheveled mess, blood streaked over his face, fangs, glowing eyes, and then her mental recognition as she put the pieces together.

Unlike others before her, her mind didn't deny what she saw. It screamed, *vampire.* No doubt or hesitation. He had to admire her for that. Her pulse thudded in her throat, drawing his eyes to her jugular.

He heard the thoughts swirling through her mind as she wondered which thing she'd said to him to piss him off. She recognized him. Not just the monster, but the man she'd known from the bookstore.

In one swift movement, he grabbed her around the waist and pulled her to him, her back pressed flush against his chest. Then he sank his fangs into the warm column of her throat.

Her blood was exactly as he'd imagined it would be. Sweet and somehow spicy, like her. He couldn't get enough. He could drink her forever and was dimly aware that wasn't possible, that at some point soon the blood would run out and he'd never drink from her again.

He could feel her beginning to die in his arms.

"Anthony . . . stop, please." She'd found her voice.

He growled, angry as he regained some sense of control. This wasn't how he'd imagined this. He flung her away from him, and she hit the soft couch, bouncing once and then lolling to the side like a rag doll.

He rushed and knelt beside her, running his tongue over the puncture marks to seal them and stop the flow of blood. He continued to lick the sealed wound until the marks disappeared from her throat.

How much had he had? Her cleaner blood ran through his system, diluting the drugs from the therian. He listened to Charlotte's heartbeat. It was slow, but there. Not yet thready. She'd be okay. *She'll be okay,* he repeated to himself as he stood and paced the floor.

What have I done?

His hands shook as he collapsed in a chair opposite from her, watching and listening for any change in her vital signs.

This wasn't how he'd pictured this. He'd had better control of the hunger for centuries. He'd imagined seducing her, fucking her, then drinking from her, but never killing her. He never wanted to kill her. She hadn't been afraid of him. Until now.

Of all the humans who instinctively pulled away, who turned and walked the other direction when they saw him coming, she'd been the only one who hadn't backed down, who'd mouthed off to him, in fact. Repeatedly, and with great abandon. If he'd liked making Greta nervous on his trips to the bookstore, he'd loved trading banter with Charlotte even more. He savored the fearless way she verbally put him in his place.

It was the true reason he'd resisted drinking from her. Although he could erase her memory, he'd never wanted to see recognition and fear darken her face because of him. He didn't want her reduced to another meal, another victim.

The drugs had shifted his desires. Yes, he'd dreamed of her begging, but not for her life. His fantasies had run more along the lines of her begging him to bend her over a counter to take her from behind. Of taking her throat and drinking just as she reached orgasm, while she begged him never to stop touching her.

He shook himself back to reality. She opened her eyes then, and he could hardly look at her. Her pulse sped, still calling to the monster inside to finish the job. He moved to her and gripped her hands; she fought him until she realized the futility of the act. She closed her eyes and looked away, tears tracking down her cheeks as she waited for him to finish her off.

He listened to her mind as it raced with horrible scenarios. Half of him wanted to act them out, and the other half was horrified he'd put those fears there to begin with.

"Look at me," he commanded.

She did, her lower lip trembling. "Anthony?" Betrayal. Hurt. Fear. He couldn't stand it.

He held her gaze, putting the full force of his power behind it. "Forget. Forget everything."

Charlotte collapsed back on the sofa, and Anthony picked her up and put her in her bed. He wanted to heal the cuts on her foot, but he knew he didn't have the control not to start drinking again. Instead, he settled for removing the shards of glass from her skin and tucking her under the covers.

When he'd left her, he found a broom and dustpan in the pantry and swept up the debris from the lamp, righting the end table as he made his way back into the kitchen to throw away the broken glass. He stopped one last time by her bedroom. She looked peaceful.

He took a deep breath and let it out in a shuddering whoosh of air. It didn't matter. She wouldn't remember what he'd done. She'd go back to smarting off to him.

He'd go back to baiting her. And the next time he drank from her would be different.

Chapter Two

She woke to the sound of a dog whining and scratching at the door. What the hell? Where was she? The next question came tearing through her brain without preamble. *Who* was she? She scrambled out of bed, her sleep-filled eyes flitting around the room seeking to light on something recognizable.

The bedroom would have been calming if not for the lack of recognition. Pale blue walls, white wicker furniture, and a handmade quilt in pale blues and lavenders with a hint of spring green filled her line of vision. Fresh flowers bloomed happily in a vase on the bureau. The room smelled like a spring meadow, courtesy of fabric softener, no doubt. Her feet sank into thick carpeting.

Ouch.

She perched on the edge of the bed and lifted her foot to find several small cuts, then limped to the full-length mirror to get a look at the stranger in the room. Red hair, green eyes. She wrinkled her freckled nose. Cute. Now who the hell was she?

She was wearing a cami top and pink capris pajama pants. There was blood on her clothing, but not in a place it could have gotten from her foot. She lifted her top and turned to see if there were more injuries. She wasn't even sure it was her blood. Had she been injured in some sort of fight?

Had she hit her head? She ran her hands over her scalp, not finding any bumps. The dog continued to whine outside.

When she opened the back door, an Irish Setter with bright eyes bounded in, his tail wagging. He sniffed her, then growled, whimpered, and went to lie on the opposite end of the floor, covering his nose with his paws.

Weird.

Her eyes scanned the room until she found a purse. Jackpot. Inside the red leather bag was a leopard print wallet. She spotted a driver's license and removed the thick plastic card from the sleeve.

633 Oak Circle. Cary Town, Washington.

According to the birth date, she was twenty-six. The name didn't feel right though: Charlotte Devlin. She didn't feel like a Charlotte. She sorted through the rest of the wallet's contents and discovered a library card that read: Charlee Devlin. *Better.*

"Now what?" she said to the dog. "I don't suppose you have ID too?"

He slunk warily to her, looking as if he expected to be tackled to the ground. Charlee hoped she wasn't a dog abuser. She didn't *feel* like a dog abuser. When he reached her, she felt around his neck for his collar. The word "Sammy" was engraved on a shiny gold heart, with a phone number underneath it.

"Sammy. At least I'm a responsible pet owner. Now I know two names. I can totally build a life with this."

She went to the kitchen and filled a cereal bowl with food she assumed she liked and sat at the table with it. A light from a gray box blinked in the corner.

"More clues." She pressed the button on the answering machine, and a stilted automated voice came on.

"You have seventeen messages. First message 9:30 am: 'Charlee, where the hell are you? You were supposed to open the store. I got here, and there was a line down the block. Call me if something's wrong.' "

Beep.

"Second message 9:46 am: 'This is Greta again, you're not usually this late. What's going on? The store opens at eight. Call me.' "

Beep.

Charlee glanced at the clock on the wall. Eleven-thirty.

"Third message 9:55 am . . . "

The pounding on the door overpowered the next message which, going with the odds, was from Greta as well. When she opened the door, a woman with short pixie-cut brown hair stood on the other side, all color drained from her face.

"I'm going to go out on a limb and assume you're Greta," Charlee said.

"Huh?" The brunette paused for a second, like she didn't know what to do with that statement, then rolled ahead. "At first I was just pissed you weren't there on time because I had the craziest, scariest night of my life and wanted to tell you about it. But then it got later and later, and I got worried. It took me awhile to find someone to cover the store so I could come look for you. Didn't you get my messages? Why didn't you call? You have no idea what happened to me last night!"

"I have no idea what happened to *me* last night."

"That's the second time you've said something strange and Charlee-like, but not Charlee-like. What is going on with you?"

The redhead took a deep breath. It wasn't that she wasn't freaked. She was definitely freaked. But she was in her house, everything seemed safe enough, and whatever had happened to cause her amnesia, crying about it wasn't going to make her memory come flooding back.

"I don't remember who I am. Or anything about my life. I just know my name is Charlee because I found my wallet, the dog's name is Sammy because he has a collar, and your name is Greta because you left messages on the machine. And I just woke up a few minutes ago."

"Okay, that's so completely not funny."

"Which part? That I just got up or the memory-loss thing?"

Greta's brow furrowed. "How can you be so damn calm about it? If it were me, I'd be hiding under the bed in my fur."

"In your what?" Charlee wondered what comfort a fur coat brought in times of crisis, especially with such warm weather.

"Nothing. Never mind."

"I don't know why I'm not more upset about this. I keep thinking of it as an adventure or puzzle to solve, like a mystery. Does that sound weird?"

Greta smiled. "Not for you. I was on the run for my life recently, and you were all ready to go with me. I think you wanted to start a romance book club."

Charlee nodded. "That feels right, but now I'm at a dead end. I guess I could look through pictures and home movies if I have any, and you can tell me what you know." She paused a second, thinking. "Maybe we should take me to the doctor. Isn't that what normally happens in these situations?"

"I've got someone better."

Once they'd left the safety and somewhat controlled circumstances of her house, Charlee's trepidation grew. It had been hard enough waking in a strange house with a strange dog, both of which were nevertheless comforting. But to ride through a town she couldn't recognize as people waved to her from the streets was unsettling. She'd fiddled with the radio and had leaned her seat back to listen to music for the rest of the trip. Anything to distract herself from the smiling faces that knew her.

"We're out of the area you're supposed to remember now," Greta said.

Charlee's eyes snapped open. "You know me well don't you?"

Greta laughed. "We go way back. If it makes you feel any better it took me about ten minutes to figure out what was going on, and even then it was just a guess."

"Lucky guess." Charlee put her seat back up. They were driving through a heavily wooded area now. The redwoods stretched for what seemed like miles straight into the sky around her, enclosing the long, winding road. She rolled her window down and took in the fresh air.

A few minutes later, the car stopped in front of one of the cutest cottages she'd ever seen. It looked like it could have belonged to the witch in Hansel and Gretel, minus the baked goods as building materials. When she stepped out of the car, she heard a babbling brook and birds chirping excitedly in the trees.

"What is this place?"

"Probably my new house. My lease is up soon. But I'm not sure yet, we haven't talked about it," Greta said. "Damn, I wish you could remember because I wanted you to have full back story when you got here."

Charlee moved closer to the door and stopped. "No."

"What is it?"

"Oh hell no. Nuh uh. Take me back." Her skin crawled and goose bumps popped out over her arms. It had all seemed so peaceful and nice until the moment she'd stepped closer to the house. Now the only thing going through her mind was panic. The feelings didn't match the idyllic scene in front of her. It was a paradise, but something low in her gut screamed, *run!*

"This isn't like you," Greta said.

"Then maybe we should listen to it. Something is very wrong with this house. I don't know what it is, but I can't go in there."

"Oh! Hold on a second."

Greta walked up to the porch leaving Charlee to question the other woman's intelligence. After a brief rap of knuckles against wood, the door opened, muffled words were exchanged, and then the feeling about the house dissipated. It was suddenly as welcoming in her head as it was to look at.

Greta called from the front porch, "We're going to wait just a few minutes, while Dayne straightens the house. He wasn't expecting company."

Charlee nodded. She wondered if she was insane, but she couldn't work up the fear and warning she'd experienced only moments before. She felt so stupid now.

Minutes passed and a man came to the door calling out that he was ready for them. He had dark hair and a voice that could melt chocolate. He also had a strong jaw, and his build suggested he might be preparing to star in a cologne commercial sometime soon. Charlee raised an eyebrow at Greta.

"Don't worry, we just got together. I was going to tell you about this today. You're not forgetting anything juicy, I promise."

"That's a relief. You did good. He's a hottie."

Inside the cottage, the smell of coffee percolating in the kitchen and something decidedly cinnamon-related drifted out to the entryway. A couple of comfortable-looking red leather couches stood in the middle of the room, with a table fountain burbling away, not unlike the brook outside. Soft jazz played in the background.

"You're a doctor?" Charlee asked, noticing shelves of medical books. She'd thought Greta was taking her to *someone better* than a doctor. Not that she necessarily agreed with the assessment that someone else could be better than a doctor in this situation.

"Medical researcher," Dayne replied.

Charlee noticed Greta's brows arch upward and knew there was something she wasn't being told, but decided not to press the matter.

"If you'll come with me to the lab, I can run a few tests so we can figure out what's going on with you and how we might be able to remedy it."

"Don't memories just come back on their own when someone has amnesia?" Charlee asked.

"It depends on what's causing the amnesia."

She followed him down a hallway and a sloping, winding path until they were underground where she was surprised to see a fully-outfitted lab. He must be serious about research. Probably privately funded.

There was a medical examining table, more books, charts, and a few machines. Along one wall were computers and refrigerated cases with vials of unrecognizable liquids with little labels on them. Fluorescent track lighting hung from the ceiling, illuminating the light green walls.

"Nice lab," Greta said, giggling.

Charlee's brows knit together, not getting the joke. "What?"

"Nothing."

Dayne rolled his eyes and directed Charlee to sit on the table. He donned a white lab coat and scrubbed his hands in the sink, then returned armed with a needle.

"I'm going to draw some blood and run a few basic tests."

"Aren't you going to X-ray my head?"

He looked uncomfortably over at the machine Charlee assumed was for X-raying heads. "CT scan, but it depends on what the blood work shows."

After he'd filled a vial with her blood, Charlee and Greta went up to the main part of the house and out to the garden, leaving Dayne to work.

Lush blooms dotted the entirety of the stone-encased backyard. In the absence of trees, the sun streamed down without obstruction, sparkling off the water in the bird-bath showcased in the center. It was like another world.

The two of them sprawled on beach towels with coffee and cinnamon rolls. They talked about Dayne until he returned, causing both women to blush like guilty adolescents.

"Greta, I need to speak with you privately."

Charlee looked up. "Is something wrong?"

She wondered what awful thing he could have found in her blood.

"It's fine, Charlee. I just need to borrow Greta for a minute."

Greta excused herself and the two of them moved just inside the door. Charlee waited until their voices got louder, and she couldn't resist going to eavesdrop. She slipped to the edge of the garden and hid behind a spray of greenery arranged in a large stone urn beside the door.

"You are *not* involving him," Greta hissed.

"Please be rational. I know you don't trust him, but I've known Anthony for many years. This is his mess to clean."

There was a long pause, then Greta let out a loud sigh. "Fine, but I hate it. When will *Evil Dead* get here?"

"I can't call until after sunset, but then . . . "

Charlee leaned forward too far and the urn toppled over. She raced back to her beach towel and tried to look innocent.

Dayne poked his head out the door. "Charlee, are you okay?"

"Fine." But her mind whirred with possibilities. Who was Anthony, why didn't Greta trust him, and what kind of mess had he made?

Chapter Three

Anthony chuckled as he stepped out of the black Mercedes and felt the wards encircling the cottage. The magic didn't feel foreboding to him, but welcoming. A thick fog of darkness he could get lost in. He guessed not many vampires had been near the Wickham house or Dayne would have plugged the security hole by now.

The sorcerer hadn't been forthcoming on the phone. He'd just said he needed Anthony there immediately and that it was of the highest importance. He rolled his eyes.

Humans.

Wickham might have a longer lifespan than the rest of them and a few extra perks from the magic, but he still thought like a human. Everything was life or death and potentially world-ending for them. When you'd lived as long as Anthony had, you stopped listening to dire warnings of doom. These things usually had a way of working themselves out.

And 'lo, the world still stands. Funny how that worked out.

The only reason he'd come out to Deliverance country was curiosity. He assumed there was still poison in Greta's blood and he'd been called to drink again. His memories of the previous night were chaotic at best. Despite the temptation of her blood, if that was what Dayne needed, he'd have to find himself another vamp.

Starting now, Anthony was adopting a strict *just say no* policy. It was too close to the tournament to be so careless. He'd worked too hard. He wasn't risking a full century for one more drink of therian blood, pleasurable though it was. When he became the coven's king, he could have the stuff shipped in. Hell, he could have a personal stable of therians if he wanted.

Greta opened the door, and he couldn't wipe the leer from his face fast enough. She drew back, frightened. His jaw clenched at her reaction, far less amusing tonight than normal.

He dragged his gaze over her body. "You look fine to me. No horrible side effects from last night, I presume."

She glared. "I was against you coming here. And it has nothing to do with me."

Dayne came up behind the brunette and opened the door wider, gently moving Greta to the side. "Do come in. We can speak downstairs where it's private."

Anthony nodded and crossed the threshold.

The door to the garden opened and Charlotte entered the room, a guarded expression on her face. Anthony reached out his senses to read her, upset by the confusion and anxiety she projected. He clearly hadn't done a very good job with it. Was the woman he'd known lost for good after what he'd done? Perhaps a part of the brain couldn't forget. He ground his teeth together.

"This is the psychiatrist that's going to help you," Dayne said. "I need to speak with him privately. We'll be back in a moment. Anthony, shall we?"

The vampire had only been there two minutes and already he could tell he wouldn't like where any of this was heading. Psychiatrist? Was he kidding?

"I'm going too," Greta said.

Anthony zoned out while Greta and Dayne argued about the rudeness or lack of rudeness of leaving Charlotte alone. He absently regarded the redhead, becoming increasingly irked as she edged farther away from him.

This was all Dayne and Greta's fault. He indulged briefly in a fantasy of snapping their necks, but was brought back to reality as images of how it would affect Charlotte entered his mind. If he wanted her back to the snarky smartass who told him off, killing her friends in front of her probably wasn't the way to go.

He was drawn back to his surroundings by the dull thud caused by Greta tapping her foot on the carpeted floor. He couldn't read her, but her body language projected everything he needed to know. Her arms were crossed over her chest, while her lips sat in a determined line.

"I have other things to do tonight," Anthony said. "I don't see why we can't just discuss whatever needs to be discussed right here."

Both Greta and Dayne looked at him aghast as if he'd suggested slicing up a puppy and cooking it over an open flame.

"We're sorry to leave you alone," Dayne said, directing his attention to Charlee. "It's incredibly rude." He speared Greta with a glare.

"No, it's fine," she said, oblivious to any subtext.

Anthony winced, knowing he made her nervous, and she just wanted him out of the room. He turned and headed for the basement, wanting to get the discussion over with as soon as possible so he could escape the suffocating blanket of Charlotte's fear.

When they reached the underground level, Dayne bolted the door behind them and took a book from the shelf. He chanted for a moment then turned his attention back to Anthony. "The room is sealed; it's safe to talk. I had hoped Greta would stay upstairs with Charlee."

Greta glowered at both of them.

Anthony sighed. "Whatever little psycho-drama you all are acting out here, kindly get on with it. I have things to do. You know I'm one of the favorites to take over as coven leader, and I don't need these petty distractions. I'm not available anytime you can't handle something on your own. I'm not your personal vampire on call."

"This isn't my problem," Dayne said. "It's yours. Greta brought Charlee to see me today because her memory has been wiped."

"Clearly not well enough," Anthony said, still resentful Dayne had put him in this position to begin with. "She fears me. She never feared me before."

"Maybe she *should* fear you," Greta said.

Anthony hissed, baring fangs.

"Enough," Dayne said, stepping between them. "Her memory is completely gone. She doesn't even remember her own name. Greta tells me she had to get it from a card in her wallet. I used her blood for a spell; it led me to you. You've done it, and now you have to undo it."

Anthony had a vague sense of what had happened the night before; how he'd almost killed her, the guilt, wiping her memory. He supposed he might have done the memory wipe a bit more forcefully than was necessary, but he hadn't been himself.

"I can't undo it," he said.

Greta poked a finger in his chest, "Well, you better figure it out, buddy, or I promise I will find a way to unmake you."

Anthony retreated a couple of steps. "When did the kitty get claws?"

Dayne smiled. "I suspect she always had them. You will need to figure out what to do about the girl."

Vampires routinely took and manipulated memories. Millions of people all over the planet who didn't believe in their existence had been fed on. Many of them more than once. Every human had a different flavor, and most vampires had favorites they fed from multiple times. Unless the human was kept with them, they were never the wiser for it.

Vampire fangs could kill, but vampire saliva healed at a rate impossible outside magic. After feeding and sealing the wounds, there was no trace of physical evidence. After wiping the memory, there was no evidence at all. But no vampire had ever returned a memory. As far as Anthony knew, it wasn't possible.

Sure, he could implant false recollections until she had a more-or-less intact memory from her perspective. But it wouldn't be hers, not her actual life. Though he'd been inside her mind, read it and manipulated it previously, Anthony had never watched the full movie of her history. What he didn't know, he couldn't replace.

"I'll talk to a couple of vampires older than me and see if there is a way to bring them back, if you'll keep her here with you. I'll be back in a few days."

This was going to take away from the time he could be using to prepare for the tournament. His taking leadership wasn't preordained. The coven was large and spread over several states, and many vampires were coming in from out of town, some of them fierce competitors.

"She can't stay here," Dayne said.

"Why in the hell not?"

Greta poked Anthony in the chest again. "Because, moron, she believes he's a medical researcher. He put a big glamour over the magic dungeon here and kept it going long enough to draw blood and get Charlee upstairs. Now it's gone. He's barely holding onto the glamour on the rest of the house that covers up the magic books."

Anthony growled. If the therian poked him once more, he was going to unmake *her.* "Well, she can't be left unsupervised."

"Why not?"

"Linus would take her."

Dayne understood, but Greta didn't. Anthony figured Dayne would fill her in later if he cared to. Linus was one of his rivals and older by a few centuries. He would arrive soon for the tournament and had a particular interest in mistakes and failed experiments. Anthony wasn't aware of another vampire having taken a full memory before, but if his rival found her, he would take her for his collection.

Linus had a menagerie of girls whose memories hadn't been properly erased, girls with permanent scars because an inexperienced fledge hadn't healed them properly, girls who'd been tortured by sadistic vampires who didn't clean up after themselves. The list went on. It was his collection of other vampires' messes. He got off on making these women live in a state caught between grateful and terrified.

If Charlee was running loose, Anthony's signature could be found just as easily as Dayne had found it. Easier in fact. A vampire only had to taste a human's blood to instantly glean a full mental history of his or her previous experiences with their kind.

"Then I suggest you move her in with you," Dayne said.

"Absolutely not," Greta said. "He's already done enough

damage. I thought he was just going to come over here, reverse it, and leave."

The vampire turned sharp eyes on her. "I'm sorry, little one, how long have you lived in our world? Have you really survived this long with such a simplistic understanding of it?"

Greta changed tactics, this time addressing Dayne, practically pleading with him to see reason. "Are you really going to let him take her?"

"We don't have a choice. Linus is bad news."

Tears began to well in the corners of her eyes. She pointed an accusing finger at the vampire. "He'll hurt her. Look at what he's already done."

Anthony's fangs were out, and his eyes glowed red. He wanted nothing more than to drain the life from the irritating little therian. He couldn't believe he'd bothered to save her life. And now he had complications to deal with as a result of that choice.

"Anthony." Dayne's voice was even. The vampire took a deep breath and allowed his eyes to melt from red back to blue and willed his fangs to recede into his gums. He sent a derisive look toward the therian.

"If I wanted to hurt her, I'd hand deliver her to Linus, not insist she be kept from him. I don't want to hear any more of your tantrums."

She had her hands on her hips and was about to open her mouth again.

"Greta, don't," Dayne said. "I'm barely holding onto the glamour. I can't keep Anthony off you at the same time."

The vampire smirked.

"I don't love the plan either, but it's all we've got."

"Why can't we just drop the glamours and tell her everything?" Greta said.

Anthony growled softly. "Because it's against the law. The preternatural council will excuse your carelessness in letting a human in on our secrets because you were under duress at the time, and your life was in danger. But it would not be forgotten nor forgiven a second time.

"If I win the upcoming tournament, I'll be on that council. Something you might keep in mind. You know if she were to learn all of this, her memory would have to be wiped again. I fail to see how you, as her friend, could justify such an act when her mind has already been so damaged."

He might as well have lifted further accusations from her mind by the look in her eyes.

"I'm taking her with me and that's the end of it. Dayne is right; she's my responsibility. Should I not find a way to return her memory, I will return her safely to her home the moment the tournament ends and Linus has left town, assuming he doesn't win and become the next leader. If he does, we've all got far bigger problems than one girl's amnesia."

Chapter Four

Charlee crouched on the other side of a weather-beaten door at the foot of the stairs leading to the lab. The tall blond man—Anthony was it? They'd said he was a doctor there to help her. If that were true why had her stomach clenched in anxiety when he'd stepped through the doorway? It was the same type of fear she'd experienced when she and Greta had arrived at the cottage several hours earlier. Surely she had to know him to react so strongly.

The wooden door before her was thick with knotholes, but it was old and falling apart. There were wide spaces between the slats, and she was sure she'd be able to see through into the lab. But when she looked through the gaps there was nothing but blackness, as if a thick velvet curtain had been put up for privacy.

She pressed her ear against the door but found that did no good either. Charlee wondered if they were standing at the far corner of the lab next to the refrigerator full of strange vials, whispering about her. What was so secret they couldn't just say it in front of her? It was her life after all.

She let her legs come out from under her, unfolding herself from her crouched position, and slumped, frustrated at her inability to discover what was going on. An orange tabby wound its way down the stairs and let out a little "mrarrr," before settling on her lap and purring.

Great. The cat probably knew more about Charlee than Charlee did. She was caught up in the self-pity loop when the door swung open. The cat made an unearthly howl and skittered away into the darkness.

"Let me help you up."

Charlee's head rose to find Anthony towering over her in the doorway, his hand outstretched. He had the face of an angel, no doubt a body to match. And aside from his all-black ensemble, he appeared magnetic but nonthreatening. As enticing as the light a moth flits to. Yet every muscle in her body was poised to run, and every synapse in her brain agreed.

She crab-walked backward and used the crevices in the stone wall to hoist herself up, ignoring the offered hand. She began the journey up the winding staircase, refusing to look behind her to see if the man was following.

When she got to the living area, she went straight to the bookcase, needing a distraction to keep her gaze from drifting back to the terrifying stranger. She scanned the titles of the medical books, trying to look natural, then reached out to pluck one off the shelf.

"Don't touch that."

She turned, startled to find Dayne standing behind her. He reached over and pressed the book back in line with the others.

"Sorry," she mumbled.

It was just a book on anatomy. Maybe it was rude to go through other people's books, but it was at least equally rude to leave an amnesiac alone in a strange house and then go off to have a secret meeting about her.

The blond man sat in the center of one of the red leather couches, his arms stretched on either side of him across the back of the seat. His long legs were splayed casually, the way some men sat, as if trying to stretch to fill the entire room with their presence. Anthony didn't require a special seating position to accomplish that effect.

Greta sat on the opposite couch, glaring at him.

"Why don't you have a seat?" Dayne said, gesturing to the place beside Greta.

Not knowing what else to do, Charlee took the seat and looked down at her hands, uncomfortable that these people she couldn't remember, but must know, were deciding her fate.

"Charlotte." Anthony's rich baritone pierced the silence.

She avoided his gaze. "Yes?" Her voice came out more cracked than she'd intended.

"Dayne and Greta have asked that I put you up at my place for a little while for observation."

"Wouldn't it be better to take me to the hospital if I need to be observed?" Charlee directed her words to Dayne who still stood beside the bookcase. He looked tired.

Anthony answered for him. "You don't have insurance, and I'm a friend of Dayne's. No charge."

Charlee wasn't so sure about that. "But I don't feel bad. I've just lost my memory. Isn't it better that I be around my things so I can remember?"

Again the question was directed to Dayne, and again Anthony intercepted it. "We'll stop and get your things."

Charlee looked desperately to Greta who clutched the sofa arm nearest her, gritting her teeth. Her eyes went back to Dayne, who looked as if he might collapse any second. He seemed deep in concentration and not altogether there.

"Why can't I just stay here?" This time she made the mistake of looking at the doctor. A smug look crossed his features and sent a shiver of something she didn't quite recognize shooting down her spine.

"Come here," Anthony said.

She didn't know why she stood and walked the few feet to where he sat, still smirking up at her. She felt like an insect caught in a spider's web, unable to take her eyes off him.

He reached out and took her hand. Immediately, peace and comfort washed over her, and she knew she must have misinterpreted her feelings before. Maybe even Greta's reaction.

A new scenario presented itself, filling in gaps where no memories lived. Maybe she'd been in love with Anthony and he'd broken her heart. It would explain why it felt so right when he touched her and why Greta didn't want her to stay with him. With no memory, she must have felt more fear than the circumstances warranted.

Anthony's voice cut through her inner monologue. "That would be quite impossible. Dayne is feeling ill at the moment and needs to rest."

Dayne looked more faint than he had even a few moments before.

"We must leave now," Anthony said. He stood, pulling an unresisting Charlee with him.

"Okay." Her voice carried a dreamy lilt she barely recognized as her own. She would be fine with Anthony. Whatever was in their past, he'd put it aside to help her. She was sure of it.

During the drive to Charlotte's house, Anthony made sure he was touching her. One hand guided the steering wheel, the other rested on the seat next to her, his fingertips just grazing her thigh. If he were an ordinary man, she would find the touch inappropriate, especially coming from someone claiming to be acting as her physician. She would have moved the few inches necessary to be out of his easy reach.

It was a simple matter for a vampire to control the mind and actions of another, but to guide emotion was more difficult. The fight-or-flight instinct so ingrained in humans could not be so easily shut down. A vampire had to be touching his prey to influence emotion.

Anthony had to be careful with this one. He couldn't upset her, with later plans to erase the event from her memory. Her mind was already too jumbled and damaged. Further memory wipes could make recovery impossible.

If it's not already. His jaw tightened, angry at the thought.

He popped a CD into the player and classical music drifted out of the speakers. When he'd calmed, he found himself distracted again by the racing of her pulse. It had sped considerably in the last few minutes, though not from fear.

He caught her eyes and smiled, then tuned in to her thoughts to find she'd convinced herself the reason she hadn't pulled away from his touch yet was because she found him attractive. He'd promised himself he would try to avoid controlling her thoughts and behaviors, but emotions were another story. This he could work with.

Why do I even care how she feels? She's human. Yes, he found her amusing and admired her fire and the way she'd stood up to him before the incident, but he didn't regularly concern himself this strongly with the affairs or well-being of a mere human. No one was that interesting.

Though he did wish to avoid creating an unwanted enemy this close to the tournament. While he believed on an even playing field he stood a strong chance against Wickham, now was not the time to test the theory.

Take her, his mind whispered. He turned his attention back to the road, ignoring the insistence of his darker side that wanted to stop the car and have another taste of her blood this instant. Rain had started coming down, and though his visibility wasn't impaired, he flicked on the windshield wipers.

His eyes drifted every few minutes to her throat, his ears tuned in to the thrumming of her pulse, the sound almost dwarfing the music. He wasn't sure if it had been the drugs in his system the night before, or if Charlotte was one of those humans that just tasted better. Like gourmet chocolate after a life of Hershey.

His fangs twitched and sought to push through his gums, but he forced them to recede. Biting her now would only make things worse. The tournament was too close to introduce new variables.

There were many contenders for the title of vampire king, but Anthony was most concerned about Linus. If Linus got control of the coven, it would be the vampire equivalent of the Dark Ages. As much as his kind loved and thrived in darkness, there were limits to everything. And now Anthony had this little human to contend with, a mess Linus would love to take away from him and use to his own advantage.

Fuck. How will I pull off acting human? He'd have to control the speed with which he did things in his own home and moderate his strength. He'd have to be sure he didn't let her see how unnaturally keen his senses were. He'd have to partake in real food. He'd have to be careful not to look at her as if she were a piece of veal if she happened to cut herself.

"How did you know where I lived?"

Anthony looked up. He'd driven on auto pilot to her house. And . . . he'd have to stop doing that.

"Your friend gave me directions."

"Oh."

He heard the disappointment in her voice and shuffled through the thoughts tumbling through her mind to find their source. If Greta had given him directions, they hadn't been a couple. He felt her anxiety rise as she second-guessed her earlier theories.

Anthony allowed his fingers to press more firmly against her thigh. "Let's go get your things."

Charlee jumped as his fingers pressed harder into her flesh; her entire body was flushed. That couldn't have been an accident.

As they'd driven away from the cottage, he'd told her his full name but insisted she call him Anthony. *Doctor Burgess* felt more appropriate under the circumstances.

She was still unsure what their history together was, but she had a hard time believing he'd broken her heart, at least directly. Maybe she'd had a crush and he'd never known about it. It would explain the X-rated thoughts that had been running on repeat in her brain since they'd gotten out of the forest.

She looked up to find him watching her with an amused grin on his face as if her brain were a Teleprompter.

"Sorry, I was thinking."

She reluctantly moved, breaking the contact his hand had made with her upper thigh. She was embarrassed she'd remained as still as possible in the car, not wanting him to realize he was touching her and pull away. He had to have known, yet he hadn't moved either. Why did she feel suddenly like she was in junior high? *It's probably for the best I can't remember junior high.*

There were good points to amnesia. You didn't remember every time you'd made a fool of yourself. Or the stupid, hurtful things you'd said to others. Or love lost. It was a fresh slate to start all over on.

She looked up to find Anthony standing beside her door, ready to open it. Man, he'd moved fast. She got out of the car to stand beside him.

If she had to guess, he was about six foot four. His shoulder-length blonde hair was swept back into a low ponytail. On Fabio, Charlee found it a ridiculous hairstyle. But it definitely worked for Anthony.

She spotted the Irish Setter running toward them. "Oh." She'd forgotten the dog in all the amnesia. "I can't leave Sammy. Who will feed him?"

When the dog got closer, he took one look at the doctor, then whimpered and ran into the woods. Charlee started to go after him, but Anthony put a hand out in front of her.

"No, let me. It's dark out. All sorts of nasty things run around after sunset."

Before she could protest, he darted into the wooded area after the dog. She didn't blame Sammy; she'd felt much the same way when she'd met the man earlier. Maybe she and Anthony had no history at all. If Sammy reacted that way, it might just be a vibe he gave off, and then once you got to know him it went away. Though, weren't dogs supposed to have good instincts about people?

Before she could follow that thought trail further, Anthony appeared again with the dog in his arms. Sammy's tail wagged happily as he licked Anthony's face like they'd been best pals for years. Very strange.

Chapter Five

A ritzy six-story apartment building rose out of the center of downtown Cary Town. The building was from another era, full of old-world elegance where time moved at a more leisurely pace. It seemed out of place standing next to more modern architecture and buildings that didn't rise above three stories.

Charlee tried not to gawk at the luxury surrounding her as they finished loading her bags onto a gold-gilded rolling cart. The lobby ceilings were high, and crystal chandeliers flooded the room with light that bounced off mirrors and shiny tiled floor. Anthony hurried ahead to the elevator and jabbed impatiently at the button.

She glanced around, searching for the source of his agitation. Finding nothing unusual, she shrugged and headed for the elevator. He held the door while she pulled the cart in behind her.

"Are you sure this is okay?" she whispered, nodding toward the dog as she got on the cherry-paneled elevator. Sammy was lying at her feet as the doors slid shut, panting happily.

"I'm renting the penthouse. It's fine."

The metal doors opened on six to plush hunter green carpeting which led to a single matching door at the end of the hallway.

The penthouse was lavish, as expected, and very male. Dark colors. Thick fabrics. Not a flower or doily in sight. The windows were odd, though. They were thin, narrow panes up near the high ceilings.

Charlee wondered what kind of person would want to pay outrageous sums of money to live in what amounted to a cave with tiny strips of light filtering in. In fact, the furniture seemed to have been strategically positioned to avoid all sunlight.

Anthony interrupted the mental calculations in her head. "I sleep during the day. This was an ideal living situation." It was like he'd read her mind. But then she figured she probably hadn't been very covert about the window assessment. Between that and her pathetic attempt at eavesdropping back at the cottage, stealth just wasn't her game.

"I thought you were a psychiatrist."

"You think mental disturbance stops after the sun goes down? That's generally when it begins. I get paid a premium to work the graveyard shift. I'm afraid I won't be able to entertain you during the days, but there is a private pool on the roof. You're welcome to use it while you're here."

Back at her house, he'd suggested she pack a swim-suit. She'd assumed there was an apartment community pool she could use, but a private one for the sole use of those in the penthouse was even better. Lying on a towel and baking in the sun sounded nice right then. She wondered if he missed the sun working at night. That couldn't be normal.

She excused herself to drop her bags off in the guest room, still unsure how he'd be able to help her. Curiosity compelled her to take a quick peek at his bedroom, as well as the bathroom.

When she returned to the living area, Sammy was sprawled in the middle of the couch with his head on Anthony's lap.

"You don't have a bathroom mirror."

He appeared uncomfortable, and she immediately felt bad critiquing his choice of design. The man was letting her stay in this amazing penthouse rent-free while she tried to sort out her memories. He was giving her free psychological care to help facilitate that, and she had to commentate about his weird, short windows, and lack of bathroom mirror.

"I'm a guy. I live alone. I know what I look like. Are you ready to go?"

Charlee was startled by his abrupt tone. She glanced to the clock on the mantle. It was nearly ten-thirty. "Go? Go where?"

"To the all-night grocery. I'm afraid I don't have any food in the house. I eat out a lot."

"Whatever you have is fine. I don't remember what I like anyway."

Anthony pushed Sammy's head off his lap and rose to go to the kitchen. She followed. He opened the cupboards, fridge, and freezer. There literally was nothing there, not even so much as a tin of coffee grounds.

"I haven't lived here long."

"Okay."

The weird, anxious feeling she'd felt on first meeting him started to creep back in. She couldn't think of a logical reason for it. Maybe it wasn't Anthony. It was entirely possible he just happened to be there when she started doing this meltdown thing she did.

For all she knew, she had a history of mental disorder that hadn't taken a vacation when her memory had. Good thing she was staying with a shrink.

They'd gotten a cart with a squeaky wheel and had spent fifteen minutes in complete indecision standing in the produce aisle staring at the fruits and vegetables as if neither of them had ever eaten food before. Finally, they agreed to toss things in and sort it later. If they didn't, they'd never get out of there.

As they squeaked up and down the aisles, Charlee felt tense again. She chanced a look at Anthony and the mystery of why was solved. His jaw was clenched tightly as they walked along, anger radiating from his eyes.

"Did I do something?"

He rounded on her, his arms gesturing as he spoke. "Yes. This . . . this isn't you. You don't behave this way."

"How am I behaving?"

"You're behaving like a little mouse, and it's driving me up the wall."

He could have said a million things and each of them she would have been prepared to handle, except this. "As a psychiatrist don't you think you should be a little more understanding? I don't even know who I am. How am I supposed to know how to act? I can't even remember if I like oranges.

"Tell me, doctor . . . is that normal? I've never heard of a case of amnesia where a person can't even remember what food they like. I've had people acting weird around me all day with clandestine meetings held behind closed doors. About me, I might add. And blood drawn and the results not explained to me. Then you show up, all dark and brooding with your coat flapping out behind you like a comic book villain, and you're upset I'm not acting like me?"

She took a deep breath and continued on. "I didn't even know that we knew each other before today. But apparently so. No one has taken the time to bother to tell me much of anything except for how they're all going to take care of it." She was flushed and angry, her hands gripping the cart as if for her life.

A third shift stock boy and a college girl had poked their heads around the corner to witness the display. Anthony stood with his mouth hanging open; then he burst out laughing.

"God, that's better. Let's finish shopping shall we?"

He managed to wrangle the cart from her tight-fisted grip without any trouble and started down the next aisle, whistling. Charlee stared after him, trying to assess *his* mental condition.

It took two rolling carts to get the bags to the penthouse. Charlee had offered to pay for the groceries with her credit card, but Anthony had declined. It was probably for the best. She didn't know what kind of money manager she was. It would be mortifying if her account showed she didn't have enough of a balance to buy all that food.

"So, how are we going to do this?" she asked while they were finding homes for the groceries. Sammy trailed behind them, wagging his tail and waiting for someone to drop something he could easily tear into.

"How are we going to do what?" Anthony was reading the instructions on the red coffee pot he'd purchased. "This smells awful. This new smell. I don't know how you hu . . . I don't know how you stand it."

Charlee had been busy organizing cereal and other dry goods in the pantry. She ignored his weird comment about the coffee maker. Hadn't he ever used a new appliance before? Yeah, there was a smell, but it wasn't like it knocked you over or anything.

"Helping me. I thought the reason for my staying here was to help me get my memory back. How exactly are we going to do that? I thought memories just naturally came back on their own." The whole scenario was sounding stranger the longer she thought about it.

Anthony finally looked up from the coffee pot. "We are not drinking this swill. I'll brew another pot after this one. I'm sorry, what?"

"What do I need to be observed for? You guys said I needed to stay here for observation."

"Oh. That. Yes, well, you're very disoriented. You don't have any family locally. Greta is the only person you're really close to, and Dayne is sick. It would be a good idea if someone were with you to keep an eye on you and help you along until your memory either returns or you get oriented to your surroundings."

Charlee thought about that while she lined up the canned goods. Finally, she turned back to him. "How do we know each other? Or is there some rule you can't tell me anything about my life?" There was an edge of irritation in her voice.

"No, I can tell you. I'm a regular patron at Lawson's Bookshoppe, where you work with Greta. Her mother, Jaden, owns the store. Though Greta may become the new owner. Jaden seems to have run off. You used to smart off to me a lot when I came in."

Charlee looked horrified. "How did I keep a job that way?"

Anthony chuckled. "Oh, believe me, I had it coming. I provoked, you retaliated. It was a little game we played. We both liked it."

"Oh." Charlee felt her face growing hotter. "So that's all of it? Our only interactions have been at the bookstore?"

Anthony's eyes seemed to darken for a moment, then his face shifted back to the calm mask from before. "Yes."

A cell phone in his coat pocket rang. "Hello?" A pause. "Linus. No, that would not be convenient. I am indisposed at the moment . . . Yes, something like that. I would prefer to meet you. Do you know the diner three blocks from my building? There. Twenty minutes would be fine."

"I could leave if you need to meet someone here," Charlee said when he'd disconnected the call. She regretted she was interrupting his schedule. "Are you supposed to be at work now?"

"Fortunately, I have the week off. This was an emergency call. One of my patients. He's a bit unbalanced to put it lightly, and I wasn't comfortable having him near you."

"Oh." Charlee wasn't sure doctors were supposed to call their patients unbalanced in front of others. Wasn't that part of doctor/patient confidentiality? Or at least good taste?

Anthony grabbed his keys from the counter. "Will you be okay alone here? I have satellite television if you aren't yet ready to sleep."

She started to open her mouth to reply, but he was already out the door. *Hello, rhetorical question.* She finished with the groceries and put the plastic bags inside the pantry. She found it odd he'd not bought a single grocery item for the place until now.

He'd said he'd just moved in, but the apartment, though tidy, looked lived in. Charlee's eyes scanned the penthouse looking for details that would confirm his "just moved in" story. A few weeks worth of newspapers sat stacked in the corner. That wasn't *just moving in.* Not unless he toted old newspapers around with him, which seemed like strange behavior, even for him.

She went back to the bathroom and stared at the space where the mirror should be. No mirrors in the house. No food in the fridge. Night schedule. Furniture arranged where no sunlight could reach. Sammy freaked out. She freaked out.

"If I didn't know any better, Doctor Burgess, I'd say you were a vampire."

Immediately she regretted saying the words aloud, as if speaking them made them real, or as if someone could possibly hear her all tucked away in the penthouse of the Cary Town Luxury Apartments.

She had to have a mental disorder, otherwise why was being under observation so necessary? Maybe she had delusions. Or was paranoid. Both seemed to fit the bill. Vampires weren't real. He'd probably laugh or put her on a Thorazine drip if he knew the path her thoughts had just tumbled down.

Sammy followed her into the guest bedroom while she unpacked and slipped into pajamas. The guest room looked as if it had been decorated by the staff and had been left in its original state. Something about it screamed *hotel chic*, as if a thousand rooms just like it must exist.

Neat, orderly, even luxurious, but no personality. It looked to be designed by robots instead of human hands. There was an old-fashioned floor lamp in the corner with a red damask lamp shade, a couple of Botticelli prints on the walls, a TV, and a cherry dresser that matched the cherry from the elevator with too much precision to be accidental. A king-sized, four-poster bed with intricately carved scrollwork took up one corner of the room. No mirror. In the space a mirror would have gone was one of the framed Botticelli prints.

Charlee went through her belongings, trying to recognize something. She inhaled the scent of freshly laundered clothes and the faded perfume from a pair of jeans she must have worn once since the last washing.

She sifted through a pile of books she'd brought. Romance. Was she the kind of girl who believed in romance? Or did she read them to mock them? She didn't know.

She'd hoped contact with one of these objects would trigger a memory and some small piece of who she was would come flooding back, but it didn't. Her makeup and skincare products, her clothing, her books, all these things were the belongings of a stranger.

Charlee sighed and went to the kitchen to make a mug of hot chocolate. When she returned, she got underneath the covers, and Sammy snuggled in next to her. She dug around in the bag of books until she found the one book that might help, a thick leather volume she'd found beside her bed. Her journal.

Chapter Six

The all-night diner's blue flashing neon sign was missing letters. It was supposed to say, "Spare Ribs on Sale, half off." Instead, it said, "Spare Ribs on off." Quite confusing for anyone newly literate.

Inside, the diner was as run down as it was outside. The centerpiece was the fading Formica counter tops with retro chrome edging. Only it wasn't retro. The diner had been there, nestled underneath a giant hackberry tree when retro was *new and improved,* or at least new. Spinning bar stools that creaked when you tried to swivel on them were bolted into the floor running the length of the counter. The pale blue vinyl covering had faded even lighter over the intervening years.

The place was dead tonight, as it was most nights. The only reason it was kept open was that the varied and sundry preternaturals of Cary Town preferred to take their late night meetings here. For therians, the third shift cook, Al, made a great rare steak. For Anthony, the place was just close and convenient when another of his kind dropped in unannounced.

Even without Charlotte there, he wouldn't have wanted Linus in his personal space. The Cary Town Luxury Apartments at one time had been a vampires-only establishment. In fact, the place had been cloaked so only vampires noticed it was there.

Then management changed hands and they got the brilliant idea to integrate humans into the clientele. Perhaps with the perverse mission of having humans on tap for vampires too lazy to go out hunting, Anthony was never sure, but it seemed to him that over the years the place had gotten more human-friendly and less vampire-friendly.

Some rooms had full windows installed, though all nocturnal residents were assured it was special glass that prevented even the slightest bit of UV radiation to penetrate. Anthony still preferred the darkness and had refused the *better* windows in his rooms.

The most telling change had been the mirrors in the lobby. Vampires didn't avoid mirrors because they cast no reflection, quite the contrary. It was once believed by the superstitious commoners that mirrors didn't reflect the person, but the soul. No soul, no reflection. The villagers had been half right.

Vampires had a soul, but it wasn't very pretty. And while humans could hide their inner darkness from a mirror, vampires could not. After many centuries he'd grown uncomfortable looking into the reflection of his own eyes, seeing only the shadow of humanity under the surface of the demon.

Linus was already sitting in a booth at the back, watching the door, waiting for him. Anthony took an unnecessary breath and made his way to the table.

The other vampire was an inch shorter than Anthony, but broader. He too wore all black. He was olive complected, with his short black hair slicked away from his face. They looked like mafia hit men about to go out and whack someone. They needed a new vampire uniform.

Linus looked up from his plate of half-eaten waffles and sticky syrup.

"Anthony."

Anthony slid into the booth across from him, looking disgusted. Why Linus ate was anybody's guess. A petite brunette wearing a short pale blue dress, apron, and a silver name tag that read, *Tina*, appeared with a full pot of coffee.

Linus placed his hand over his cup. "I'm fine, thank you, dear."

She turned to Anthony. "And for you, sir? What can I get you?"

"I don't think what Anthony wants is on your menu," Linus said.

The waitress blushed, assuming sexual innuendo.

He shook his head. "Nothing, I'm fine."

When Tina had retreated out the back door for a cigarette break, Linus leaned in closer. "I thought you were feeding when I called."

"I said, 'something like that.' If I had been feeding, do you think I'd take a call from you? You're important but you aren't that important." Anthony impatiently drummed his fingers on the table. "So what do you want?"

"Can't competitors have a friendly meeting before the big tournament? These are fantastic waffles, by the way. You should try some."

Anthony just stared at him.

He pushed his plate aside and sipped the coffee. "Fine. I'm offering to make you my second-in-command, if you withdraw your name from the competition."

"No." Anthony stood, wondering if he could catch Tina out back before she finished her cigarette.

Linus placed a hand on his arm. "You know I'll win. You can live and be at the top of the new order, or you can die."

Anthony raised an eyebrow. "Or I could win. Or one of the forty-something other competitors could win. But you only see me as competition, otherwise you wouldn't be requesting my withdrawal. I think I'll take my chances."

He removed his arm from Linus's grip.

"Don't be so glory-happy. I'm creating a brave new world with or without you, my friend."

"We stopped being friends a long time ago. I expect not to see you again until the tournament."

He'd left Charlotte alone without her memory for this. Linus was barking mad. Vampires had cleaned up their act over the past several centuries. A bit less killing and mayhem. A lot more discretion. For these new efforts, no one hunted them.

They'd done so well at becoming well-blended shadows that no one even believed in them anymore. Under the current order, vampires cleaned up their messes. If they killed, they made damn sure it looked like an accident or a human cause. Otherwise, they wiped memories. The few that couldn't follow those rules were hunted by other members of the coven and eliminated.

Now, after a century, it was time for a change of the guard. Linus wanted to take them back to the former reign of terror. He wanted big, beautiful messes where his menagerie of found mistakes would be commonplace, where people knew what lurked in the shadows and their fear flowed even faster than their blood.

Anthony managed to catch Tina before she went back inside. She found him attractive, so it was easy to flirt with her and get her away from witnesses. He didn't have to enthrall her. Even in today's age, women still trusted beautiful monsters because they couldn't believe anything evil could ever be wrapped up so pretty.

Fortunately for Tina, she'd been led away by Anthony and not Linus. Linus had no problem killing the humans. Sometimes he kept them for awhile, but it usually ended in their death when he got bored. Anthony fed, erased memories, and moved on.

He couldn't be sure exactly why he did it, except that disposing of bodies was more work, and wiping memories was far cleaner. With the recent exception of Charlotte. After centuries of not killing, he'd grown accustomed and lost his taste for it. He was, perhaps, a domesticated breed now.

Like modern humans, the hunt had been conditioned out of him by the necessary way of life. Humans didn't usually hunt their food anymore either. Most didn't even grow it. Instead, they went to the store and bought lumps of red or pink, wrapped in plastic with a bargain price sticker and a USDA-approved label. It was as far removed from a living animal as it could possibly be.

A small group of vampires didn't believe in taking from human necks. Some of them fed from animals, while others got their blood from blood banks. There was much about their way of life that hung in the balance. Gregory, a proponent of the bagged-blood group, was competing in the tournament.

If he won, would Anthony become an outlaw to continue the hunt? He believed that he would. But he didn't think a vampire subsisting on bagged blood could win. It wasn't alive. There were no emotions. No vampire living on that swill could hope to be strong enough to win, let alone defeat someone as savage as Linus.

He led Tina away from the diner, down the road toward a nearby abandoned park. He felt her growing trepidation so he took her hand and smiled at her. She relaxed, and they continued on.

When they reached the park he let go of her, and her fear came pulsing back. He smiled, this time letting her fear flow over him like a summer breeze.

Emotions were like flavors. Fear, sadness, anger, lust, happiness. He'd caused and fed from each of them and tonight he craved fear. Perhaps he was as bad as Linus.

After all, he opposed Linus's way—his new order as he called it—not because it was immoral, but because Anthony believed it could upset his own way of life. He didn't want to have to hide in dank crypts like in the bad old days.

It was nice to be able to live in one place for awhile and enjoy the fact that no one would try to stake you in your sleep because no one believed you were more than a fanciful myth. Now Hollywood was on his side since vampires had risen to the status of sex symbols.

Tina started to run, but he knew this hunting ground well and was far too fast for her. He caught her and clamped a hand over her mouth to stifle the scream.

A favorite human pet's happiness or sadness was far richer than a stranger's. He inhaled her warm fragrance and sank his fangs in deep, savoring the taste of her. When he'd drunk his fill, he sealed the bite marks with his tongue and licked the tears from her face. "Shhhh."

As strange as it seemed, a vampire's bite wasn't painful unless pain was a flavor the vampire enjoyed. Pain was an acquired taste, and lucky for Tina, Anthony had never acquired it. He read in her mind the confusion over the lack of pain, the fact that she was still alive, and her internal debate over whether she was going crazy.

"No, you're not crazy."

He released her, and she edged back from him, looking around her, gauging distance and her chance of escape.

"Don't bother. You can't outrun me. I'm taking you back to the diner."

She raised her hand to her throat, unable to believe there would be no scar. "You're not going to kill me?"

He shook his head. "More trouble than it's worth. I'll erase your memory when we get back."

They were walking back to the diner when she asked the question few thought to ask him. "Is this the first time, with me?"

"No," he admitted.

"Oh."

He didn't know why he said what he did next. "When you're happy you taste like strawberries. When you're sad, like peaches and cream. Tonight, you tasted like caramel apples."

An involuntary shiver. "You're really a fan of fruit."

He chuckled. "No, that's just you. You're always fruit."

When they got back to the diner, they stopped by the trash cans where Tina had smoked her cigarette. She took another one now and lit the tip.

"Don't go anywhere alone with Linus, the other man that was with me in the diner. Don't make eye contact. Don't let him touch you."

"Why not?"

"He doesn't think it's too much trouble."

She nodded, as the realization that he was probably saving her life sunk in. "But I won't remember . . . "

"I'll let you keep a healthy fear of him."

As Tina went back to work, Anthony wondered if he would have moved her into his apartment if he'd given her amnesia instead of Charlotte, why he'd never drunk from Charlotte before the previous night despite fantasizing about it, why he'd hated her fear despite loving the taste of it, and if killing her wouldn't be far less trouble than keeping her alive.

He stood by the window, watching the waitress as she kept a good, safe distance from Linus. He'd done the best he could. If Linus killed one of his favorite snacks, he killed her. Anthony wasn't in the business of saving humans, though the redhead in his penthouse belied that fact.

He cared what she thought about him, that she'd feared him. He'd never wanted that from Charlotte.

The dog slipped from Charlotte's room to greet Anthony when he came in. The animal's earlier fear had been completely erased, no longer registering the vampire as a threat. *Stupid dog.* Then he heard her. She was trying to be quiet, but of course his ears picked up the soft crying.

"What's wrong?" he said when he reached her bedroom doorway.

She looked up, her face red from her distress. "I'm insane."

"What?"

She held a thick old-fashioned book in her hand.

"My journal. One of the last entries I wrote something about Dayne being a sorcerer and Greta being a werecat. But that stuff isn't real. If I get my memory back, will I be crazy again?"

Anthony let out a tired sigh. He didn't need this on top of the tournament. When he'd searched her mind to erase it the night she'd tried to help Greta leave the city, why hadn't he thought of something like a journal entry? She'd known about their world for several days before he'd gotten to her. He should have searched her apartment for any remaining evidence, but he hadn't. And now the mess was larger.

"I don't feel crazy right now. So how can I be crazy with my memory but not crazy without it?"

Anthony stared hard at her and lifted the interior monologue running through her head. She was second-guessing her crazy status because earlier she'd thought he was a vampire. He sifted through her thoughts about his kitchen and lack of mirror to the point she'd dismissed it all. He moved to sit on the bed and wrapped an arm around her, considering his options.

He could kill her, but then he had Dayne and Greta to contend with if she went missing. And as simple as he wanted that solution to be, he couldn't seriously entertain the idea of a world without Charlotte in it. He could erase her memory again, but that might do greater damage.

Who was he kidding? She hadn't lost her memory through natural means. It wasn't just going to come back on its own. If such a thing could happen, his entire kind would be endangered.

There was no known way to return a memory. So he was back to killing her. Perhaps he could convince Dayne and Greta it had been a mercy killing, or that Linus had gotten to her. They'd known Linus was a risk. It was the entire reason Anthony had brought her to his penthouse.

She was practically already dead. He felt as if he'd taken more than her memory. Except for the outburst at the store, this wasn't the sassy smart-assed Charlotte he adored. He couldn't restore her. His fangs itched inside his gums, begging him to finish her, to not leave a mistake sitting around, something that would fit in Linus's twisted menagerie. Or something Anthony might keep himself out of weakness.

Her head was on his shoulder, her tears wetting his shirt. She didn't know he weighed the value of her life as his fingers stroked absently through her hair. He thought of all the ways he could do it. He could drain her quickly or he could snap her neck and never have to hear the thoughts of betrayal go through her mind again, thoughts he'd suffered through the first time he'd drunk from her.

He could just *give* her to Linus.

As soon as the idea entered his mind, it was met with such revulsion he thought he might vomit. Why did she affect him this way? What made her so different that he couldn't kill her and make easy work of a complicated mess that had arrived at the most inopportune time?

"Shhhhh." He had no other choice. "You're not crazy."

She looked up. "But . . . I wrote those things . . . and earlier . . . I thought you were a . . . Oh my god, you won't believe how crazy I am. The thought actually entered my head that you might be a vampire."

"I made a mistake."

The strange admission stopped her crying for a moment as Anthony got up and went to the closet. He pulled out a large mirror and took down the Botticelli print. "Close your eyes."

Charlotte looked at him, hesitating for a moment. Then she did what he asked, and he exchanged the print for the mirror.

"Keep them closed." He took her hands and led her to face the reflective surface, holding her back firmly against his chest. "Open them."

Chapter Seven

Anthony wrapped his arms around her, and immediately Charlee felt the peaceful calmness she was beginning to associate with him. Safety. Comfort.

The feeling was short-lived. Upon opening her eyes, her first instinct was to scream. Anthony's hand came over her mouth to silence her, and she bit down. Still, he held tight.

His eyes met hers in the mirror. "Do not do that again."

She nodded and whimpered against his hand. Something dark and twisted, black with silver waves, rippled over his skin. His face was demonic; his eyes glowed red. His teeth were wolf-like. She saw the wicked-looking claws resting against her cheek but only felt the softness of his fingertips.

She turned in the tiny amount of space he'd given her to look up into his face. When she did, she saw Anthony. Beautiful face, crystal blue eyes, long blond hair. She whirled back to face the mirror and was greeted again with the demonic visage. If she looked hard, she could still see Anthony. But the demon overpowered his reflection, making it clear he was more monster than man.

"If I remove my hand will you promise not to scream?"

She nodded, and he took his hand away from her mouth. "Which one is real?"

"Both. The human face you see is more or less what I looked like as a human. Just a bit more perfect. The other is what joined me when I was turned. People see a flicker of it before a bite. My eyes glow and my fangs come out, but only the mirror reveals the whole picture."

She felt suffocated, as if there was no air left in the room to breathe. "Why do you keep a mirror in the closet?"

He held her gaze with his. "Because I used to love the look on your face right now." He bent his head while Charlee watched his reflection and trailed his tongue lightly over her throat. He murmured against her skin, "You've got to calm down. You smell so fucking good."

She closed her eyes and leaned against his shoulder. Her thoughts flitted back and forth like a schizophrenic butterfly torn between terror she might only live a few more minutes and an odd certainty that wasn't the case. The hand that had been over her mouth moved to stroke through her hair.

"You're lucky I'm not hungry."

Charlee blushed as he stepped away from her. She'd stood in the arms of a predator without the will to even scream once he'd caressed her throat with his tongue. It seemed an unnecessary added perk. He already had too many advantages. She swayed on her feet, but before she could collapse, a chair was slipped beneath her.

Anthony turned the chair to face him and made himself comfortable on the bed.

"You're the reason I can't remember my life." The words came out dull and flat when she said them, a statement of fact, as if she'd mentioned a bill she'd gotten in the mail or a bank statement. "Can you fix it?"

Anthony looked down at his hands. "No."

"So that's it. It's just gone then. It's like I was born yesterday." She tried to think what that meant. No hope of remembering the past, only being able to move forward. A clean slate if she'd been bad, but a waste if she hadn't been. Somehow she doubted there was much she wanted wiped away.

"Yes. That's right."

She'd known the answer before he said it, but still the loss washed over her. Family, friends, memories she'd never know. Did she have parents? Brothers? Sisters? Where had she grown up? What was her childhood like?

Greta could help put some of the pieces together and lead her to others who could fill in the remaining gaps, but none of it would ever belong to her. Not really. It could be anybody's story and it wouldn't make any difference.

"I'm sorry."

Charlee looked up. He *did* look truly remorseful. She couldn't resist stealing a glance at the mirror for a second opinion, but the demon's eyes revealed much the same as Anthony's human face. Guilt and regret.

"Why?" If vampires erased memories, surely they did better and more localized jobs of it. No one else seemed to be running around with amnesia. Not that she'd had much of a chance to see the city, but Dayne and Greta had at least behaved as if her circumstances were peculiar.

"What you said about the last pages of your journal about Greta . . . A few days after that, you tried to help her escape town. You failed, and I was called in to erase your memories of the preternatural world. Later Dayne asked me to siphon drugs from Greta's body. Her blood affected me, twisted my desires." He looked away as if unable to stand the scrutiny and judgment behind her gaze.

"I came to your house. I terrified you and drank from you, and afterward I wiped your memory. I couldn't stand for you to remember me as a monster when you'd never feared me before. I took too much."

Charlee stared at her hands, letting his words settle around her. "I don't know what to say. Why did it matter to you? I'm sure I'm not the first person to be scared of you." She couldn't imagine anyone who wouldn't find Anthony terrifying.

He shrugged. "I saw you several days a week at the bookstore. I liked your spirit. You made me feel like a person, and I missed that feeling. You smell and taste so good when you're afraid, like the finest wine. But at the same time I hate it from you. I don't want you afraid of me."

"So you're not going to kill me?"

"It would make things easier."

Charlee's lip trembled, and she fought to stop herself from crying. She still wasn't out of the woods with him. She flinched when he reached toward her, but he only rested his hand on her knee, sending a sense of calm through her. It wasn't real, but she'd take it.

"No, I won't kill you."

"Then I can go?"

"I didn't say that."

"Dayne and Greta won't let you keep me here against my will."

"Is that why they let me take you? They know what I am."

At least the mystery of why Greta didn't want her to go with *Doctor* Burgess was solved. "You're not a doctor are you?"

He shook his head. "I'm somewhat relieved you know. I have too many things to worry about to have to hide my nature from you as well."

"If I'm allowed to know, then why take my memory after I helped Greta?"

"You're *not* allowed to know. But since you're my guest at the moment, it doesn't much matter. I've taken responsibility for you until after the tournament, at which time I'll erase your memory again and send you on your way."

Anger gathered from somewhere deep inside her at his flippant plan. "Well, I'm glad you've got it all worked out."

She stomped past him to one of her suitcases and retrieved a swimsuit. The only place she knew to go to get away from him that he would allow her to go was the rooftop. And she wasn't altogether sure he'd allow that.

She was afraid he'd follow her, but after five minutes with no sign of him, she felt safe to change clothes.

Charlee dove into the water and began swimming laps, making smooth strokes, even as her thoughts grew more turbulent. Keeping her prisoner until after *the tournament* was he?

He must not be too put out about her amnesia if he planned to take her memory again. Then just what? Deposit her on the doorstep of her house without any clue of what she should do next? If Dayne was a sorcerer why couldn't he just magic her memory back?

What bothered her most was that she'd had feelings for the vampire. Her journal had made that painfully clear. She dove under the water as if by doing so she could escape the words she'd read in her own handwriting, words she couldn't now erase from her mind.

Anthony was at the bookstore today. He's such an ass, but he's an ass in that way I like. I swear to god, telling him off is like foreplay. The crush caught me off guard but now I think it's developing into something more. Is that possible when we've never kissed?

Or maybe I'm reading too many romance novels. Maybe I need to get out more. I keep thinking he's going to come in and sweep me off my feet.

He looks at me like I'm a main course. So why hasn't he made a move yet? Am I just imagining all this? He makes me feel light-headed. I haven't felt this way since I was fifteen with that stupid high school boy that we so aren't going to talk about here.

I shouldn't have told Greta, though. She said, and I quote: "Anthony is not a good guy. Trust me, you don't want to go there."

A freaking vampire. Yeah, that pretty much qualified as *not a good guy*. She broke the surface of the water in time to hear the metal door clang against the outside brick. Anthony emerged wearing a pair of black swim trunks. His face was tight.

Charlee looked up, afraid, but intent on masking it with annoyance. "Did no one ever introduce you to the broad spectrum of wardrobe color choices?"

"That's my girl." He smirked and got into the pool.

She tried to tamp down the flutter in her stomach at hearing him reference her as *my girl*. "Did you come to check on me? Did you think I'd jumped off?"

He smiled. "We didn't finish our conversation."

"It seemed pretty finished to me. 'You're my prisoner until after the tournament, cue evil laughter.' What tournament?" Now hardly seemed the time for sports.

"That would be the unfinished part. A tournament will be held in a few days which will decide the coven leader for the next century."

"Huh?"

He grimaced. "King of the vampires. In this country, at least. Competitors are arriving in town as we speak. My most dangerous opponent would take you if he knew about you."

"And why exactly is that?"

"Because you're a mistake, and he collects them. He doesn't have anyone with full amnesia in his collection. He'd use you to get to me."

"Why would it get to you?"

"Oh, for fuck's sake. Because I love you."

Charlee looked up sharply, *No, please no. Don't say that, not now.* Anthony's face held the same shock she knew hers did, as if it were as much a revelation to him as it was to her. An awkward silence descended. Thunder rolled in the distance, filling in the spaces where the words had died on their lips.

Seconds later the rain poured down on them. Anthony was out of the pool so fast he was a blur, then his hand was outstretched to help her out of the water and back inside.

The sky lit up through the weird thin windows, and the penthouse was flooded in darkness. She heard his footsteps recede into the bathroom. Moments later a thick towel was wrapped around her.

Her teeth chattered as he picked her up and carried her through the darkness. She'd lost sense of what direction they were going in. When she landed on a soft bed, she didn't know if it was his or hers. Her head was swimming. He'd said he loved her. They'd never even been on a date. How could he love her?

Maybe he could. They'd known each other for months. And hadn't her journal reflected a similar feeling growing inside her? Could you love someone before you really knew them? If you could read their thoughts and sense their feelings? If you'd drunk their blood?

Hadn't she suspected he had some sort of romantic feeling for her when he'd said the thing about not wanting her to fear him when he didn't seem to mind it from others? Her mind kept chanting at her, *He's a vampire. He stole your memory. He stole your life.* Could any feelings she might have developed in that other life make up for what he'd done and what he was?

She was under the blankets now still in her swimsuit, though she had no idea how she'd gotten there. In the dark with her mind so jumbled, she couldn't catalog the physical sensations around her.

She felt Anthony curl his body around hers. She wanted to protest but couldn't find the words.

"Relax, Charlotte. I'm just warming you up."

There were benefits to being in bed with a mind reader. She blushed as that thought fully bloomed in her mind. Anthony chuckled behind her.

"Get out of my head."

The warmth of his skin had shocked her. She'd expected cold and clammy, like death, like a vampire.

"I recently fed. I'll be cold again soon. Enjoy it for the few minutes it lasts."

She tensed, thinking of the life he might have taken.

"I didn't kill her."

"I swear to God, Anthony, if you don't get out of my head . . . "

"You'll do what?"

She sighed. "I'll be really annoyed."

"I quiver in terror."

She couldn't stop replaying the spontaneous love confession in her head. Anthony hadn't repeated the sentiment, nor had he denied it. And since he couldn't seem to give her brain any privacy, he had to know it was running on a loop in her mind. Yet he ignored it, forcing her to say the words aloud.

"Did you mean what you said out there?" She didn't know why it mattered. She could never love him, not if a thousand years passed. Not now. Still, if he felt for her, she might survive longer.

"I don't know. I've never loved anyone, not since I was turned. I didn't know I could. I can honestly say I'm fond of you. I'm intrigued by you. I find you attractive. But I'm not sure why I used the word love."

Well, that cleared things right up. She wasn't sure if he said it to freak her out less or because it was true. She had to admit, she *was* a little less disturbed by him being fond and intrigued and attracted. Especially since when he said it, he didn't sound like he had a shrine built to her or anything.

"I don't want to be a vampire," she blurted into the stillness. It seemed like a good thing to get out of the way up front, in case he'd had any intentions in that direction. She didn't want living inside her the same thing that rippled beneath Anthony. It had unnerved her to see that thing looking out at her from the mirror. Though, if possible, the demon seemed fond of her too.

"I hadn't intended to turn you into one."

"Okay."

As long as that was clear.

Chapter Eight

When the sun rose, the mystery of which room he'd taken her to was revealed. His. Small bits of light from other parts of the house trickled into the master bedroom, but the windows in his room had been blacked out with paint. She wondered if the management knew about that.

He looked so peaceful in sleep, almost innocent. She'd laid her head against his chest most of the night listening to his slow heartbeat. It wasn't what she'd expected from a vampire, though he appeared dead now. The stillness of his body was interrupted every few minutes as his chest rose and fell.

"Anthony." No response. Sammy's ears perked from his position lying across the vampire's stomach.

He was like a hibernating bear, and it struck her how completely helpless he was in sleep. He'd said he was immortal and not all the myths were true, but sunlight would obviously hurt him, judging from the blacked-out windows. And she didn't know of anything that would survive decapitation, no matter how bad ass it was.

He'd said she was only his *guest* until after the tournament. The seething anger that had curled in the pit of her stomach the night before fluttered to life again at the memory. *He almost kills me, then takes my memory, and now I'm his prisoner? Maybe he could chop off my hands or something later to round out the week.*

Something inside her screamed to kill him. He was dangerous. There was no way to know what he'd do in the next few days or if he'd keep his promise. And if he did erase her knowledge of the preternatural world and return her to her home after the tournament, what then?

He could come to her and feed from her and do whatever he wanted and then just erase it from her mind. He could violate her in any way he chose, and she'd never even have the knowledge of it. She still found him as attractive as she'd found him in the pages of her journal, but he was the enemy.

She went to her room and returned with a silver cross. His hand was splayed on the pillow next to his face.

Without stopping to think, she pressed the pendant against his skin and jerked it away, disgusted when smoke rose off his hand. Sammy whimpered and darted out of the room, making her suddenly ashamed of her behavior.

She dropped the necklace on the floor and backed away. What was wrong with her? She'd slept in the vampire's arms all night, and he hadn't made a move to harm her. As far as she could tell, aside from giving her amnesia, which he hadn't meant to do, and drinking from her—and hey . . . *vampire*—he hadn't threatened her.

She just needed to know what would work against him. If he were to turn on her, how could she protect herself from someone so strong? How could she survive him?

The burn flared bright red against his pale skin. She bent to pick up the cross and slipped it into her pocket, then paced back and forth, eyeing the burn. How long would it take to heal? Would it heal before the sun set? And if not, what then?

She shuddered to think what he might do if he found out she'd been experimenting with ways to end him while he was incapacitated. He'd trusted her not to hurt him during his sleep. And she'd betrayed that trust.

A voice whispered in her mind, *The motherfucker erased your entire life. He was out of control. He could have killed you that night. He didn't care. He's not the victim here.*

A tear slid down her cheek as she looked down at him. "I'll never love you." She had to hear herself say it out loud. He had ridiculous amounts of power, and he could get inside her head. "I don't want this."

The vampire slept on, oblivious to her words. She reached into the pocket of her jeans and clutched the cross, then released it, comforted by its presence. She had to get out of there.

On her way through the lobby, the front desk clerk stopped her. "Ms. Devlin."

She was shocked he knew her name. "Yes?"

"You're Ms. Devlin staying in the penthouse with Mr. Burgess?" He looked to be in his late forties. He was wiry with thinning hair and glasses perched on his nose. An olive green sweater vest was buttoned over a linen shirt.

She hesitated. "Um, that's correct."

"Mr Burgess left instructions for you to be given this, and also to remind you to be home by dark." He paused for a second and met her eyes. "He would find you, you know."

Charlee knew the person behind the desk couldn't possibly be a vampire, as he wasn't hibernating. But what exactly he was, she couldn't be sure. The look in his eyes was too knowing. She wondered why, if he suspected what Anthony was, he didn't just go upstairs and kill him while he slept.

She took the crisp ivory envelope from his extended hand and opened it. Five new-from-the-bank one hundred dollar bills. She blushed, wondering if the front desk clerk thought she'd done inappropriate things to earn it. She quickly shoved the money back inside the envelope.

He continued to give her that smug, knowing look.

"You don't care if he hunts me down?" She asked.

"What matter is it to me?"

"You know what he is?"

"Of course. Vampire."

A young couple milled about the lobby, and she looked for their reactions but found none. They hadn't heard. Or else they themselves lived with or were guarding vampires.

This conversation was becoming surreal. "What are you?"

"A guardian."

"You're human?"

"No," he said very slowly as if talking to the mentally deficient, "A guardian. I look human, I can walk around during the day, but my entire purpose in this realm is, as it sounds . . . to guard. So I wouldn't go getting any funny ideas, Ms. Devlin."

Charlee slipped the envelope into her purse and backed out the door into the bright sunlight, for the first time unsure she was safe in the day.

She wandered down the street taking in everyone that passed. Probably there weren't hundreds of guardians running around during the day. Right? And they seemed mostly passive anyway. Just . . . guarding, as he'd said. What else?

How many witches, wizards, and sorcerers were there? How many werecreatures like Greta? She couldn't help wondering if every person she passed was as human as they appeared, or if they were something else altogether.

She'd spent the previous day thinking sooner or later her memory would return and everything would be back to normal, whatever normal was. She was now faced with being a twenty-six-year-old baby in a world much scarier than the one she was supposed to know. She knew who the president was and all about current events; she just couldn't pull a personal memory out of her head.

Was this what death was like? All that time spent scurrying around doing things, only for it all to be gone with no matter that it had happened?

"Watch where you're going!" Charlee looked up to find herself nearly colliding with a teenage girl in all black with a nose ring and bright pink hair.

"Um, sorry."

The girl continued on, then Charlee said, "Hey wait, do you know where Lawson's Bookshoppe is?"

She turned, an annoyed expression painted on her face and pointed down the street. "Five blocks that way."

"Thanks." But the girl had already disappeared into Anthony's building.

Charlee had planned to track down Greta, but she couldn't stop herself from following the strange girl back inside. The guardian at the front desk merely raised an eyebrow, then went back to the stack of papers in front of him.

She ran toward the elevator. "Wait!"

One scuffed *Doc Martin* slid between the closing doors.

"Thanks," Charlee said when she got in.

The elevator's other occupant nodded and moved to the corner, leaning against it with her arms crossed, chewing gum. On closer inspection she looked to be early twenties. Not much younger than Charlee. She'd taken on a bored and disaffected look, her eyes going to the little numbered circles, watching them light in turn as the elevator lurched upward.

"Do you live here?"

"Do you?" She retorted.

"I, I'm staying here for a few days. In the penthouse."

The girl raised an eyebrow, then let out a low whistle. "Nice. I'm staying on the fifth floor. We're just in town for the tournament."

"So, are you a . . . guardian?"

The girl snorted. "Haha! Yeah, no. Though I guess I serve the same purpose. I'm with Gregory Michaels. He's competing. I'm Jane, by the way."

She'd worked hard to live above the plainness of her name. She was dating a vampire.

"How old is he?"

"Like a hundred and eighty. Or something. They preserve well don't they? I keep begging him to turn me, but he gets all emo about it and says in this dark brooding voice, 'Trust me, you do not want this curse.' Yeah, sure. Curse. Let me know when the curse part kicks in, right?"

The elevator stopped on five. "You want to come in?" Jane asked.

"Sure," Charlee said, not at all sure. But if Jane's vampire was anything like Anthony, he wouldn't be getting up anytime soon.

"Help yourself to anything in the fridge."

Charlee dropped her purse on the couch and went to the kitchen. She let out a startled cry when she opened the refrigerator door. Stacked in neat rows on the top shelf were clear plastic medical bags of blood.

Jane poked her head into the room. "Oh, yeah. Guess you're dating a real vampire. Greg won't drink straight from the source. He says it's immoral and that vampires could be out of the coffin if they all bagged it."

So was Charlee staying with a *bad vampire* then? Despite wanting to kill Anthony less than an hour ago, now that she was labeling him as such, she couldn't quite get behind it. Like maybe he wasn't goodness and light, but surely he couldn't be the worst out there either.

"I'm not dating him." She reached behind one of the bags for an apple and a jar of peanut butter. Not exactly breakfast food, but it looked good.

"Oh. Sorry. So you're like a pet then? Does your master have other pets?"

Charlee whirled around at that. Was this chick serious? The pink hair dye must have rotted out her brain. *Pet? Um, no.* "I'm not his pet." *Gross.*

She got an awful image of a glassy-eyed woman with multiple bite marks wearing lots of red and black latex. She was most definitely not Anthony's pet. He hadn't even bitten her, except for that one time she couldn't remember. Well, probably the one time. Damn, another point for *not that incredibly evil.*

"You're his what then?"

"I'm not his anything. I'm just staying with him for a few days. Look, could we not talk about Anthony?" She'd found a knife and cutting board and busied herself cutting up the apple.

"Anthony?"

The tone of Jane's voice was so sharp, Charlee missed and sliced her finger. "Ow!"

"Damn, Anthony. He's on Greg's list of top five bad guys that should *not* get into power. I hear about it on a nightly basis."

Charlee bent over the counter, holding her hand with her eyes tightly shut. When the initial pain subsided, she rinsed her finger under the tap, hissing as the pain flared to life again. Then she wrapped it in a damp paper towel and took her apple and peanut butter to the table.

"Holy crap!" Jane squealed a few minutes later. She looked up guiltily from where she was bent over the spilled contents of Charlee's purse. "I went to sit down, and it fell over. And holy crap this is a bunch of money. Like hell you're not his pet. What did you do to earn this?" She looked up, accusation in her eyes.

Charlee was sure her face was completely blanched, and was even more sure that if Jane, Miss My-boyfriend-is-a-vampire thought she'd done special favors for the money, the guardian probably thought she had too. Just great.

And judging from her attire, who could she blame? Apparently she really dug the slutty look. It was all that had been in her closet. She was wearing hip-hugging blue jeans and a low-cut red halter top. The outfit said *come bite me.*

She'd added a pair of sparkly silver flip flops to try to tone it down some. The effort had obviously failed. Probably no one's eyes were making it all the way down to her feet.

"Man, I'm sorry. I didn't mean anything by it."

She took a deep breath. Jane was nice enough, though she clearly had a couple of issues. Charlee could see immediately why she'd thought the woman was younger than she was. The punky look she sported would fit better on a high school student. Her manner of talking and walking all broadcasted a lack of maturity most women in their twenties had outgrown. She wondered what had caused Jane to become so stunted.

"It's no problem. He just gave me some money. I have no idea why. I didn't *earn* it as you put it. I said I'm not his pet."

Jane nodded. "Not his pet. Got it. We could get out of here and go shopping if you want?"

Why not? Everybody seemed to think she was his little concubine. She may as well be compensated for the embarrassment.

Chapter Nine

Anthony **rolled over, jolted from** sleep as a wet slobbery tongue explored his face. He shoved the dog off him and sat up groggily. Why was he still tired? Vampires weren't tired when it was time to get up. They just got up, wide awake. Unless they'd been injured.

The clock on the bedside table said 8:05. *Shit!* Anthony leapt out of the bed and ran a hand through his hair.

The sun had set over an hour ago.

"Charlotte?"

The penthouse was silent.

He was starved. What the fuck? He'd overslept; he was tired; he was hungry. This hadn't been normal since his fledge days. "Charlotte!"

Her bedroom was empty. He caught his reflection in the mirror, the demon rippling over him, as a glowing red light emanated from his hand. He looked down to see an ugly red cross-shaped burn. Charlotte? Would she do that?

He didn't know who the hell else would have done it. He tried to think why, other than the obvious *vampire* part. Maybe he would have been better off erasing her memory. It wasn't as if the problem could get any worse, and it wasn't possible for it to get better as far as he knew.

The hunger burned and writhed like a living thing inside his belly.

He had to find Charlotte. He'd told her he loved her. How could he have said something so stupid? What was he thinking? He couldn't love her. He was fond of her, yes. But not love. That was insanity. He quickly threw some clothes on and headed for the elevator.

He was sure he'd be able to track her; he just hoped it wasn't too late, that something else hadn't gotten hold of her first. He could still smell her scent in the hallway. She had to have just been there. Then he heard her laughter and let out a breath. She was in the building, one floor down. Excellent.

When he reached apartment 5D, he banged on the door. "Charlotte! Open this door."

There was a scuffling sound and sharp whispers. He could smell Charlotte's fear, then heard Gregory say, "It's all right, dear, you don't have to go with him. You're safe here."

Like hell she could stay with the bagged-blood reject. Anthony banged on the door again. "This is not your business, Gregory. How would you feel if I were holding your girl hostage?"

The other vampire spoke in a placating tone through the door. "She is not a hostage; she's perfectly welcome to leave at any time."

"Open the door or I'll go to the front desk and get a key."

"How very civil of you. Wouldn't want to rip the door off its hinges in front of the girl."

Anthony gritted his teeth, holding back a growl. He could feel his fangs pushing through the gums, his hunger tearing through him. He kicked the door in and made a beeline for the refrigerator. He took a bag of blood and ripped through it with his fangs, gulping the cold liquid, then a second and a third.

Finally, he stopped and wiped the blood from his chin with a dish towel. "I don't know how you drink this shit. I think I might vomit."

Gregory stood in the kitchen doorway, Charlotte hidden protectively behind him with a second girl that looked like a vampire groupie. Boy had she picked the wrong vamp if that was her thing.

Gregory gaped. "Why . . . why . . . " He pointed at the blood bags lying on the table and the small drops of blood that had found their way to the linoleum.

"Why . . . why . . . what? I was hungry. Starved, in fact." He tossed a glare toward Suspect Number One for the cause of his hunger. "Charlotte, let's go."

She stayed hidden behind Gregory. "I don't know if I should."

Anthony rolled his eyes. "Has he told you why I'm the most evil of all the evil vampires except Linus?"

She hesitated, "Yes, but . . . " He caught her looking at his hand. It wasn't as if there had been any question who'd done it, but the confirmation she'd tried to harm him when he'd been resting, rankled. He would never have done the same to her.

"I explained to you last night why you had to stay at the penthouse. Gregory wouldn't be able to protect you."

The other vampire dropped into a fighting stance and kicked out. He may as well have been a human the way he telegraphed the movement. Anthony reached out and grabbed his ankle, twisting until he fell to the ground. He bent and wrapped his hand around Gregory's throat.

"As I said . . . he wouldn't be able to protect you." Then to Gregory, "You may as well withdraw from the tournament now. You have zero chance with your diet."

He stepped over the prone vampire, and Charlotte backed away. The anger over the burn receded. He held up his hand and she shrank back as if he might hit her.

"It's already starting to heal. It'll be fully repaired when I drink from a source." She moved her hand to cover her throat. "Not you," he clarified. "Now, let's go."

She hesitated for a moment, then grabbed her bags and preceded him out the door to the elevator. He took a deep breath and counted to ten.

He'd wanted Charlee to be taken care of if she needed anything during the day. The money he'd left for her was a drop in the bucket, but the fact she'd go shopping with it, after burning him . . . His fangs started to press through his gums again.

The metal doors closed behind them as he put the key in next to the number six and pressed the button. Halfway between floors he stopped the elevator and turned to face her, his arms crossed over his chest.

"Why weren't you home before dark?" he demanded.

He watched the confusion cross her face. That wasn't what she'd been expecting. He watched the thoughts tumble through her mind. She'd been scared about the consequences for burning him.

"Forget my hand. I told you it will heal. I'm pissed off about it, yeah. I trusted you. I didn't enthrall you because I didn't think you'd do something like this. Maybe I'm getting foolish in my old age. I told you to be home by dark."

"I was in the building." Charlotte crossed her arms protectively over her chest, her lips drawn down in a petulant pout.

"But not in my home, not where I can keep an eye on you. In fact, you were with one of my competitors. You're lucky it was that pussy, Gregory and not someone you'd have to worry about, like Linus."

She lifted her eyes to his, all thoughts of self-preservation tossed aside. "I'm not your pet." Behind the brave facade was the question, wondering if that was how he'd classed her.

He made a sound of disgust. "Vampire groupies. Don't listen to anything that girl has to say. No, you're not my pet, Charlotte. If you were my pet, you'd be enthralled. And if I'd trusted you enough to leave you to your free will, you would be in severe trouble for this."

He raised his hand again, displaying the burn mark. The bagged blood working through his system had healed it a bit further but not enough.

He leaned in close to her and inhaled. He nuzzled her throat, his tongue creeping out to trail down the side of her neck, the tips of his fangs barely skimming her tender flesh. Then he was on the other side of the cramped elevator. He gripped the railing for support and looked up, shocked. She held a cross in front of her, her hand shaking.

Her other hand covered the place where his fangs had almost penetrated, as if by covering it, he could no longer smell the blood rushing by. "You said, not me."

"Put it away, Charlotte."

"And be dinner? Gee, I'm thinking no."

"Charlotte. I didn't mean . . . It's a small enclosed space."

"Then you should have waited 'til we got out on your floor for this discussion. Start the elevator."

He inched over to push the button that would take them up to six. The air sizzled around him, charged with an unpleasant electricity caused by the close proximity of the cross. She had a point about talking upstairs. He'd been determined to use her fear of him against her so she'd know how serious he was about her being in by dark.

The door slid open. "Put that away," he said, still eyeing the cross she held out like a protective shield. With a holy object mere feet from him, he couldn't enthrall her, and she was avoiding his eyes anyway. Jane must have educated her about eye contact and vampires during their spend-all-the-vamp's-money shopping extravaganza. But he could still read her mind, especially when the volume of her fear made her thoughts so very loud.

"Get out," she said, holding her ground.

In his mind, he saw her intentions. He'd get off the elevator, then she'd close the door and escape. She'd decided he was too dangerous. Well, he'd give her points there.

Gregory's little speech had made an impression, and Anthony's apparent lack of self-control with her had led them to the current standoff. If she wouldn't be in danger out there, he'd admire her. This was the woman he knew. The one he loved. He pushed that thought away. Not loved.

"You're forgetting I can read your mind, and you've pretty much laid out your plan. You first. Get rid of the cross."

She shook her head firmly, tears prickling at the corners of her eyes.

"All right, look. You can keep it in your pocket and use it later if you need to. You can stay up all night and go to sleep when I do. That way you know I can't get to you. Fair?"

"You're going to trust me not to burn you?"

He knew she wouldn't burn him again unless it was necessary for her survival. She was practically throwing her thoughts out at him. He couldn't fault her for trying to protect herself. That's what he admired so much about her, that she was so strong. He was going to have to start making her feel like she could defend herself.

"I know you won't do it again." He tried to make eye contact to let her see his sincerity, but she didn't even trust him that far. He sighed.

Several minutes passed before she returned the cross to her pocket.

Once inside the penthouse, Charlotte took her bags to the guest room to unpack. They'd only been there a few moments when Anthony realized something felt off. The dog was hiding; normally he ran out to greet them.

Linus stepped out of the kitchen, two other vampires in tow. Both, Anthony recognized. One was his body-guard, Slade. The other was Linus's lover, and—Anthony scented the air—claimed mate now. Well, wasn't Callie just the little social climber?

She must be betting Linus would win the tournament. The little bitch wanted to be queen. She'd always said she was headed for big things.

"What are you doing in my home?" he practically growled.

"I just came by to see if you'd decided on a vampire mate yet. In the unlikely event that you win, you'll need to claim someone to reign as your queen. The coven won't fully accept a bachelor. It would create too many political problems."

"I'm touched you care so much," Anthony said, making sure to convey how much he wasn't.

Charlotte picked that moment to come out of the bedroom.

"This must be your pet," Linus said.

Charlotte looked like she was about to object. But she made the mistake of meeting Anthony's eyes for just the barest moment in her uncertainty. It was enough. He gripped her mind with the full thrust of his power. "Yes. She is." Then to Charlotte, "Come here, my pet."

He slipped a suggestion into her mind, and she put a little extra sway in her hips as she glided across the floor toward him. She was going to be royally pissed when this was over. It would get him nowhere in the trust department, but the stakes were far too high to give her the illusion of independence right now. He trailed his fingers through her hair and she sighed and rubbed against him like a contented cat.

Callie moved to sit in the overstuffed leather chair, her long legs draping gracefully over the arm. Linus remained standing while Slade stood just off to the side and a few paces closer to Anthony than his boss.

"Pretty," Callie said. "I'll bet she tastes divine or you wouldn't keep her." She licked her lips, making her intentions clear.

"Yes," Linus agreed, placing a hand on his mate's shoulder, "How about sharing with a few weary travelers? Holing up in hotels for days away from our homeland has been quite exhausting. We'd like to . . . play."

Anthony gritted his teeth, trying to rein in his temper. Three against one were not good odds. Especially when at least one of them was his equal or better in a fight.

"I would prefer you didn't. I don't share what's mine." Like hell he was letting them *play* with her. That could go to several bad places. He worked to maintain a mask of calm.

"Now that's just rude. You know we share pets. There is no claim on them," Linus said, the picture of reason.

Anthony couldn't deal with the issue at hand and maintain a grip on Charlotte's mind, especially when he hadn't drunk from her in a couple of days. His control snapped.

He didn't have time to be impressed with her ability to break his hold so quickly because things were escalating too fast. He gripped her wrist hard, warning her. He wanted to slip into her mind to see how much she'd been able to process, what she knew about what was going on around her, but there was no time.

A moment later, he was pushed away from her while Linus backed up several feet as if he'd come across a rattlesnake. She held the cross out, putting every ounce of her faith behind it. Her eyes were determined, though they carefully avoided the eyes of any vampire in the room. She threw a disgusted look Anthony's way for what he'd just done to her.

"LEAVE," she shouted to the interlopers. Despite her lack of eye contact, she was putting on a rather impressive show of being in control.

"How did you get into my apartment in the first place?" Anthony asked. For the moment things seemed under control, or at least as under control as they were likely to get.

"I got a key from the front desk. They aren't as stringent about their policies here as they used to be," Linus said. "There was a time they only employed guardians both day and night. Now they're letting humans run the night shift, and well, you know about the weakness of humans."

Anthony held his breath as he watched Linus. He knew he was trying to bait Charlotte into looking at him. The other vampire shrugged, as if giving up that plan, and reached into his pocket, pulling out a gleaming revolver.

"I used to just count on my fangs to help me out in a crisis, but I've since embraced weapon technology. It allows for greater reach." He pointed the barrel of the gun at Charlotte; a gruesome grin painted his face. "Now, be a good girl and drop the cross or I'll have to pull the trigger. Blood is all the same to me. I'll get it either way."

Charlotte's hand started to shake. Anthony saw her new plan unfurling, to rush the vampire with the cross. He shook his head.

"No, Charlotte, that'll never work."

"Be a good pet now, and drop the cross. Kick it across the room where it can't get in our way."

Callie had taken her legs off the arm of the chair and was leaning forward now, a look of feral amusement on her face. Slade remained in place, his expression and stance ever stoic, waiting to jump into the fray if needed.

Tears began to track down Charlotte's face, and her hand started to shake more noticeably. She turned to Anthony, desperation and anger warring in her eyes.

"I hate you," she said. She dropped the cross and kicked it across the room.

As soon as she'd done it, Anthony was on her, his fangs in her throat, drinking. He nicked his tongue and sealed her wound with his blood. It happened too quickly for Linus to react. Anthony turned to the other vampire and raised an eyebrow, having found the one way to best him at his own game. Vampires didn't claim humans. Didn't mean they couldn't. They just didn't. He'd worry about how he'd fucked up his life later. For now he was the victor.

"Well, she's mine now," he said, wiping the blood from the corner of his mouth and sucking the remains off his finger.

He released Charlotte and she fell to the floor, a horrible shrieking scream tearing out of her throat.

Chapter Ten

It had happened too fast. She'd been holding the cross, knowing whatever was about to occur it wasn't going to be quick, and she likely wouldn't survive it. Anthony's warning against her thoughts had scared her sufficiently to do what Linus had said. Why the fuck did he have to be in her head?

The room was loud, too loud. Then she realized the noise was coming from her own mouth. She couldn't stop the screaming. There was too much in her head now. Memories crashed over her in waves, trying to fit together with the past two days of nothing. Her normal memories sat as a blurry background that barely felt real, playing second to the night Anthony had bitten her.

All she could remember, all she could think about, was the pain. She finally managed to stop screaming, her throat raw as she wondered if she'd ever get sound from it again. Her forehead rested on the floor, and she sobbed quietly.

She was dimly aware of voices carrying on in the background. Linus was laughing, that horrible vampire laugh that sounded like he'd spent centuries making it just creepy enough to give everyone he met nightmares.

"Well, guess you showed me," he said.

Charlee listened more closely now, not bothering to move. She heard the sound of high heels clicking over the hardwood floor toward her, and she cringed.

There was a protective growl. She didn't have to guess who that was.

"You touch her, and Linus is out of the tournament," Anthony said.

"She's not a vampire; she doesn't count," the vampiress whined as if a toy had been taken away. Charlee realized with revulsion that it had been. God, she hated vampires.

"She's mine. You touch her, and I kill you. I'll be well within my rights."

Heavier footfalls moved to where Callie's had stopped.

"Don't, Callie. The elders won't be happy. However . . . unusual it is. I hope you realize what you just did, Anthony. If you win, the coven will never support you. They'll never accept a human queen. You may have done me a favor. And if I win, you know this claim won't stop me. Well, goodnight then."

When the vampires had filed out of the penthouse, Charlee wiped her eyes. She couldn't stand to be alone in the same room with him. She'd been about as close to love as a woman can get to a man she's not dating or sleeping with. Her diary hadn't done the situation justice.

"Oh, bite me," she said.

"Some day, definitely." He smiled at her, a world of sexual promise in his gaze that caught her off guard for a moment. Then she bounced back.

"Have you had all your shots? I'd hate to get rabies."

He put his hand over his heart in mock offense. "You wound me."

"Yeah, I'm dangerous that way."

"Not half so dangerous as me I'd wager."

She laughed. "Just because you've got that coat that makes you look like a comic book villain, don't think that makes you bad. Fashion rarely frightens me."

"We'll see."

Her heart dropped into her stomach at the way he said 'we'll see'.

'Do it, ask me out,' her mind screamed at him. 'Let's take this beyond the bookstore . . . out there. You know we'd be great together.' She wasn't sure how long she could keep the banter up before she just threw herself at him.

Her former feelings for him battled against the current reality. A reality so scary she was glad vamps wiped memories. She wouldn't be able to handle being a human in a vampire world, knowing what lurked in the night.

"Charlotte."

She felt him moving closer to her and scooted away. "Don't. Don't touch me."

"Just tell me what happened."

She looked up sharply. Something had changed. He couldn't read her thoughts now. She felt as if she'd just won the battle but lost the war.

"What did you do?" she asked.

His response was calm, matter-of-fact. "I claimed you. Now tell me what happened. I can't read it straight out of your head anymore, but I can make you talk."

He sat Indian-style next to her, and she looked into his eyes, letting him have the full force of her loathing. Finally, she spoke.

"I thought I was going to die . . . "

"Charlotte, I wouldn't . . . "

" . . . From the pain."

He was confused, or he was pretending to be. She wasn't sure which.

"It's not supposed to hurt. It was fast, but I was in control. I wouldn't have done that to you."

"No . . . not tonight, the first time. I thought I was going to die from the pain that night." *That night* was playing over and over in her mind. She'd been so surprised to see Anthony on her back porch.

She'd half expected him to kiss her or ask her out, but then she got a closer look. There was blood on his face, and he looked . . . frenzied, angry. The rest she tried not to think about. She could still feel him tearing into her throat and hear her own soft pleading. Then his tongue was sealing the wound shut, and for one brief moment she felt the kind of bliss women only felt in fairy tales. Then he'd made her forget.

If it was possible, even more color drained from his face. "Charlotte, I'm so sorry. That night, there were drugs. I was out of my mind, I . . . Wait . . . you remember?"

"Everything. Did you know I had feelings for you?"

Anthony sighed. "Yes."

"But you didn't do anything about it."

He gesticulated wildly around him. "Well, look how well *this* is turning out."

"Just take out the memories of you and take me back home. After Linus is gone, I mean."

"I can't do that now. What I did, claiming you, I can't undo it."

He moved closer and cradled her in his arms. He might not be able to read her mind anymore, but he seemed able to do all the other vampire things, including touching her emotions, manipulating them.

She felt indescribably happy, calm, warm, safe, loved in his arms. And though she knew these weren't the normal things she felt about him now, his skin pressed against hers made her forget the part of her brain that couldn't cope with the way reality had shifted.

He rocked her like a small child. Then he slipped a finger underneath her chin, raising her face to his, and kissed her. His tongue invaded her mouth with smooth expertise, and if she'd felt a thousand happy thoughts before, it was more now as arousal joined the mix. She wasn't sure if it was real or if he was using the vampire mojo.

A moan slipped past her lips as she remembered all the times she'd thought about this moment. It felt like a dream. Only she knew she wouldn't have imagined it this way, with a bite mark on her neck. His hands had slipped beneath her shirt, and she felt him fumbling with her bra. A part of her wanted to let it happen, feel his cool, soothing touch against her skin and forget the horrors of the past few days.

Then the thought stole into her mind: *He'd erase those memories if you wanted him to.*

She pulled away from him and bolted off the floor as if she'd been stung. Her lips were swollen from his kisses. Her hands moved back to reconnect her bra strap. She wanted to look into his eyes to see what was there. Lust? Anger? Hunger? Or would he just look like the predatory animal he was? But she didn't. She didn't trust him not to enthrall her.

She could understand why he'd done what he'd done with Linus. It had been for her safety. But this world was too new for her, her life too fragile to carelessly put it into the hands of someone like him.

"Charlotte?"

He moved toward her, his hand reaching for her shoulder.

She sidestepped him. It was practically choreographed.

"Stop playing with my emotions." She was proud her voice had come out steady, calm, as if he hadn't just done some weird vampire thing. Some weird vampire thing he'd failed to explain to her. "If you enthrall me, I'll never trust you again."

She chanced looking into his eyes and saw pain.

"I can't read your mind now; it's not as easy to know the right thing to do where you're concerned. I was trying to take some of your pain away. If you'll let me, I can make this better."

She assumed he expected her to go running back into his arms, easily forgiving his indiscretion with the biting and pain and fear and almost death. Since it was an accident, all was easily forgiven? She knew he never would have done it in his right mind. Right?

He hadn't meant for it to happen. Not the amnesia or Linus or the bite he'd yet to explain. It didn't change that it *had* happened.

"I could erase it. I could replace the memories with something more . . . palatable."

Hadn't she just thought the same thing? The temptation had been there for a moment. But she couldn't stand the idea of living a fake life.

"No! Don't mess with my mind." She held her hands out in front of her, as if she could ward him away. Her eyes drifted to the cross still on the other side of the room. She wanted to line the guest room with crosses to keep him out. He could mess with her mind with the best intentions. The little place inside her that hated him grew a tiny bit more.

He held his hands up, placating. "All right. I won't. I just wanted to fix what I did."

"Too late." A tear slipped from the corner of her eye, and she swiped it away. She wasn't going to start that again. There were more important things to deal with. "What do you mean you claimed me? What were they talking about before they left?"

He crossed to the overstuffed chair Callie had been lounging in moments before, putting some much needed distance between them.

"Vampires being immortal do not often mate. Some do, some swear by it. But eternity is a long time, and few want to be tied down in that way. When two vampires decide that's what they want, there is a bite and mingling of blood that bonds them for eternity. It's taken very seriously because once blood is mixed, it can't be unmixed, anymore than you can unmake a vampire."

Charlee had moved to the couch. Her fingernails dug into the soft leather as he spoke. "And this means what for me?" Was she stuck with him until she died? A man she almost loved but definitely hated, who she'd never forgive.

"I don't know exactly. It's a vampire mating ritual. Vampires don't generally claim humans."

"So let me get this straight. You took my memory, then you returned that but took my life instead?"

He didn't respond. What could he say? She almost felt bad for making him feel worse. Almost. His hands began shaking.

"Anthony?"

"What?" He looked down.

"What's happening?"

"It's the bagged blood. My body's rejecting it."

For the first time since the claiming, Charlee could feel the invisible link, like a strong multi-strand twine that stretched between them, and it was pulling her to him. She would have been angry, but Anthony wasn't pulling on her mind; it was the link calling out to her to help him. And the part of her that had almost loved him responded.

Before she had time to think about what she'd done, she was sitting on his lap. His fangs grazed her neck, and she tensed.

"Shhhh," he whispered. "This won't hurt."

She didn't really believe him. But he was right, it didn't hurt. Inexplicably she never felt his fangs slide into the column of her throat. He growled softly, the sound reverberating against her skin, causing her body to respond in places far more interesting.

One of his hands had slipped under her shirt. She was about to protest, but he wasn't undressing her. Instead, his cool fingers rubbed soothingly over her back. From the angle she was seated on his lap, she could feel the effect her blood was having on him as his erection pressed against the side of her hip.

It wasn't as if a similar reaction wasn't taking place in her body. Still, she resented him. She tensed as he sealed the wound with his tongue. It was a vastly different experience from the first time, or the second time. This time had been . . . Oh hell, in any other set of circumstances she'd be on her back for him by now. But she couldn't pretend the events of the past several days hadn't happened.

He pulled away to look into her eyes and she averted her gaze, afraid that in his current state the temptation would be too great to bring her mind in line with her body's desires.

He sighed deeply. "You're never going to trust or forgive me, are you?"

She remained silent. It was a small relief that he couldn't read her thoughts anymore, that she'd regained some measure of privacy from him. No, she couldn't see herself trusting or forgiving him. And that knowledge frightened her more than if she could. Because either way she was stuck with him now, and there was no happy future unless she could forgive him.

There would be no other men. Somehow she couldn't picture Anthony being okay with that. Her entire life had closed off, and there was nowhere to run. So no, she couldn't forgive him for that. Not ever.

"Charlotte, if I could undo the chain of events that led us here, I swear to you I would. We're never going to have that easy way between us again, are we?"

"I don't think so, no." Those days were gone.

Chapter Eleven

Anthony stood in Charlotte's doorway, barred from entry as she slept blissfully unaware of his presence. At the first opportunity, she'd grabbed the cross and slipped the silver chain around her neck. Then she'd had the nerve to break one of his kitchen chairs.

At first he'd thought her intent was to attempt to stake him, but she'd taken some duct tape and lashed two strips of wood together into a makeshift cross. Then she'd found a way to prop it up in her doorway. He hadn't protested because it was what she needed to feel safe, and it hurt too much that he'd done enough damage to warrant this reaction.

Although a cross would burn him no matter what, it didn't have the repellent force that nearly drove him to the other end of a room, except with extreme faith behind it. Charlotte had that kind of faith. Another thing he admired about her.

He'd been sure the moment she reached unconsciousness the cross would go back to being nothing more annoying than a hot kitchen stove. He'd been mistaken. Her breathing had regulated in sleep, yet the cross guarded her more savagely than a large protective dog.

He found he was more relieved than angry about that. She'd come to him in her own time, and until then, the claim plus her faith would keep her safe from others of his kind. He made his way down to the lobby and gave stern instructions using a blend of suggestion and threats regarding who got keys to his penthouse.

By the time he exited the lobby, he was sure he smelled the acrid scent of urine on the terrified night clerk. *Good. The message got through.* He didn't care who they said they were or on what authority they were demanding a key, no one was to be given access to the penthouse floor or his suite. The place had gone downhill in the last fifty years. Replacing the guardians at night with humans merely to cut costs was poor management.

He could work up no guilt over his behavior with the clerk. This was his mate's life on the line. *Dammit.* His mate.

He'd never planned nor intended to take a mate, vampire or otherwise. The fact that he'd now taken a human was an extra layer of complication for his bid for coven leader. Linus was right. The coven wouldn't be happy about it. They viewed humans as lesser beings, not only because they were food, but because they showed such poor loyalty and displayed such consistent weakness.

He'd absently started moving toward the park. Paul was waiting for him when he got there, his legs splayed out as he sat on a manual merry-go-round. He spun a little to one side then the other, causing the metal to creak as the disc turned.

"Took you long enough," he groused. "Where the hell have you been the past couple of days?"

Anthony laughed. Paul was an impertinent little fledge. Young, cocky, but entertaining as hell. Vampires were only allowed to turn a certain number of people for obvious survival and food supply reasons.

Anthony had doubted he'd ever use up that allotment or turn even one human, but when a twenty-something boy had saved his life, he knew he owed him something in return. Learning Paul had been dying only reinforced the choice to gift him with eternal life.

"I ran into a little problem."

It wasn't standard practice for a vampire to let his fledglings in on his personal plans and goings-on, but Paul was a friend. Anthony briefly filled him in on the events from biting Greta to siphon the poison, to Charlotte holed up in her room with anti-vampire protections in place.

"Damn, Boss. When you fuck shit up, you fuck it up."

Anthony growled, but there was no menace behind it. "I wish you'd stop calling me that. It makes it sound like I hired you to work for me at the Piggly Wiggly."

The boy's brows scrunched up. "What's a Piggly Wiggly?"

"Never mind."

Paul shrugged. "I guess you don't need to feed then."

Anthony grimaced as his mind flashed to his earlier feeding with Charlotte wriggling on his lap, the air so heavy with the scent of her arousal he'd nearly drowned in it. They'd both been on the edge of throwing caution to the wind for a good old-fashioned animal fucking. But her fear and the manners he'd somehow developed where she was concerned, had put it to an abrupt halt.

Which was probably for the best. The night before the tournament wasn't the wisest time to be indulging in such things. He needed to stay focused.

"Hey, Boss?"

Anthony looked up.

"Have you considered withdrawing your name from the competition?"

He'd considered it about forty times since putting the claim on Charlotte, but if Linus won and Anthony didn't at least compete to try to stop it, he'd never forgive himself.

Linus would end their kind and all the progress they'd made. It would celebrate the worst of them and leave the weakest for the picking by junior Van Helsing or Buffy wannabes stalking the night with crosses and holy water.

"You know I can't do that."

Paul nodded in understanding and fell back into a fighting stance. The younger vamp was no match for Anthony's strength, but he had a different enough fighting style, the elder vampire believed he was gaining some benefit from the sparring.

Paul fought dirty. Being young, he just about had to. Even taken under Anthony's wing, there were times when things got ugly. Anthony was betting Linus would be fighting dirty as well, so for once he was learning from his fledge instead of teaching.

"Why do you want to lead the coven anyway?" Paul asked an hour later. He appeared wiped out, not yet having developed quite the standard level of vampire stamina. "If it was me, I'd take the girl and run."

Anthony grinned. "I wish it were that simple. She's tied to me now. If I run and Linus wins, then we're always running, for at least the next century. More, if whoever wins after Linus is someone he's groomed for the position."

The state of the vampire race had grown restless. A small faction was tired of hiding and heavily supported Linus and his policies. Anthony felt they were short-sighted, and Linus would drive them further into caves and crypts. Whereas now, cloaked in secrecy, they existed alongside the human world without incident.

There were too many young vampires who didn't remember a time when the world knew they existed and hunted them when they were most vulnerable. It would have been so easy for Charlotte to kill him in his sleep. Some of the coven didn't fully comprehend the problems that would come their way if they went back to being the horror-movie creature that lurked in the night.

"Someone's coming," Anthony said, pulling Paul into the shadows.

"Who's that?"

He realized he was growling. "Jane. Gregory's girl."

Paul scented the air. "But she's human."

Anthony chuckled. "Yeah, that seems to be going around."

"She smells good." Paul's eyes flashed and glowed, his fangs extending.

"Easy there, sport. It'll piss Gregory off."

The fledge turned with a toothy grin, his fangs flashing in the moonlight. "So? Do we care?"

"I knew there was a reason I turned you."

Paul chuckled and went to hunt his prey.

Anthony hung back and watched for awhile. He could hear the soft crying that had driven her out to this isolated place to lick her wounds in private. Then he smelled her fear. Of Paul?

Paul closely resembled a department store catalog model. Hardly threatening, even alone in a playground at night, especially to someone like Jane who'd decided to throw her self-preservation instincts to the wind and hang out with vampires as a fun hobby.

He lingered for a minute and focused in on Jane to see what he could get from her. The girl could sense vampires, handy skill for a vampire groupie. How she'd managed to fall under the radar without being enthralled to Gregory, he didn't know. But he was going to keep an eye on her.

Chapter Twelve

Charlee **woke to find herself** tangled in the bedsheets as if she'd gone three rounds with a prize fighter. She'd been sleeping later at Anthony's place with so little sunlight streaming in. Her arm dangled over the side of the bed, fumbling until she found her purse. She dug in the bag for her cell, then pressed *one* on the speed dial.

"Lawson's Bookshoppe, Greta speaking."

"It's me," she said, her voice still thick with sleep.

There was a pause from Greta's end.

"I remember everything." Somehow it sounded anticlimactic when she said it out loud. It should have felt like bigger news, but the past couple of days without her memory were starting to feel like a glitch. "Greta, are you there?"

"I'm here. Sorry, I was helping a customer and trying to figure out how to ask my next question away from prying ears."

Charlee solved the conundrum for her. "I know about the cat thing. When my memories came back I got all of them, even those Anthony erased the first time."

She was beginning to wish she'd had this conversation face to face. She climbed out of the bed with the phone still pressed to her ear, listening to Greta ring up customers.

She stopped in front of the mirror and stared at her neck. Unlike the first bite, this one had left a mark. She suspected it was the claiming, rather than the later feeding. She shivered at that last thought. *No, don't think about that.* She wasn't an expert on the ways of the vampire, but the mark seemed to say: *This one's mine. Trespassers will be shot on sight.*

"Are you okay?" Greta finally asked.

"Yeah," she lied, running her finger over the puckered mark. It wasn't discreet. What was she going to wear from now on? *Hello, high school turtleneck flashback.* Only now it could be a permanent problem instead of a temporary embarrassment.

"I've got you on the schedule for tomorrow."

"That should be fine, I guess. The tournament is tonight."

"Wait. What? What does that have to do with you? Where are you?"

"I'm at Anthony's apartment."

Greta shrieked over the phone at a decibel level that would make a banshee proud. "You're WHERE? Why are you still there? Don't you remember anything I told you about him?"

Yes, she remembered. And for once she wished she'd listened. Not that her level of listening skills had much to do with her current predicament.

"I'll drop everything and come get you."

"Calm down. We'll talk about this tomorrow, okay?"

Another pause. "Fine. But don't let him smooth talk you. You don't want to be any more closely connected with a vampire than you have to be. You're new to this world, but trust me when I tell you this."

Her finger traced over the claiming mark again. Too late for that. "Yeah, okay."

She laid the cell on the vanity and looked back at her reflection. She took the cross off, placing it next to the phone, and went to turn on the shower. She was well and truly fucked.

On the bright side, it seemed as if her jury-rigged protections against Anthony had paid off. Nothing had been disturbed. She stepped around the makeshift cross and into the living area, tripping over something in her path. She looked down. Anthony had moved his mattress to just outside her door, careful to keep it out of the path of sunlight.

She couldn't decide if it was creepy or endearing. A little of both maybe. She turned to find a wiry college boy lying on the floor with a goth chick asleep on top of him. Jane. Hmm. Weird.

Charlee glanced back down at Anthony. Almost sweet-looking in sleep, no threat to her at the moment. She wondered what it would be like to curl up with him without their baggage. She *wasn't* going to do what she was thinking about doing. She bit her lip and looked at the empty spot on the mattress.

He was in hibernation mode. What harm could it do? He wouldn't wake up; he couldn't hurt her; there was no chance she'd have to deal with sex. Having made her decision, she pulled back the covers and snuggled in with the vampire.

Before she could decide whether she liked this feeling, his arm had closed around her like the point of no return on a roller coaster ride when the safety bar comes down. Then his fangs were in her throat.

She tensed. "Anthony?" This shouldn't be happening; he was supposed to be asleep.

Then she realized, he *was* still asleep. She screamed. "Jane!"

Jane scrambled off the college guy and turned toward the shrieking.

"Jane, help. I can't get him off me. He's going to drain me in his sleep."

She rushed over. "Well hell, Charlee. I don't know what to do. He's too strong for me, too. Do you feel weak? Like you're losing too much blood?"

The panic left her for a minute, and Charlee glared at the goth. "No. He's just taking a little, but you can drain blood out of a body slowly or quickly. Either way I'm screwed if we don't get him off me."

Jane stood contemplating like she had hours to figure something out.

"My cross is on my dresser. I took it off to shower."

"Gotcha."

She returned moments later and laid the cross against Anthony's arm. It repelled him, and Charlee scrambled off the mattress. She put her hand to her neck, expecting to still be bleeding.

Images of 911 calls floated through her mind. You couldn't just hit that artery and not bleed out. Her hand came away cleaner than she expected.

"Jane, is there blood on my neck?"

"A little, but no holes. It healed."

"But that can't happen."

The goth shrugged. "You're in way deep, sister."

"No shit." Well, there went the picket fence version of her and Anthony. Not that she would have pursued it now anyway. Would she?

"Who's the guy, and how come he didn't wake up?"

"Oh, that's Paul. Greg dumped my ass, and Paul and I hooked up at the playground. He's Anthony's minion or something."

"Anthony has minions?"

"Just the one, I think."

Charlee took a quick shower and fastened the silver cross around her neck. She had no intention of removing it again. Ever. Potential hard water damage be damned. If it got tarnished, she could clean it. Her life was more valuable. If she'd been wearing it from the beginning, Anthony couldn't have gotten his fangs into her. Though he wouldn't have slipped his arm around her in that possessive/protective way either.

For a split second, before he'd started feeding, she'd felt the little flip she'd always gotten in her stomach when Anthony was near. Before all the vampire crap. That low twinge that said there were definitely sparks. At least from her end.

She lathered her hair in the apple-scented shampoo she liked. She'd instinctively reached for it on the big shopping trip when her memory had been gone. Now it felt like safety. A comforting sense memory she could lose herself in for a little while.

She wondered how she would have felt about the most recent bite had Anthony been awake. Didn't she trust him at least a little? That his mercy would always win out with her over his more primal nature? Nothing drove that home like the panic she'd felt with his fangs in her throat and him unconscious, unable to stifle instinct.

After showering, she dressed in some of the clothes she'd bought the previous day with Anthony's money and sat at the kitchen table. Jane had made them a couple of mugs of cocoa with whipped cream on top and frozen waffles with strawberries and whipped cream. Jane liked whipped cream. For this reason, Charlee liked Jane.

She dug into her dessert/breakfast with gusto. Between bites and sips of cocoa she said, "So what's the story on Gregory?"

Charlee had thought they were doing okay. Aside from his weird aversion to drinking from the source and refusing to turn Jane.

The previous day, she'd shared how they'd met. It sounded like a goth fairytale. Jane sensed vampires, and it got her hunted when one got into close enough to figure that out. Gregory had played the gallant hero and taken responsibility for her.

"Oh my god. He's such a wanker. It's bad enough he won't turn me, even though I've explicitly told him that's what I want. But last night he starts this thing about, 'I need to take my political career more seriously. The tournament is coming up, and if I win, I'll have to take a mate.' Gag. If he'd turn me like I'd asked, he could do that. But I guess I'm not worth eternity. Fine. What the fuck ever."

She dug back into her waffles then started talking again with her mouth full. "Will you go with me to get my things? I ran out of there real dramatic-like last night, and I need to get my stuff out while he's sleeping."

"Sure," Charlee said.

"I should just stake the motherfucker in his sleep. I can't believe it. You know, we've been together three years. And I get that I'm not queen material or whatever, but seriously, what a wanker. Political ambition my ass. If he had political ambition, he'd drink blood like a real vampire. That is not going over with the fanged crowd. I can tell you that much already. And I'm not even one of the sunlight-sensitive."

Charlee focused on her breakfast, wishing she'd tied a scarf around her neck. Now wasn't the time to point out that she had very close to what Jane wanted, and she'd accomplished it in less than forty-eight hours living together and no nookie. Jane might just stake *her* for that one.

She must have been thinking this really loudly because Jane suddenly came out of her funk, and looked up, alert and perceptive. "And why is there a mark on your neck? Vamps don't leave marks on their victims and pets."

Apparently victim and pet were the only two ways one could be bitten in Jane's world. Charlee didn't like it, but she didn't completely disagree either. "Ummm . . . "

Jane narrowed her eyes and looked closer. "Oh my God. I don't believe it. See, this is why Greg is so lame. How long have you known Anthony?"

"Um . . . well, casually for several months, more up close and personal, a few days."

"Exactly. In that time, Anthony knows what he wants. I can't believe he claimed you. Vampires almost never do that with humans, you know."

Charlee perked up. Jane had an unexpected wealth of knowledge. Of course she did. She'd co-habitated with a vampire for a few years. How could she not be a fount of information?

"You know about claims?"

"I've only had to hear about them daily for the past year since Greg decided he was going for this whole king thing. And really, how lame is that? King? What are we? The Tudors now? They need cooler titles. With their lifespans surely they could come up with something more interesting than *king*."

It was possible Jane could do with less sugar first thing in the morning, but Charlee was too focused on the *someone knows about claims* part of the equation.

"Anthony hasn't told me much of anything about what this means. I'm not happy about it."

Jealousy flitted over Jane's features, then she nodded. "I guess I can understand that. I've known about vampires my whole life. And knowing about them, without them being able to erase that knowledge, makes me bait. I need to be one of them or I won't survive. I'm not kidding myself here. Anthony wants to keep an eye on me so I don't screw his world up. And Paul is momentarily infatuated."

Charlee hadn't considered that. She'd thought Jane wanting to be a vampire was all an overdone punk/goth thing, some kind of social rebellion. But now she could see Jane was a survivor. She was going to have to take lessons from the goth chick if she wanted to be one as well.

"So how do I undo it?" Charlee asked. She was trying for casual because she didn't want to unleash the sugar-high angry bazooka Jane had poised and ready to go off again.

Jane picked a syrup and cream-covered strawberry off her plate, and chewed slowly. She might as well have been sitting cross-legged saying "oooooom" because clearly, she was trying to get to a Zen place before she exploded.

"I know it's a little tactless to ask you under the circumstances, but really, I can't be tied to him."

Jane sighed. "Yeah, I get it. I wish I was you, but I get it." She popped another strawberry into her mouth. "Death is the only way."

Charlee's eyes drifted back to the vampire on the mattress. "Mine or his?"

"Either."

Charlee took a deep breath. "Good to know."

But it wasn't. Not really. If she couldn't kill him the day before, she didn't see it happening now. Not when ten minutes ago she was trying to snuggle with him out of curiosity. She turned back to Jane who was looking thoughtful, an expression Charlee hadn't yet seen on the hyperactive goth.

"You can't kill him," Jane said with understanding.

"I hate him, though."

Jane nodded, wisely. "I'd do it for you, except I don't think Paul would like it. Anthony is his vampire role model. Plus he's one of the best shots we have in this tournament."

"What do I care what happens at the tournament?" Charlee had been in Anthony's world a few days and already she was sick of vampire politics. She couldn't see how their leadership issues in any way affected her. Even with her new neck decoration.

"Because Anthony is the most sane possibility that has a chance. And you don't want Linus to win. That is one psychotic vampire. All humans would be in major danger if he got control of the coven."

Before she could form a reply, Jane changed the subject. "Let's go get my stuff."

Inside the apartment, Jane made quick work of packing her bags. She slammed drawers and tossed things around the apartment like she was on a mission to ransack instead of pack. Charlee tried to keep a minimum safe distance as the clanging, clattering, and throwing of things continued.

The vampire hibernation issue was still hard for her to grasp. She kept thinking Gregory would rise out of some mist or something and start yelling at them to keep it down so he could sleep. Not that he was overly scary with his bags of blood in the fridge. Still, vampires were vampires, and from what she'd seen they just came in varying degrees of creepy, not completely safe, warm, and fuzzy.

The apartment went silent for a few minutes, and Charlee got worried. She found Jane standing in the bedroom over Gregory's prone form, with a hand-carved wooden stake poised over his heart.

She could picture Jane secretly carving it a bit at a time whenever Gregory did some boneheaded thing that was probably more from being a male than a vampire. Jane's knuckles had gone white as she stared down at him. A mask of rage covered her face, and she was crying.

"If killing Greg would break the claim on you, I know I could do it."

Charlee wasn't sure that was true. It wasn't like they were best buds or anything. For all her bravado, Jane cared about the vampire. She raised the stake dramatically like the act would save the world and give her a shiny special spot in heaven, but she brought it down almost in slow motion until the tip indented the skin just over his heart.

She pressed down, and a tiny trickle of blood ran out around the stake. "He breaks up with me, doesn't try to thrall me, doesn't even get a different room to keep me out. He sleeps without a shirt on. He is begging for death. Begging."

Charlee placed a hand on Jane's arm. "Let's just go, okay?"

"There is no court that would convict me. There would be no body. When they're dead, they just kind of rot and melt away. It's like they stopped being real when they were turned. He's dead already. This will make no difference."

For someone who wanted to be a vampire, Jane seemed to hold a dim view.

"Jane." Homicidal Slayer Jane was starting to disturb Charlee. And in that moment she knew she was never getting rid of Anthony.

Jane looked up at her then as if just realizing she wasn't alone in the room. "He deserves it. He's selfish. All he had to do was turn me."

Charlee pried the stake out of her hand. "Seriously, Jane. Let's just get the hell out of here." She led her from the room like a child and sat her down on the couch, unsure what to do next.

They were some pair. The poster children for why vampires thought humans were lame and stupid. The monsters they hated, they couldn't kill. If not for Paul, maybe they could have come up with some kind of wacky undead homicide pact. She'd off Gregory, while Jane took out Anthony.

She allowed the dark fantasy to swirl through her mind as she went through the rest of the apartment looking for anything Jane might have missed. When all the bags were lined neatly beside the door, she filled Jane's arms with bags, grabbed her share, and they made the trek back up to the penthouse.

On the elevator, Jane turned to her with a vacant expression and said, "You know, I probably could have poisoned his blood. Wanker."

Jane would make a fabulous vampire.

Chapter Thirteen

Anthony woke to the ravaging hunger again and a new burn on his arm. He was quite sure he'd made it clear to Charlotte that he'd be very angry if she engaged in such an activity again. Apparently he'd not made his displeasure clear enough, what with being busy trying to save her life and all.

Meanwhile she'd been spending his money and burning him for fun. He jolted when he realized there were people standing over him with varying degrees of worry etched on their faces. The goth girl was standing closest to him, but backed up when he scowled in her direction. Next to her, was Paul. Charlotte was hidden behind him, peeking around.

"Dude, you freaked us out. It's 7:30; the tournament starts in an hour. If you're late they'll disqualify you."

"I'm well aware of that. Thank you, Paul." He struggled to stand and swayed on his feet, dizziness overtaking him. Despite the lack of equilibrium, he made it to Charlotte in half a second. She shrieked.

"I can explain about the burn," she said, holding her arms up defensively.

"Not interested." He grabbed the wrist she'd presented —perhaps a bit harder than necessary—and pulled her toward him to feed.

Unlike the day before, he didn't particularly care about the hunger. He couldn't imagine a situation in which it would be acceptable for her to burn him a second time. He hadn't believed it was okay the first time.

Charlotte's blood flowed down his throat, warm and smooth and filled with the one emotion he hated from her. But he was pissed off enough at the moment that he could almost savor gladly the flavor of her fear.

When he felt his strength returning, he pushed her away. "You'd have no need to fear me if you'd stop doing stupid things. I am not your science experiment."

Her lip trembled as she glared at him. "Jane used my cross so you wouldn't kill me in your sleep."

Well, that was a new twist on things. Out of the million and one completely stupid reasons she could have given him for burning him again, this hadn't even been in the top hundred. "And what were you doing near my fangs while I was out in the first place?"

She looked at the ground as a flush spread into her cheeks. If not for the tournament, and his other two guests, he would have loved to throw her down on the mattress and see if they couldn't work out their differences.

"The point is, you were asleep. I thought you'd kill me, and there was no other way to get you off my neck."

Blood dripped down her hand and fingertips onto his hardwood floor. Anthony gently grasped her wrist and moved it back to his mouth. His tongue trailed languidly over her inner arm, stopping the flow of blood and healing the wound as his eyes held hers. "I wouldn't have killed you. The claim wouldn't have let me; I would have stopped."

He could get used to the flavor that now tinged her blood, a mixture of fear and arousal.

"I didn't know that. *Someone* didn't fill me in on all the finer points of being your betrothed." He allowed her to pull her arm from his grip. She looked away. "Are we going to this stupid tournament or what?"

A part of him wanted to say to hell with the tournament, kick Paul and Jane out of the apartment, and have a round of grudge sex since he was sure that was the only brand she'd afford him at the moment. The image of Linus flared to life in his mind, dumping ice water on his arousal. He sighed and went to take a rushed shower and throw on some presentable clothing.

Everything with vampires was a big display. Nothing was done without pomp and circumstance. Jane refused to change out of her goth wardrobe, though Paul had agreed to call her his pet for the evening. There would be too much going on at the stadium for anyone to care if a minor minion's pet was or wasn't dressed appropriately for the event.

Charlotte, however, was a different matter altogether. It seemed that while he was oversleeping, Paul had explained vampire etiquette to her, or at least the dress code.

She was wearing a simple black dress with spaghetti straps. Black heels set off her shapely legs, and her hair was swept up off her neck, clearly displaying his mark. That was smart. If Linus hadn't watched him mark her, Anthony would want to conceal it, just in case his opponent won. But as it stood there was no benefit to hiding it, and she'd be safe at least during the tournament if the claim was obvious.

The drive to the stadium was uneventful and quiet. Jane and Paul were in the back seat making out like a couple of horny teenagers. Charlotte sat on the passenger side, staring out the window as Anthony's hand drifted to rest on her leg.

"Don't do that. I want you to stop doing that vampire crap with me."

"And I want you to stop doing that whiny put-upon human crap. Really, this is getting old, Charlotte. I did what I had to do to save your life."

"We wouldn't *be* in this position if you'd kept your fangs to yourself in the first place!"

The lip smacking in the backseat stopped. Anthony kept his eyes on the road, his teeth clenched so firmly, one of them chipping wasn't outside the realm of possibility. If he could reverse time and undo any of the many stupid things he'd done to bring them to this moment, he'd do it.

He could understand how she felt. He'd imprisoned her and ensnared her in a world that was both more complicated and more frightening than the one she was used to dealing with. And he hadn't asked her opinion or permission on the matter. From her perspective he'd clearly toyed with her life. And the fucked-up thing about all of it was that everything he did for her benefit took her deeper into a world he'd never wanted her in to begin with.

He still wondered why exactly his fangs had been in her throat that morning. In order for that to happen, she would have had to lie down with him. But why would she do that? She'd expressed that she hated him.

He stole a glance at her. He couldn't conceive of any reason in the world she would have lain close enough for him to get his fangs in her throat, unless she didn't hate him as much as she believed.

When they arrived at the tournament, Anthony disappeared in a blur of movement without a backward glance. Charlee guessed he'd gone inside for registration or whatever preliminary issues they had to sort out. The stadium was an enclosed, dome-shaped structure that looked like it held thousands of people. Upon entering the building with Paul and Jane, it became clear that wasn't the half of it.

The stands were packed with vampires, and she had the intense urge to flee. To everyone in this stadium, she was a food group. She felt a hand on her arm and her heart rate slowed.

"Not you too," she said, grimacing at Paul. Damn vampires and their emotional manipulation.

"You were about to jump out of your skin. The less afraid you are, the better it is for you here. And don't worry, no one is going to make a move toward you. They can smell the mark if they get close enough, but we've made it nice and visible so they won't get that close. Even if you're human, it's a claim. And we respect that. Jane here is the one that has to worry."

"Gee, thanks," Jane said.

He nipped lightly at her throat with blunt teeth and grinned at her. "But don't worry, playing with another vampire's pet isn't the highest priority right now. You girls just stick with me and it'll be fine."

"I don't know why we had to come along," Jane said.

"Anthony wants to keep an eye on you, and if he wins tonight his mate has to be here. It's bad enough she's human, but if she's not here it's like she doesn't support his bid for king."

"I don't support it," Charlee said. Truthfully, she didn't care one way or the other, and thought this entire thing seemed rather insane. Instantly she wished she'd kept that thought to herself.

Paul scowled, and his eyes turned dark, very different from the *laissez-faire* college boy demeanor he usually wore. "When Anthony wins, you will stand by his side and support him, or I will drain the life from you myself. He's worked too hard for this, and he's risked his neck for you."

"Hey, back off her. She didn't ask for this shit either," Jane said. "We're going to the little girl's room."

She threw Paul a look just as threatening as his, grabbed Charlee's hand, and led her toward the bathroom. Paul stalked close behind them, the danger palpably radiating off his form.

Charlee expected there to be a line, but since few people at the stadium were, in fact, people, it was practically empty. She stood in front of one of the mirrors, her hands gripping the porcelain sink.

"You okay, hon?" Jane had a hand on her back, a touch that was comforting because it was comforting, not because a vampire was putting the whammy behind it.

She met the other woman's eyes in the reflected surface and nodded. Jane had gone for extra black tonight if that was possible. They all looked like they'd stepped out of a goth Hallmark card. Jane had decided to go with heavy black eye makeup and black lipstick. She opened her purse, pulling out several pastel-colored and flowered items before holding out a tissue.

"You have a bit of mascara starting to creep down your cheek there."

Charlee hadn't realized she'd been crying. She did a double take at the contents of Jane's purse. Pastels? Flowers? Her eyes widened as they met Jane's.

"It's not all what it looks like on the outside. Now that you're in this world, you better learn that. Let's go. Paul might come in after us if we take too long."

Paul stood waiting for them outside the bathroom, leaning casually against a wall beside an abandoned concession area. Charlee was grateful it was abandoned.

She didn't want to see corn dogs soaked in human blood being sold for five bucks a pop.

He had worked to regain his calm mask, but now that she'd seen what lurked underneath, she didn't feel so peaceful in his presence. Jane didn't have the same aversion and rushed up to him. She planted a kiss on his cheek and looped her arm through his like she was off to see the wizard.

"Hey, babe," he said, his features softening.

He led them to a gold roped-off portion in the stands. A section of a few hundred seats had been reserved for the friends and family of the contenders. Or minions, pets, and claimed mates. *Ick.*

Paul sat between them. Charlee laid her arms on the arm rests, and he placed a hand over hers.

"Anthony needs you calm for this."

"Why?"

"With the claim, he can feel your emotions. He can't be distracted by any human feelings you might have about what's going to happen here."

"Well, well, if it isn't the little human that got lucky."

Callie stood in the aisle, wearing a striking red gown and matching gloves that extended over her elbows. Charlee felt the calm Paul was pouring into her. Her emotions were like a lake unfettered by a single ripple, but her thoughts still spiraled through her mind, detached and chaotic.

She wondered if vampires felt like this. This eerie, calculated calm. Did they feel this when they hunted and fed? Anthony seemed more animated, so she assumed it was just the false serenity Paul was sending through her.

Callie leaned close to her ear, her voice lowering. "You might wear his mark, little one, but the moment Linus wins, you're ours. My guy has experience with failed experiments. You'll make a stunning addition to the collection. We're going to have so much fun playing with you."

Charlee knew she should feel terror, unease, something. It disturbed her what Paul was doing to her. She felt like a computer cataloging emotions. Fear, anger, revulsion. All just descriptive words with nothing more attached to them.

With creepy calm, she turned to the vampire and smiled. "When Anthony wins, I'm sure he'll kill you for that."

Callie looked as if she'd swallowed a live and wriggling fish. She turned, holding her back ramrod straight and made her way up a few rows to her seat, her entourage trailing behind her.

The words were something she would have thought in regards to Callie anyway, but she wouldn't have had the nerve to say them if not for Paul's steady hand covering hers.

"Way to go, girl," Jane said.

This no-extreme-emotions thing had its benefits. But she'd still be glad when it was over. The thought flitted through her mind that this sort of thing might never be over, and if not for Paul beside her, she knew she would have been more upset by it.

The lights dimmed giving way to a large spotlight illuminating the ring below them. For the first time, she turned her attention to where the action would take place. It was the size of a football field and had probably been used as such, though now she could swear she was at a Medieval Times. There were several vampires in the ring with horses. The space had been set up for . . . jousting? They had to be kidding.

A hush fell over the audience and a booming voice sounded over the loudspeaker.

"This century we have fifty-one competitors. As we've done in the past, we'll use a jousting event to open the tournament. Drawing blood, death, or being knocked from one's horse is grounds for disqualification. We will continue until we're down to the final ten. Good luck competitors."

Even without Paul to steady her emotions, Charlee wasn't sure what she would have or should have felt about Anthony down in the ring. He was attractive as ever, wearing a dark silk shirt and slacks, sitting astride a black horse. She was thankful for the emotion muting, because otherwise she would have felt arousal and would have been mortified that every vampire sitting near them could smell it.

She'd expected the jousting and sword-fighting to take a while, but with vampire speed, everything moved so fast the event passed in front of her eyes in a blur. Within minutes, they were down to ten.

The ring was littered with the bodies of injured and dead vampires. The dead were decomposing, flesh rotting off bone, and bone crumbling to dust. As Jane had said, in a sense they were already dead. Once the demon stopped animating the human, the body's decomposition went to warp speed to catch up to the state it should have been had natural causes been at play in the victim's death.

There was a brief intermission while minions cleared the ring of vampire dust and removed the jousting paraphernalia and swords. Others then entered the ring with various odd objects, including large hollowed-out logs and small sheds. It was like a theater set.

"And now," the announcer began, "for our favorite event. We've tested our competitor's fighting skills, agility, and courage." *In ten minutes?* "Now it is time to test their senses and how well they hunt."

She felt Paul's grip tighten on her hand. This had been Anthony's primary concern. Five humans were herded into the ring. One of them screamed. The others were begging for their lives no less fervently but with less glass-shattering volume.

Charlee looked on dispassionately, little thoughts rumbling through her mind, reminding her that when Paul removed his hand from her skin, she would care about this and care deeply.

The announcer spoke again, "It would be to your advantage to not scream or make any sound at all. In fact, you should probably hide."

The vampires on the other end were blindfolded. She wasn't sure if they could see through the cloth barriers, but it was clearly part of the test. A few of the humans tried to escape the ring altogether but were dragged mercilessly back to the center. They scurried to find hiding places among the set props that had been laid out. When they were in place, the blindfolds were removed, and the lights went out.

Chapter Fourteen

The lights had been extinguished for five seconds. And although Paul kept a tight grip on Charlotte's emotions, Anthony could feel the faintest tinge of fear and disgust. Who could blame her? She'd watched five of her species herded into a ring like cattle to be hunted by creatures she hated because of him.

If he won, he wasn't sure she'd stand by him. And then what? It wasn't much to build a hundred-year reign on. Hell, if he won, he ran a serious risk of being overthrown in a couple of years anyway. Given the mess he'd made with Charlotte.

The stadium was bathed in a level of darkness few vampires experienced on a day-to-day basis. He wasn't sure of the visual acuity of his opponents, but Anthony could see the barest outlines of the various props that had been set out for this task.

And he smelled the blood.

In her desperate need to hide more fully, one of the humans had cut herself, probably on the jagged edges he'd noticed on one of the logs before the lights had gone out. He scanned the space in front of him.

Ah. There. At the edge of the stadium near the bleachers.

On his way to his quarry, he was knocked on his ass. *So, we're playing this way, are we?*

It wasn't enough to hunt prey and be the fastest. Some genius had gotten it into his head to start taking out the competition in the dark while the judges were too far away to clearly see what was happening. Fine by him.

He leapt up and pulled a stake from his pocket. Nondescript Competitor Number One wasn't the only one who could play dirty.

The two grappled in the dark for what felt like a brief eternity, but by Anthony's calculation was probably thirty seconds. Thirty seconds in which another vampire could have caught Anthony's prey. He thrust the stake into the other vampire's chest, praying it was Linus now dying. For Charlotte's sake.

He wiped the spray of blood from his face as the other vampire groaned and crumbled to the ground. The stench of the rotting corpse reached his nostrils, and he nearly gagged. It had been an old one.

He could hear the human's heartbeat, thudding against her chest like a steel drum. Her crying was soft and controlled as she tried desperately not to let him hear her tears and give her location away. He reached inside the log and dragged her out, kicking and screaming.

Anthony was glad what he had to do, he could do under cover of darkness. If Charlotte had to watch, it would bring back too much of the night he'd fucked up royally. As it was, he wasn't sure they'd ever get past it.

He sank his fangs into the girl's throat and drank. He stopped a few moments later and sealed the wound. He could only be grateful that the past two centuries running this test had comprised of later enthrallment, rendering the former hunt-and-kill method awkward.

A few minutes passed, and the lights came up. Anthony blinked as his vision adjusted. Five vampires including himself had a victim they'd fed from. Two of the competitors had been left off to the side, beaten and bloody in the fight for a human, but alive. The other three no longer existed, except for three piles of dust at various points in the ring.

Anthony held the girl in his arms. She was still trembling, but since he'd put his hands on her, she'd calmed considerably. He turned her in his arms, and she turned her head away, avoiding his eyes. Smart girl. Unfortunately her intelligence regarding vampire thrall wouldn't keep him in the competition.

"I'm going to make this simple for you. Do exactly as I tell you, or I'll kill you. I have no problem causing your horrible death if you cause my elimination. If you do what I say, I'll let you live. Do you understand?"

Her eyes met his. *That a girl.*

He took control of her mind, sifting through her thoughts, then implanted the command for her to wrap her arms around him and kiss him. She complied, her tongue sweeping into his mouth with the kind of enthusiasm he might have enjoyed if it had been real. He sighed against the woman's lips. Just one more thing for Charlotte to be pissed off about.

He looked up. The judges nodded. While not a horrific display, kissing your captor and meaning it passed muster. His competition hadn't been nearly so classy in their requests and though Paul kept a steady rein on Charlotte's emotions, Anthony could palpably feel her disgust at the hypnotized orgy.

All five of the vampires passed on to the next round. It had never really been in doubt. This part of the tournament's purpose was to feed the normal lust that blood lust caused in most vampires. Anthony had restrained himself, in part because of Charlotte's presence, but also because if he won, he had much easier access to the respect and cooperation of the older of his kind, by showing self-restraint.

When the test was finished, the remaining vampires snapped the necks of their victims and let the bodies fall to the ground. Anthony had loosened his mental hold on his victim after she'd completed the task. She turned in his arms, a mask of horror over her features, as if she'd been lied to.

"Go," Anthony said. Regardless of whether they liked it, this wouldn't disqualify him. When she got to the edge of the ring, a guard blocked her path. Anthony said, "Let her pass." The guard made a disgusted snort but stepped aside.

He took a deep breath. And now to the fun part. While his attention was focused on getting the young woman out of the ring, minions had stepped forward to bring out five chairs. Nice of them to think of the comfort of the competitors for the next round.

The announcer took the microphone again. "And now, for one of our less tasteful tests. The vampire who will lead us for the next hundred years must display many qualities that have already been tested; endurance is next. Competitors, have a seat." The remaining vampires took their places.

Anthony wasn't shocked to see Linus among them. He was, however, surprised that Gregory had made it this far. It struck him at once that Gregory had fed. From a throat.

Under cover of darkness, he'd abandoned his supposed principles with regards to drinking from the source so he could stay competitive. Gregory was a true politician.

He caught the look of guilt etched in the other vampire's eyes. Gregory was sorry he'd killed his victim. He'd been out of control. The blood was too strong, and he wasn't used to it. For a moment, Anthony felt sorry for him. Then there was no time to feel sorry for anyone.

The announcer spoke again, "The rules are quite simple. You are free to leave your seat at any time, but getting up, you forfeit your right to be king."

"Sounds simple enough," Gregory said.

Anthony chuckled. Gregory knew as well as he did what was next.

Five werewolves in black hoods rolled out carts with tureens of holy water and golden crosses. The Weres wore the hoods because relations between them and vampires were strained to begin with. This way they wouldn't be hunted down later and paid back in kind for the pain about to be delivered.

The wolves worked as a choreographed unit, each using the same amount of holy water, or pressing crosses against the same expanse of flesh. Five minutes passed before the first vampire dropped out.

Another ten minutes and they were down to three. Linus, Gregory, and Anthony. He had to admit, he was impressed with Gregory's ability to withstand all this, and a grudging respect grew. A couple more minutes and Gregory was eliminated.

Anthony sighed. Linus turned to him, a dark grin on his cross-burned face. He'd known it would come down to them, as if the other events and competitors had been mere window-dressing of the inevitable. The implements of torture were taken away, as were the chairs.

"There will be a brief intermission as competitors prepare for the final test."

Numbness wrapped around Charlee. She could barely feel Paul's grip on her hand and was sure by now all the circulation had left it. But she couldn't find the energy to care.

"Are you okay?" Jane leaned over Paul to examine her face.

"Fine." There had been a few moments when she'd felt Paul's control slipping and her own emotions spiraling out of control. Too many confusing thoughts and feelings.

The vampire was getting tired from using so much energy to calm her emotions for such an extended period. Nothing could stop the dread that had gnawed inside her stomach when the lights came on, when that girl had curled against Anthony as if they were lovers and mauled him with her mouth. Was that jealousy that had stabbed her gut?

She hated him. What did she care if some enthralled woman gave out fake affection? She'd had to close her eyes at the animalistic fucking that had taken place in the center of the ring with zombie humans. Paul had whispered in her ear to reassure her Anthony hadn't followed the pattern of the others.

When it was over, she'd opened her eyes too soon to see lifeless bodies being dropped without care. She'd looked to Anthony and mentally she'd chanted, *Please don't kill her. Don't kill her. I won't be able to stand you living if you kill her.* As if he'd heard her, he let the girl go, and Charlee released a breath she hadn't realized she'd been holding.

"Jane, I need you to do me a favor," Paul said.

"Name it," she replied with the same fake adoration she'd used with Gregory—until she'd obviously believed it—and now was using with Paul.

"I need you to go into the ring; tell them you're there as Anthony's second. You won't have to do anything but hand him his sword. I need to stay with Charlotte."

Jane hesitated.

"I'll be fine," Charlee said.

When Jane had left them, Paul turned in his chair to face her. "If Anthony loses and Linus becomes king, we have to leave this place immediately. There is a car waiting. For whatever reason, Linus has become obsessed with having you. I'd just as soon not make waves, but Anthony is my friend."

Charlee's fear was beginning to become overwhelming for a drained Paul. She wondered if this would affect his ability to help her escape. But she knew if he didn't keep doing what he was doing it would distract Anthony, and they'd have to find out. So she took a few deep, calming breaths to try to lessen Paul's psychic load.

"And if Anthony wins, you will march down there and support him," the vampire added.

Charlee bristled. It reminded her of why she hated Anthony. Either way her life was on the line. The only real decision was whether it would be the greater or the lesser evil she was saddled with. For either victor, somehow she'd become the prize.

The lights dimmed, and a bright spotlight illuminated the ring. Charlee felt her stomach tighten.

"Close your eyes," Paul said.

"I can't. I'll be more tense."

"Your call."

There was a drum roll in the background. "And now, Ladies and Gentlemen, the competition has been narrowed to two very worthy opponents. Anthony Burgess turned in 1546. And Linus Renard turned in 1312. In the human world we might vote, but in our world, we fight to death."

Charlee had pretty much figured those were the stakes. She zoned out as the announcer went on describing rules and calling for swords to be brought out. She turned in her seat to find Callie staring at her with a vicious sneer.

She nudged Paul. "How will we get past her?"

He gritted his teeth against her assumption of Anthony's death. "She'll have to go down with her entourage. It's not allowed to bring anyone else into the ring for the coronation. We can get out if we're quick."

Both vampires were expert swordsmen. It made sense as old as they were, but Charlee wondered who stayed in practice like that for centuries. She winced as Linus's blade whipped out and caught Anthony's cheek. Her hand came up to her own cheek, and she couldn't resist the urge to look to make sure she wasn't bleeding. Of course, her hand came away clean.

Anthony feinted to one side, dodging a strike that would have sent his head rolling across the ring. He twisted and took advantage of his opponent's lack of center and drew his sword out in a wide arc, wanting his rival's head but gashing his shoulder instead.

Linus laughed as blood gushed from the wound. If he hadn't moved so quickly, he'd be minus one arm. Unfortunately for Anthony, it wasn't the arm he was fighting with.

Anthony's movements slowed. *Something's wrong.* The thought grabbed hold of Charlee and wouldn't let go.

Paul lost his tenuous control and her pulse raced, her emotions flooding out of her. She flinched when Anthony looked in her direction as her feelings swamped him. In that moment, Linus's sword jammed into Anthony's gut. He doubled over, and Charlee felt like the world had gone on mute, everything shifting to slow motion.

Her attention went to Linus as he turned toward the cheering crowd, holding his sword in the air, being a pompous ass, ridiculously sure of himself and his easy victory. So sure he could turn his back on his opponent.

She felt the rage surge through Anthony as he watched Linus's display. He got his bearings back and rushed the other vampire, driving the sword into his back, and tackling him to the ground. While Linus lay shocked, the wind knocked out of him and his face in the dirt, Anthony slid the sword out and decapitated the vampire cleanly.

He looked up in Charlee's direction, getting to his feet, clearly stunned he'd won so quickly and equally confused by Linus's odd display of bravado at such a crucial moment.

Linus's head and body began to rot.

Behind her Callie screamed, "NO!" There was murder in her eyes. "Fucking bitch!" She tried to climb over the rows of vampires below to get to Charlee but her entourage held her back. Charlee wasn't sure why they prevented Callie from killing her; she was only a human. The claim couldn't be *that* important.

Then she remembered what Anthony's win meant. Callie couldn't kill her because she was the queen and it would be *off with her head.*

Anthony's sword fell with a loud clang in the stillness, and a sharp, unified gasp went up from the audience. Charlee turned in time to see Anthony stumble and fall.

Callie let out a peal of laughter. "Oh yes," she bellowed from six rows up, "Your vampire got cut on Linus's sword. Poison on the tip. One of the few that affects our kind. Guess you don't get to be queen either."

"I don't want to be queen, bitch," Charlee said. Then she thought better of it as she realized that if Anthony died, nothing would stop the crazed vampiress from descending on her.

"Go to him," Paul said. "As his mate, your blood might save him."

Charlee stood on shaking legs to make her way into the aisle.

"Wait!" Callie said, "You'll be tied to him forever. Your life entwined with his will stop your aging. You hate him for doing this to you, don't you?"

Charlee wasn't sure if she hated him enough to let him die, but it was true she hadn't asked for any of this, and she hated how he'd taken away all her choices.

Callie collected herself and was back to the elegant temptress, a mask which suited her far better than the hysterical loser. She slipped out of her row and descended the steps to calmly speak with Charlee, as if her spastic outburst hadn't just taken place.

"This isn't your concern, little human. No one wants a human queen. It will shame and undermine his reign. Let him die with dignity at least, and no harm will come to you. The claim will break, and we'll let you go free."

Charlee highly doubted that would be the case. Seeing her doubt, Callie lifted her voice to the crowd, the sound carrying farther than it should have out of such a tiny body.

"If Anthony dies, I have offered his little claimed human her freedom. Stand if you'll support this decision."

A murmur went through the crowd, and slowly, thousands of vampires rose to their feet. A door leading out of the stadium was less than ten yards from where Charlee stood. And beyond that, the circular lobby, and then the fresh air, and freedom on the other side. This entire nightmare could be over.

She started toward the door. Anthony was a monster; he'd likely killed thousands of people. He'd destroyed her life. She could walk away. No doubt someone from Cary Town's finest organized troupe of vampires would find her and erase her memory. She wouldn't have to carry this. Her life would be normal again. No vampires. Just a blissful, sweet ignorance.

Paul's voice cut through the stillness. "How can you do this to him? He's done nothing but thought of your safety. He shouldn't have bothered."

Charlee turned slowly. "I'm sorry, but I can't live like this. I have to be free. I could never forgive him."

It all seemed so easily laid out. So simple to execute. The perfect solution to the tangle that had become her life.

But then she felt it, the invisible twine stretched between her and Anthony. In a single day, it had almost started to feel a part of her. Now she felt it weakening, untangling, thread by invisible thread, and she made the mistake of looking into the ring.

He was doubled over on the ground, fighting to survive. Her feet stopped moving toward the door, and instead, she found herself turning and moving down the stairs.

At first she moved slowly as if she couldn't quite believe she was doing it, arguing with herself the entire way. Every step was an effort, a temptation to turn back and run. Then the threads began unraveling faster, and a sense of purpose attached itself to her as she moved down toward the ring with more speed than she thought she possessed.

"Stop her!" Callie shrieked.

But no one started to chase her. The only explanation for why the insane vampiress hadn't given chase herself, was that someone must be restraining her from doing it. Charlee got to the circle and slipped her arm underneath Anthony's mouth. He'd lost consciousness.

Somewhere along the way she'd started crying. "You stupid vampire. Don't you dare die on me!"

He remained unresponsive. Her eyes flitted back and forth between the two swords lying on the ground. Which one had the poison, and would it affect a human?

"Anthony's is the one with the sapphire handle," Jane shouted from the sidelines.

Charlee slid the blade across her arm and cried out. She'd expected it was going to hurt, but holy shit. She knew he wasn't dead yet because she could feel the single thread pulled almost taut between them, a moment from breaking, but still there. That and his flesh hadn't started melting off his bones yet. She shuddered at the thought.

She pried his lips apart and smeared a finger through the blood and put it in his mouth, trying not to think too hard about what she was doing. If she thought about it too much, she was bound to pass out. She'd barely made it through dissecting frogs in science lab.

She repeated the procedure three times before his mouth latched around her finger, sucking the blood off. She shoved her bleeding arm in front of him and almost cried with relief when his fangs extended, and he latched on.

She ran her fingers through his hair as he drank. The invisible cord between them tightened, the threads reweaving together, the connection growing so strong she knew she'd never be rid of him. For some reason she couldn't seem to get worked up about that.

He ripped his mouth from her arm and crushed his lips against hers. She could taste her coppery blood on his tongue. His hand drifted to her breast, stroking under the fabric of her dress.

She jerked away from him. "Anthony! Public place! Public place!"

He removed his hand and waggled his eyebrows at her. "That's what makes it fun."

Then he turned serious. "Why did you come back for me? I was still conscious when Callie made the offer."

"I love you, too. I should have known when I hated you so much. I couldn't let you go."

Anthony rested his forehead against Charlee's, his hand cradling the back of her neck.

The loudspeaker crackled and the announcer spoke again, "Well, this is . . . unprecedented. I think there is no question Anthony's mate supports his reign. So I give you your new king, Anthony Burgess, and his human queen."

Anthony rose, his strength revived, gripping Charlee's hand in his own. He stood with a kind of confidence she hadn't seen on him before.

But the stands remained quiet. A single vampire stood and started clapping. Charlee couldn't be sure, but he came from the gold rope section, so it was probably Paul. A minute or so passed, then a few more vampires stood. Then a few more, until the entire stadium erupted in applause.

Anthony let out a breath and turned toward her. "They'll accept you. What you did was damn impressive. I don't think any of them believed that given your chance at freedom you'd choose to throw in with the vampires."

"I didn't. I chose you."

He smirked. "Let's keep that between us, shall we?"

Epilogue

Greta padded to the kitchen to pour a glass of milk. Today Charlee was coming in, and she could find out why she was still hanging around the vampire. She might have to detach that girl with a crowbar.

"Morning."

Dayne planted a kiss on her lips that left her breathless and started the coffee maker. "Did you have a good hunt last night?"

"Mmmhmm."

Greta's eyes caught the answering machine blinking on the counter. "When did we get a call?"

"It must have been late last night, I was downstairs working. Didn't hear it."

Greta pressed the button.

Beep.

"Hey, it's Charlee, I just wanted to call and tell you," giggle, "Anthony, stop that, I'm on the phone." There was a pause, then Charlee's voice came back on the line. "I just wanted to call you to tell you I might be a couple of hours late tomorrow. There's weird paperwork I have to fill out." Anthony's voice was muffled in the background. "I just wanted to let you know I'm gonna be a little late but I'll be in."

"Next message."

"Greta, it's me again. Sorry. Anthony wouldn't get off my neck, and I couldn't think . . . Stop, that tickles . . . The reason I'll be late and have to do paperwork is because I'm queen of the vampires now."

"What!?!" Greta shouted at the machine.

"Next message."

"Me again. Sorry, Anthony thought that last message might not have been specific enough. I'm not a vampire or anything. He just claimed me. Details at work. Within reason. Later, babe."

Click.

"End of messages."

Part Three:
MATED

Chapter One

I f **Jane Tanner's life could** be summarized on a bumper sticker, it would say: "Be small. Don't look threatening." An odd life mantra for a 24-year-old woman who was five foot three, and one hundred and ten pounds soaking wet. But sensing vampires in a world where such beings were a well-kept secret wasn't great for survival.

Jane huddled in her coat and scrunched behind Paul as he led her into the smoke-filled club. There was snow on the ground, but this wasn't about the cold; it was about being invisible. Lately, the goal had been to be invisible from Paul. Over the past six months, he'd become what every vampire before Gregory had been with her. A monster.

To the average human, Paul would appear handsome, nonthreatening. His frame was slight, his height only five foot nine. But in that compact form, he held the strength of an immortal. And although he was still a fledgling by most vampiric standards, he was still about ten times stronger than Jane. A fact he reminded her of often.

While other humans saw a handsome face, hair that glinted gold as if touched by the sun, and perfect creamy skin, Jane could only see his good looks as a passing shadow. Instead, what she saw when she looked at Paul—and every other vampire—was coal-black skin that glistened like a snake, with shimmers of silver where the light hit it, and eyes that glowed like doorways into hell.

His fangs remained hidden inside his gums. When they were out they showed on his human visage, and vampires preferred to keep a low profile.

Which was why they hated her.

She could see them without being one of them. She'd begged countless times to be turned, but Gregory wouldn't curse her, and the other vamps wouldn't reward her.

Paul held her wrist in a punishing grip as he dragged her through the bar. The smoke of countless cigarettes was a thick haze that had her eyes watering. It had to be the control of all the preternaturals because Cary Town was the only place she'd been in a long time where you could still smoke in a bar.

The establishment was run down, but it was obvious it had been the spot in its heyday, maybe sixty years ago. Back then there had no doubt been live singers and performers of jazz and blues, instead of the canned music that was being piped out now through a cheap sound system.

Jane scanned the bar quickly, noting her surroundings. Paul seemed unwilling to protect her from others, so she had to stay aware. There were vampires, some demons, a few humans, and a wolf.

Demons were a hard sort to recognize. If they mingled in the human dimension, they looked like humans. But there was something *other* about them. They often incited that fearful gut instinct most people feel stupid for feeling, then ignore.

Demons also tended to stare quietly and made plenty of eye contact . . . something most humans didn't do with strangers. The humans were easy to pick out because they were just plain clueless. Laughing, talking too loud, drinking too much, completely unaware of the danger around them.

Considering the desire of the preternaturals to remain secret, one would think a lot of humans would mean safety, but with so many vampires present who could easily perform memory wipes, that bet was off.

And finally, the wolf.

Jane was glad Paul was dragging her to the back room because the wolf scared her more than the others. There was no particular defining characteristic that made him obvious to her as a wolf. His eyes didn't glow, and she couldn't see fur, for which she was grateful. She knew him from his picture.

Cole Riley. The alpha of the local wolf pack. The strongest werewolf pack in North America, fifty-three members and living right here in Cary Town. No one could find their den. They seemed to move in and out of the city at will without the need to go through the border patrol, and no one knew exactly how they were doing it. Underground tunnels maybe?

The wolves were a law unto themselves, anarchists except within their own group. So far the other preternaturals couldn't bring them to heel. Which made them dangerous. Anthony said Cole had been the alpha for twenty years. For a wolf to remain in power that long, well, nobody crossed him.

The back room was sectioned off by heavy burgundy drapes. The walls were a rich mahogany wood paneling, accented with posters of pin-up girls from the forties. While time had been kind to the walls, the carpet was threadbare and in desperate need of replacement.

Vampires filled the room, and the alcohol flowed freely. The last thing she wanted was for one of them to get it into their head to get her drunk or shoot her up with something just for kicks. But then she noticed the other humans, vampire groupies . . . or pets. They blurred together now. She let out a small sigh of relief that she wasn't the only human amusement.

In the middle of the room sat a large table made of dark gleaming wood. A few vampires in biker jackets sat around it, already dealing cards. There were chaise lounges against the walls in the shadows away from the one light that shone over the table center. Several vamps lounged about, a few with humans draped over them in a way that veered toward NC-17.

"Take off your coat and stay awhile," Paul said.

Jane jumped as his voice cut though her mental cataloging.

The other vampires looked up, interest in their eyes. None of them felt much older than Paul. Though that would only be of benefit if she had a useful superpower. All her powers, if they could be called that, were the kind that put her life in constant danger. She could see them; she could feel them; sometimes she got vampiric memories. She didn't want to speculate what *that* was about. They couldn't get inside her mind or thrall her. Vamps hated that.

Reluctantly, she removed the coat. It was one of those Eskimo-style coats, with the fur-fringed hood that a person could easily get lost in. Though not real fur. Under the coat she wore black leather pants, a black leather halter top that was cut high to show her stomach, and black boots. The cherry on the sundae was hot pink hair and a nose ring.

At first glance, this wasn't a look that matched the *be invisible* mantra. But you had to know this crowd. Looking around the room, Jane saw the other humans were wearing black too, including black lipstick and eye makeup. A couple of them had light face make-up that made them look dead, and they each had a different rainbow color in their hair. One of the girls had blue hair, another green, and one had short, spiky crimson.

This was exactly what crayons would look like if they were produced by a group of goths.

Jane didn't wear the white make-up; her skin was naturally pale. Living with vampires in the dark and on Vampire Central Time since she was sixteen pretty much guaranteed she'd look like one of them.

One of the vamps looked at her appreciatively with a raised eyebrow. It was ridiculous, but many of them preferred naturally pale women instead of the groupies that wore makeup. They claimed the make-up altered the flavor of the blood, but Jane thought it had more to do with feeding their egos, the thought that some human would willingly give up the sun just to be in their precious presence.

Then again, maybe he was looking at her neck.

She could still feel where Paul's fangs had pierced her throat earlier in the evening. He'd sealed the wound so she wouldn't bleed to death but hadn't healed it fully, preferring to see her wearing his mark. He wouldn't give her a true mark, a claim. He just wanted to piss on his territory a bit.

Paul finally took an empty seat at the table and patted his knee. Jane sat on his lap as he picked up his cards and placed his bet. "Front me some chips, Rayne?"

The vampire sitting across from them snorted. "Where's *your* money? Thought you had an endless supply?"

Paul slammed his fist on the table. "Anthony's gotten too big for his britches now that he's king. He's cut me off. Says he won't pay any more of my debts and that he better not hear I've been stealing off humans. He's not cleaning that mess either." Paul said it in a snotty sing-song voice.

For about the millionth time, Jane wished she could get into his sleeping chamber to stake him at noon when his sleep would be deepest.

Anthony's fledge or not, Jane couldn't see how he would mind her getting rid of the wanker. All Paul did now was cause trouble, threaten her, and make the new administration look bad.

"So, why don't you earn some money?" It was the eyebrow lifter. The one who'd given her *that look*. And now she could almost see the cogs turning in his creepy little brain.

Paul let out an exasperated sigh. "I'm not getting a job. I'm a vampire for Christ's sake."

The other vampire at the table hissed on hearing the C-word. Maybe a superstitious one.

The eyebrow-raiser pressed on. "I was thinking you could put your girl there to work. I know I'd give you a few chips for a taste . . . or a ride."

Jane worked hard to keep her face blank. She'd survived it before; she could survive it again. There had been the brief reprieve with Gregory, and while Paul had been a right bastard, he hadn't shared her with anyone. He hadn't gone out of his way to protect her, but he hadn't passed her around either.

Yet.

Paul ran his hand over her arm. If she were any other human, she'd be feeling calm at his touch, maybe even horny. The idea would be sounding good to her right now. She wished she were a regular human so she could hide in the oblivion like they did.

"You know what she is, right? You can feel it?"

The other vampire nodded, "Kindred, but . . . not. She's human, but she feels like vampire."

Paul snorted. "She's an insult, is what she is."

"But she's different. You have a commodity here. Something unique you could sell if you had a better business head on ya."

Jane stared at the cards in Paul's hand, avoiding looking at the vampire with the entrepreneurial ambitions. She wouldn't cry. She wouldn't scream. She wouldn't give them anything that would make them want to come back and get more.

"Get up," Paul said.

Jane's head snapped around to him, not really believing this was happening, even though she'd been mentally preparing for the possibility. "What?"

"I said, get your ass up. Now!"

She stood and braced herself against the table as she felt her legs begin to liquefy beneath her.

"I'll front you the chips to start if you let me take her home with me tonight," the vamp said.

By now, the vampires lounging about the room had stopped feeding and fucking to watch, intrigued by the human in the room that wasn't quite what she appeared.

"Okay," Paul said, "She's yours for the night. Jane, go over there."

Humans didn't question. Mainly because they couldn't with a thrall on them. "Paul, no. Don't."

It would have been better for her to go to the other vampire than to piss him off by embarrassing him in front of his friends. Before she could track the movement, Paul had left his seat and backhanded her. His claws sliced her cheek, and she went flying.

She landed on an empty couch that was just soft enough to break her fall. The thought crossed her mind that Paul had the foresight to aim for the couch so she'd be able to do whatever he was going to force her to do later in the night. She remained absolutely still, her eyes on the floor, knowing every glowing eye was on her . . .

the girl with the fresh blood flowing down her cheek in a den of monsters.

Jane heard the drapes ripped to the side, followed by a low growl. "Paul!"

She looked up to see Cole standing in the doorway. His eyes flicked momentarily to her then back to his prey, the vampire.

"You got my money?"

Jane chanced a look at Paul. If possible, he was even paler than before.

"No . . . I . . . um . . . not yet. Give me a few weeks. I'll get it."

Jane felt the tears running down her cheeks, mixing with the blood that still flowed freely. She knew how he'd get that money now. The thought of being passed from vamp to vamp again would have been enough to empty the contents of her stomach if she'd eaten recently enough.

Rayne, who'd been silent during the pimp business plans, rose smoothly to his feet and turned toward Cole. "Get out. It's vamps-only in here tonight."

Cole strode forward, put his hand on Rayne's shoulder, and forced him back into his chair as if he were a kitten trying to climb out of a basket. "Sit. Down. My business is with Paul. Don't make it become about you."

The wolf moved past Rayne and stopped in front of Paul, "That's what you said a few weeks ago. I'm going to have to collect something now. You understand that, right? If I just let you walk, it makes me look weak." He wrapped a hand around Paul's throat. "Would you like to be an object lesson?"

Jane should have been jumping up and down to see the vampire who'd been lording it over her, stink with fear of his own. If she could sense it from him, she knew the vamps could as well. But all she could think about was how badly he would take it out on her later. She was only human, but he'd find ways to make sure she survived whatever it was he was likely planning for her now.

"If you kill me, you'll start a war. You know who my sire is."

Cole rolled his eyes. "Yes, I also know your sire has cut off the money tree to his beloved fledge. Trouble in paradise?"

"It's that fucking human he's with," Paul snarled.

Cole loosened his grip. "Be that as it may, you owe me ten grand, and my patience is up. Think fast. How are you going to make payments?"

Paul's eyes drifted to Jane, and the world stopped. He wasn't going to pass her around to all the vamps to raise money. That would be too much work for Paul. He was going to try to give her outright to the wolf.

She wanted to beg him not to do this to her. The wolves had an even worse rep than the vampires. Judging from Paul's earlier reaction, it would only drive him on, so she remained silent as she watched the transaction.

"How about a trade, call it even?"

Cole looked as if he might be considering it. "A trade? What do you have of any value to me?"

Paul gestured to Jane with a wide sweeping motion that made him look like a game show host. She can be yours if the price is right. "Jane. She's a little banged up, but she fucks like a dream."

Cole turned toward her and she looked away, unable to take his calculated glare. "Well, if you're just 'giving' her away, she must not be worth much to you. Looks to me like you're trying to get off easy."

"I could keep her and make the money if you want to wait a few weeks. I've got vamps here who want a piece of her. Right, boys?"

The other vampires all nodded their agreement, a couple rustling through pockets to produce cash, as if to prove how serious they were about their purchase.

Cole's eyes narrowed. "Is that right? If that's the case, how do I know you won't just gamble away the profits instead of paying me?"

Jane shrank back as the wolf moved toward her. She expected him to jerk her up by the arm or yell at her or say something horrible, but he scooped her up carefully and headed for the door.

"If I can't get money, at least I can close off your earning potential. Have a nice unlife, Paul. And if I see you again, I might kill you whether or not it means a war." Then he nodded to the other vamps in the room. "Gentlemen."

Chapter Two

Ten *fucking grand. **What are** you doing, man?* Cole sat in his cherry red Mustang, his head on the steering wheel. He'd gone in with every intention of collecting his money or at least beating some sense into that insufferable little fledge of Anthony's. Paul was right. Cole couldn't kill him without starting a war, but not because he was the favored fledge of the vampire king. Interspecies killing among the preternaturals was a no-no.

And now he had this tiny human who thought God only knew what about what he was going to do with her. Good question, actually. What the hell *was* he going to do with her? And why had he taken her as payment? It wasn't like he'd starve, but it wasn't pocket change either.

The smell of her blood mixed with fear would have sent any other wolf into a frenzy, but he, of course, was the alpha and above such weakness. His claws lengthened as fur started to crop up on his hands. Shit. *Go to the happy place, Cole.* It wouldn't be ideal to eat the payment. That's one damn expensive meal.

He heard the click of the lock's release as the woman —Jane was her name?—reached for the door.

"Now wouldn't be the best time to do that," he growled around elongated fangs. "It's the blood and the fear."

His voice softened. "Nothing to do about the blood just this second, but try to tone the panic down a notch."

He watched her squeeze her eyes shut and intentionally slow her breathing. Smart girl. She knew she couldn't outrun him and was intelligent enough to know not to lead a wolf into a chase. While she was engaged in deep meditative breathing, Cole matched the pace of her breath to calm himself and get the beast to go back and take a nap.

The claws receded, and the fur went back into its hiding spot. He lifted his hands to see the claw marks in the steering wheel. "Dammit. This is new leather interior." Jane jumped in the corner of his peripheral vision. His voice was calm when he spoke again. "If I wanted you dead, little lamb, you'd be dead."

He ran a hand through his hair. "I'm Cole, and I'll be your captor for the evening." He watched her eyes grow large and her body tense further. He shook his head and sighed. "It'll be funny later, I promise."

The girl looked doubtful.

He didn't blame her, but she unnerved him as much as he unnerved her. For one thing, there was the eerie silence. Maybe it was his experience with the pack, but he'd never seen a woman so quiet. Sure, he'd seen women afraid before. Being the alpha, he'd seen a lot, but he'd never seen one like this.

She looked out the window, away from him again. She'd buckled her seat belt and had curled her body into a tight ball like a porcupine. She was still breathing slowly, in and out, the effort to remain calm obviously taking all her concentration. This was some pickle she'd gotten herself into.

As he pulled onto the highway he said, "What did you expect being a vampire groupie? Vampires are not a friend to humans."

"And werewolves are?" She kept the tears out of her voice. But he smelled the salt.

He'd wanted to piss her off, find some fire in there somewhere. Instead, he'd made her cry.

"I'm sorry. But you have to see my point. Hanging out with vamps. Dressed like a goth. Really, what did you expect would happen?"

Cole zipped through traffic like a lunatic, but Jane seemed too upset to notice. If it were possible, she was crying more now.

"You don't know anything about me." She flinched after she said it as if just remembering who or *what* she was talking to.

Fabulous. I've got a mental case on my hands. He growled.

Her fear escalated, and he flipped through his mind to find out why. Had he just growled? What the hell was he going to do with a human in the hive?

The hive was the term the wolves had affectionately given the network of interconnecting caves the pack lived in. The network of interconnecting caves that was absolutely off-limits to humans. Of course, he'd instituted that rule. Still.

The pack had been on him about finding a mate for the past five years when they decided as a group that, at thirty-three, his bachelorhood wasn't cute anymore. Rhonda, the pack omega, had done her best to snag him herself. But they'd grown up together.

He swerved between then past two cars that were going a ridiculous 70 mph on the freeway and glanced at Jane. She had pink hair for god's sake. The pack was going to love this.

Cole reached across her for the glove box. She jumped, and he put his hand back on the wheel. "Okay, I need you to do something for me. There is a thick, dark piece of cloth in there. I need you to cover your eyes with it."

Her hand shook as she reached for the compartment.

"I can't have you seeing where I'm taking you."

Her heart rate skyrocketed. That sounded worse than he'd meant for it to sound.

The blood on her cheek had started to clot, making it possible for him to hold onto control. He was glad it wasn't the full moon. "What do I have to do to convince you I have no intention of harming you?"

She was holding the cloth in her hands as if it were soaked in a deadly poison. "Let me go." Then she added quietly, "Please."

"No."

"Why not?"

"You're worth ten thousand dollars to me right now. Letting you go isn't an option."

"What are you going to do with me?"

"I don't know." He eased the car to the shoulder and turned toward her. "I can't go any further until you do as I asked."

She stared at the offending object in her lap, running her fingers over the thick black wool, her hand still shaking.

"Listen, the safety of the pack is my responsibility. Vamps and werewolves aren't exactly best friends. Bringing you with me is like bringing an enemy into the camp. I can't put any of them at risk."

She took a few shuddering breaths and looked out the window down the road, no doubt trying to measure her potential for success if she ran. Finally, she turned back to him with a pleading look in her eyes that caused his chest to tighten and made him want to reach out and comfort her.

The moment passed, and she put the blindfold on without further argument. She was silent the rest of the way.

Jane felt like he'd doubled back, maybe more than once. She couldn't be sure what direction they were heading in anymore. And what kind of idiot did he think she was?

Not going to harm her? In his book, not beating her probably equaled not harming her. Maybe if she was lucky, he wouldn't pass her around. She thought back to when she'd seen his photograph for the first time.

She'd thought he was almost unbearably hot with jet black hair that fell in a disheveled sexy mop over his eyes and a white T-shirt that molded tightly to the muscles of his upper body. That was before Anthony had labeled him Prime Enemy Number One and given her a crash course on werewolves.

It wasn't that she'd never heard about werewolves or their reputation before, but Anthony had gone into grisly detail. Now Prime Enemy Number One seemed set on keeping her as payment. How was he going to get ten thousand dollars out of her? With the same plan Paul had? Or would he just use her himself? Would he let her go when he felt he'd gotten his money's worth? Or would he kill her or pass her on to someone else like a used book?

In another set of circumstances, if he wasn't a werewolf, if he wasn't the *leader* of the werewolves and hadn't taken her as payment for a gambling debt, she could see herself falling into those warm brown eyes.

She felt the fleeting temptation to reach out and touch him. He'd be warm. She'd never slept with anyone warm before. It had all been vampires and death for her. She could barely remember making out with her first serious boyfriend when they were sixteen.

She'd been so close to giving it up at a college party they'd snuck into. Until the vampire showed up. He'd killed the guy and taken her. In the small moments when she wasn't trying to find a vampire to turn her so she'd be safe, she dreamed about what it would be like to sleep with someone warm, what it would have been like to have that one experience without the monster showing up and ripping her life away from her.

Cole had turned quiet since she'd put on the blindfold. She was glad. It gave her some peace to think. She just had to get to a phone. Anthony wouldn't let a wolf keep her, not Prime Enemy Number One. They'd find her.

But did she want to be found? Maybe Anthony didn't see a problem with how Paul was treating her. Maybe he just didn't care. Which would be the lesser evil? Cole or Paul?

There was a sound like a steel door whooshing open, and she tensed. They were getting closer to wherever he was taking her. In a tunnel maybe? Five minutes passed, and the Mustang stopped.

Another few minutes and she heard the car door open, causing her to nearly jump out of her skin. Then his hand was on her arm, gently guiding her out of the vehicle and toward God only knew where.

He must have sensed her growing anxiety now that they'd arrived at their destination because he said, "I'm not going to hurt you, Jane. I promise you'll be safe."

She heard a sound like a code being pressed into a computer, a decidedly unsafe sound. Moments later she felt herself being ushered into a temperature-controlled room.

"You can take off the blindfold now."

She reached behind her head to remove the fabric. It was insane, but there had been a sense of safety behind that cloth barrier. As long as he didn't touch her or talk to her she could pretend she was somewhere else, doing something else. When the blindfold came off, she was jolted back to her new reality.

It looked like a cave. They were in a large circular room with stone walls and a dome ceiling. Vents near the ceiling piped in air. She felt as if the air had heated and was pressing in on her, trying to suffocate her.

"We're underground, aren't we?"

Cole nodded. He was standing about eight feet away, his arms crossed over his chest, observing her like a bug under a glass.

She sat on the black leather couch behind her—more like collapsed—and put her head in her hands. "Please let me go. I'll find a way to get you your money. I can't stay here." She looked up at him, her eyes pleading.

"I said no. You're staying with me."

"But it's underground. I can't . . . " She started to hyperventilate.

He was beside her in less than a second, but she couldn't think about that now. The walls were closing in.

"Claustrophobic?"

He didn't say it with a mocking tone or an evil sneer, just a question.

"Yes. Please, you can't keep me here."

He knelt on the floor beside her and took her hands in his. Not threatening, not sexual. Comforting.

He'd taken her hostage, and now he was comforting her?

"Look at me."

She did.

"Now, take a deep breath in very slowly. Good. Now, out."

She breathed with him. It was so ridiculous. She was with a werewolf and the thing that put her over the edge into complete hysteria was being underground.

"This place is big. There is plenty of air. The system we use is state of the art and has security you wouldn't believe. Even if the vent stopped—and you'd know it instantly—you'd have a day's worth of oxygen. Maybe more. But a day's worth at minimum."

Jane looked at him warily. He was being so nice. It had been ages since anyone but Charlee had been this kind to her. She wanted to believe it. But if he were really a good guy, he'd let her go. Besides, this wasn't the first time someone had been nice to her just to screw with her later.

But weren't head games a vampire thing? Werewolves didn't do that, did they? From all she'd heard, wolves weren't big on subtle. They were supposed to be more about the mauling and tearing limbs off.

"Are you okay now?"

She nodded.

"I'm going to take a shower. Feel free to look around the den."

He got up from his crouched position on the floor and disappeared into one of the doors in the stone wall, leaving Jane with her thoughts.

Chapter Three

The hiss of the shower was strangely soothing but even more comforting was having a moment alone. Paul had never left her alone, going so far as to put a guardian watch dog on her while he slept. *God, Jane. Think.*

The knowledge about the vents had calmed her enough to stop the hysteria. Though even without that knowledge, she would have gone into survival mode and forgotten the claustrophobia panic. Maybe.

There are bigger things to worry about than walls closing in. She shouldn't have thought that. She dropped to the ground on her hands and knees as memories of enclosed spaces slammed into her so hard she could barely breathe. She squeezed her eyes shut, trying to block the images of the past, and forced herself back to her feet. She fought back a wave of dizzy nausea and gripped the arm of the sofa for support.

The walls were a dark gray stone, probably natural to the area. The furnishings were minimalistic and modern.

Her eyes scanned the tops of the walls. Nearly a dozen large flat screens encircled the cave. He hadn't been kidding about the security. When anyone got near, there was probably a loud 'Security breach in Sector Five' warning with buzzers and flashing red lights.

There were six doorways around the circumference of the cave's main living area. Two of the doors had security panels and were made of steel. One she'd been led through. She didn't know where the second went.

The other doorways were empty spaces carved out of the stone. No privacy. Not that she'd expected any. One of the doors led into the bathroom where the shower continued to run. She peeked inside the others to find a bedroom, kitchen, and an office.

She spotted a phone on the desk in the office and rushed to it, her heart racing. Instead of a dial tone she heard, "Please enter your security code to make an outgoing call."

She fiddled in her coat pocket and came out with Paul's cell phone. Only two bars left. By tomorrow night it would likely be dead. This might be her only opportunity. She hadn't expected to get a signal. The wolf must have a tower. Of course he did. He lived in the Fortress of Paranoia.

Could the coven trace the call?

She took a deep breath and dialed.

"Jane?"

"Yeah, it's me. You have caller ID; who else would I be?"

There were tears in Charlee's voice. "Oh my god, you're alive. Paul said you'd been killed. When we tried to get more information out of him, he said it was a werewolf. Where are you?"

Jane's stomach roiled at Paul's lie, but she chose not to address it. Getting to safety was the priority. Her eyes roved over the walls of the office, looking for anything that might give her a clue to her location to help them start a search.

"I don't know. I'm in their den, I think. Cole has me."

"Cole? Jane, you've got to get out of there."

She gritted her teeth. "No, I thought it would be fun to hang out a while. If there was a way out, I would have taken it. I . . ."

The phone was pulled out of her hand. She spun to see Cole pressing the *end* button. He was standing in a towel, dripping from the shower. Her tongue darted out to wet her suddenly dry lips.

"No phone."

She moved behind the desk to put something between them. Not that a puny little desk was going to stand in his way if he was going to go psycho over her trying to call for help. Before she could think of anything placating to say, the phone rang again. He answered it.

"Hello . . . Yes, this is Cole Riley . . . Yes, I have Jane . . . No, I won't release her to you . . . the debt is ten thousand dollars . . . Oh, you think you can get Anthony to give you the money? Does Anthony have limitless supplies of cash to cover the gambling debts of his fledge? Let me talk to him."

Cole's back was to her as he spoke. Jane sank into the chair and watched the water droplets trail their way down his skin, trying to convince herself it would be fine. Maybe he wouldn't physically hurt her. She could have sex with him if that was what he wanted from her.

Oh, God, could she have sex with him. She worked to push the images of their bodies sliding against one another out of her mind. He'd kidnapped her. What was wrong with her? What if he passed her around, shared her with the pack?

She shuddered, her fantasy appropriately doused with a bucket of cold reality.

"Anthony, congratulations on the tournament. I haven't had a chance to call you and congratulate you personally . . . Yes, well, I've been busy . . . you know how it is . . . Better you than Linus . . . all right, fine. Yes, I have Jane, and no, I'm not returning her."

There was a long pause while Anthony delivered what must have been an impressive monologue.

"Have you taken a good look at her lately? She's got some pretty deep bruises, and on her lower back I noticed what could only be knife wounds. Purposeful, lined up knife wounds. She's not a cutter unless she's a contortionist . . . "

So he'd noticed that. She wanted to melt into the floor.

" . . . She's got a bite mark on her throat. You and I both know vampires only leave marks when they want a mark left . . . and it's not a claim, or he would have protected her. So why exactly do you want her returned? You want to have her abused some more? . . . Fuck you. I've never abused a woman. I don't care if she's human . . . I don't care if she's part of the coven. Let it go, Anthony. Tell your human she can't have everything she wants just because she's mated to the vampire king . . . Trust me, she's safer here. The coven is no place for a human, your mate notwithstanding . . . Goodbye then."

Jane felt the tears stinging her eyes when Cole turned back around. He slammed the phone against the wall, and it shattered. "Fuck!"

She flinched, and he cursed again.

"Do you realize I almost got into a war over you? What the hell is wrong with me? Are you some kind of witch?"

Jane watched as he melted down in front of her. This wasn't a good sign. He seemed to be talking more to himself than to her, so she stayed quiet and tried to blend into the background, a skill she'd perfected over the years. Except now pink hair and black leather didn't blend.

Finally, she found the strength to speak. "Anthony wouldn't pay you the money?"

Cole stopped pacing and braced himself against the wall facing her. "We didn't discuss the money. The conversation got sidetracked. You heard it. I can't believe I'm helping a vampire groupie."

"Excuse me, but how are you helping me? You're keeping me prisoner."

"You're safer with me than with them. Clearly."

She decided to let that one go. So far he hadn't hurt her. And although *benefit of the doubt* wasn't the normal operating procedure with preternaturals, Gregory had been decent to her, and he'd swooped in to her rescue, too. He'd been good to her until his political aspirations had overshadowed his concerns with her safety.

"I'm not a vampire groupie. I hate vampires."

He crossed his arms over his chest and sized her up. "Well, I'm sure you hate vampires now that they haven't lived up to your romantic fantasies of them." He pushed off the wall. "Come with me."

She stayed in the chair, her face wary. "Where are we going?"

"To clean up your face."

She followed him to the bathroom where he ran a warm damp cloth carefully over her cheek to clean the blood that had dried there. "We should have taken care of this first. It might still get infected," he said. He placed one hand gently on her shoulder, while using the other to smooth ointment on her cheek.

She took in a sharp breath. He was so warm.

"I'm sorry, does it hurt?"

She blushed. "No. I'm fine." What was she going to say? Keep touching me because I can't remember what warm skin feels like on mine? *Yeah, that'll convince him I'm not a vampire groupie.*

He cleaned off the bathroom counter, tossed the empty ointment tube into the trash can, and returned the first aid kit to the medicine cabinet. "When was the last time you ate?"

Jane shrugged. She couldn't remember, but now that he brought it up, she was starving.

"Did they not feed you? Honestly. You can't keep a human and drink their blood and not feed them. And you want me to let you go? Back to that? Back to Paul?"

She looked away. "I don't want to go back with Paul, but I have no guarantee you're safer. Werewolves are the bad guys."

He sighed and led her to the kitchen. "No, vampires are the bad guys. They're trying to force us into a police state here. Not that it's just them. The last werecat tribe leader contributed as well. If it takes off in Cary Town, it's only a matter of time until it spreads. Sit." He indicated the chair.

She sat. "Well, I'm human, so you're both bad guys."

Cole nodded. "True enough. But I don't allow my pack to hunt humans." He took a couple of large steaks out of the fridge. "If you're a vegetarian you'll have to get over it."

She wrinkled her nose. "I don't like red meat."

"Tough. It has B-12 and iron. And you've been a vampire snack for how long?"

Jane looked away. "I was taking supplements."

"Uh huh." He seasoned the meat and put it on the grill. "Trust me, you'll like this."

Jane had her doubts about that, but he didn't seem to be in meltdown mode, so why screw with a good thing?

Her gaze raked involuntarily over his body. He hadn't yet had a chance to dress, and only a towel stood between her and the full monty. A black tribal tattoo snaked around one of his biceps, and she had the sudden urge to trace the design with her tongue.

She watched the muscles of his back bunch and relax as he busied himself with the food preparation. Occasionally a drop of water from his still-wet hair made a daring trail down his back, disappearing into the towel. Jane blushed, trying to remember the circumstances of their meeting and why she shouldn't be having naughty wrong thoughts about him.

When he put the plate in front of her, she carefully cut off a piece of the meat and took a bite.

"This is actually really good."

His mouth quirked on one side, revealing an unexpected dimple. "Told you. It's all about the seasoning and not overcooking it until it's shoe leather."

He didn't seem to be eating much himself. A sudden stray thought slid into her mind. *Did he put something in my food?* She berated herself silently for being so paranoid. Why would he need to? He had her locked up with no hope of escape, and it wasn't like she could overpower him. Maybe he was drugging her so she wouldn't kill him in his sleep.

"What's wrong?"

"Nothing," she said, taking smaller bites.

"No, something's wrong. Is it the food?"

"It's nothing." It probably *was* nothing. She didn't feel funny. Well, she felt different, but that was from eating a decent meal. She tried to change the subject. "Why aren't you eating?"

He looked at the plate of barely touched steak. "I prefer my meat raw, but I didn't want to gross you out. I'll hunt later." His eyes narrowed as he looked at her, and she dropped her gaze back to her plate, unable to take his intense stare any longer. "You thought I put something in your food."

She shrugged, embarrassed now. "What are you going to do with me?"

"I don't know."

"Are you going to hurt me?"

He stood and paced. "Did you not hear me tell Anthony I don't abuse women?"

She mumbled, "Just because you said it to Anthony doesn't mean it's true."

"Fair enough. But have I given you any reason to think I'm going to start beating on you or cutting you or anything else?"

"No."

"Okay."

She was silent for a few minutes, "Do I have to sleep with you? N-not that that would be horrible if you weren't hurting me or if you didn't share me with anyone."

His jaw clenched. "Ask me again why I'm not sending you back there."

She looked at him expectantly.

"No! Rape is abuse. See earlier statement. And even if I would sink so low, you don't know werewolves as well as you think if you think we share. I'll sleep on the couch. You can have the bed."

He left her alone in the kitchen then. She was mortified by how the discussion must have sounded to him. How she must have looked. She wanted to believe she was safe here, but it seemed highly unlikely he'd just blow in and rescue her. She replayed the scene from earlier in the evening.

When they'd first seen each other in the bar, he'd given her a look. What was it? Interest? Curiosity? Was it sexual? She couldn't remember. The second she'd recognized him from his photo she'd looked away.

Why would he take her instead of ten thousand dollars? Especially when he said he wasn't going to use her to pay off the debt. She took her plate to the sink and rinsed it off. Cole's steak sat barely touched. She went through the cabinets until she found some plastic wrap and put it in the fridge. Then she finished straightening the kitchen.

"You don't have to do that."

She looked up to see him standing in the doorway. He'd changed into a pair of pajama pants. Cole didn't strike her as a pajama-pant-wearing kind of guy.

"Well, what else am I supposed to do? How many years of housework will pay off Paul's debt?"

He growled. "You're not a slave."

"Then why am I here? Why take me instead of the money?"

He ran a hand through his hair. It seemed to be something of a nervous tic with him, not that she could throw stones about nervous tics.

"I knew I'd never see that money. If I hadn't taken you, he would have whored you out for it. I would have felt responsible. I couldn't have taken money like that, even assuming I could intercept it before he gambled it away. And now I can't let you go because you'd just go back to him. Abused women always do."

Jane shook her head. "It's not a matter of going back. It's a matter of him not letting me out of his sight. He'd hunt me. And anyway, if it wasn't him, it would be another vamp. They always find me. I can see them, and they'll never forgive me for that."

Chapter Four

Cole tossed and turned on the couch. It was large, but not nearly large enough for his frame. His original intention had been to share the bed with Jane, but that would have created all sorts of problems. For one thing, he wasn't sure if he could keep his hands off her, even if she had pink hair. And for another, whatever she'd been through, she didn't need to feel that threat like she was constantly two seconds from attack.

Why did I make this my problem. I can't save everyone. He'd never wanted control of the pack to begin with. He'd killed the former alpha in a mad rage when he'd caught him raping his mother. Then he was stuck with it. And the pack needed him.

The former alpha had been sadistic and cruel to nearly everyone in one way or another. It had taken almost a year before they'd felt safe again. Now he had Jane on his hands, another person who needed him. Another responsibility he hadn't asked for.

She'd said she wasn't a vampire groupie, she hated vampires, and she could see them. He'd flipped those three sound bites over and over in his head for the past hour trying to figure out what it meant. He should have asked for clarification. What the hell did she mean she could *see* them?

He stared at the ceiling of the cave, counting the little natural indentations. Almost as good as sheep. Sheep.

Damn, now I'm hungry. He listened to Jane's breathing. She was asleep, but not deeply. Best to wait awhile.

He flung the cover to the floor and padded to the office. He'd do a bit of work, then if Jane had hit REM, he'd go hunting. Cole found the shattered cell phone on the floor and bent to pick up the pieces. No wonder he was freaking her out. He needed to get a grip on himself if he was going to have a human living with him.

"Stop obsessing over what you did, and deal with the choice now," he said to the empty room. "No sense going over and over it. You rescued a human from a vampire in lieu of ten grand. You're insane. Let's move on."

Satisfied with the self-talk, he dropped the cell phone bits into the trash bin and settled into the big leather swivel chair to work. He typed theriantype.com into the browser window and logged in as an administrator. If half the people who did business with his site knew the owner was a werewolf, they'd flip their lid. He filtered most everything through Mick.

He opened a second window to check email.

"Dammit, Dayne. You little whiner," he muttered. There was an email from the Board of Magical Merchants showing Dayne Wickham had filed a discrimination claim. It was absurd. Was it discrimination when you didn't sell a handgun to a career criminal?

Cole had only been a child when Dayne had gone on his psycho killing spree with the werecat tribe, but any ninny knew he was bad news. Freaky old hermit living out in the woods waiting for Hansel and Gretel to stumble upon the place.

He sent an email back to the board explaining his side of the situation. He didn't have proof of the sorcerer's misbehavior, but everybody knew he'd done it. It wasn't as if they could keep records as closely as humans could without detection.

It was ridiculous to Cole that the preternaturals were so afraid of the humans finding out. But due to the human fear of the unknown and their increased techno-logy, it wasn't a war many felt they could win anymore.

If they could have gotten over their squabbles and joined together in the Middle Ages during the last major supernatural panic, they could have won. But the preter-natural factions had been too divided back then.

The vamps had spent the last three centuries organiz-ing and trying to make friends with everyone else. It had worked with everyone but the wolves. That bitterness ran deep.

The second email was from Mick:

Hey Bossman, um, Dayne was complaining that nothing had been done about his ordering issues with us. He filed a complaint six months ago, but we didn't get it. It must have gotten lost. So when it was resent and finally reached the board and us, he was very put out and demanded we mention his complaint on our site. Instead of just the Lucinda Clearwater issue. Don't be mad.

Mick

Cole growled and went back to the site to find Dayne's complaint along with a response alerting and warning people about him. Oh, that was going to go over well.

If they had all been human Dayne could probably sue them, but he was the one who'd insisted they list the complaint. At least Mick wasn't letting the sorcerer bully him.

Cole checked sales and handled the other complaints that had been forwarded. By the time he'd finished, another hour had passed.

He listened for Jane's breathing again. Good. Deep sleep. His stomach was growling at him, and being in the same cave as a human wasn't the wisest move at the moment.

Once outside and safe under the cloak of trees and darkness, he stripped his clothes off and buried them in the dirt. He turned his mind to the moon, his focal point for the change. The forest swirled around him in a blur of deep green, as his spirit was ripped away then slammed back into the new wolf form. He shook himself and fought back the sense of vertigo. Unlike most of his kind, he knew he'd never get used to the way shifting felt.

As a wolf, Cole was solid black, something he loved for the way it helped him blend in dark places. He'd planned to go hunting out of town. But first, since Dayne lived in this forest, he might as well sniff around the place and see if he could pick up the scent of anything interesting he could use to his benefit should the board not be satisfied with his word on matters. The smell of roasting werecat perhaps?

He slowed as he neared the cottage. The place was heavily warded. Even he would have thought twice about coming this way if he didn't know about Dayne, assuming his primal instincts were warning him of a large, impending threat. He pushed past the feeling and crept to the back of the house. He smelled salt and heard a woman crying.

I knew it! Then there was a second female voice.

"Charlee, please calm down. I understand with Anthony," she said the name with revulsion in her voice, "that you're on a vampire sleep schedule, but you have to understand I have to open the bookstore in the morning. In six hours."

"I know, I'm sorry. I just . . . He could do anything to her, and I can't help. I should have paid more attention to what was going on. I knew Paul was bad news, but I didn't want to believe he was hurting her. If I'd listened to my gut I could have kept her away from him, and this wouldn't have happened."

A chair creaked as one of the girls sat down. Where was Dayne in the middle of this sobfest? And why was there a human and another girl hanging out in the evil sorcerer's lair, anyway? He took another whiff. A werecat? Why was a werecat making herself at home in Dayne's cottage?

"Can't Anthony get her back?"

More crying.

"Cole won't give her up without a fight, and Anthony can't get into a war over a human. He's having issues with a few members of the coven who don't support him having a human mate to begin with. It's my fault. If he wasn't with me, he could get Jane back. He told me he thought she's probably safer where she is. He's just making excuses. I can't believe I saved his life."

Cole's furry eyebrow rose. Oh really? He hadn't heard that part of the tale. Charlee had saved Anthony's life? Seemed a lot of humans were saving him, and he was supposed to be the vampire king.

"Anthony's not that bad. Let's not forget he helped save Greta." Dayne. What the hell? Had Cole landed in an alternate dimension? Was he being Punk'd? He looked around for hidden cameras.

"Yeah, and then the second he had my blood he went straight for Charlee. He could have killed her," the werecat said.

Okay, that was it; hearing and smelling wasn't good enough. He had to risk a window seat. Cole slunk around the side of the house to the first available window.

The crying redhead sat at a bar stool drinking something out of a mug, her unruly curls covering much of her face. Dayne stood behind the werecat with his arms wrapped around her, his chin resting on the top of her head.

"I mean, Jane and I weren't best friends or anything. She's a little hard to get to know. But still, I liked her . . . like her," Charlee corrected. "You have to help me rescue her."

The dark-haired woman pulled out of Dayne's embrace and rested a hand on the crying woman's arm. "The wolves are like shadows. No one can follow them to their den; the trail just ends."

Charlee turned imploring eyes to Dayne. "What about a spell? You can track Jane with a spell. I've got stuff of hers."

"Perhaps," he said, doubtfully.

Cole was glad, not for the first time, that he'd thought to add a magical barrier of security. Some of the pack had argued hard with him ten years ago when he'd insisted on wards to protect the den, claiming it was too much work and expense, that no one could find the den with magic because no one would have any of their personal belongings.

Even if the cave was camouflaged and locked up tighter than Fort Knox, it was an extra measure of protection knowing they couldn't be tracked through a spell. Least of all through a spell from Wickham.

Dayne looked right at him, and he moved away from the window. The sorcerer didn't have fancy eyesight; there was no way he could have seen a solid black wolf outside at night. Still, he must have sensed the magic coming off him. Well, he'd been standing there for fifteen minutes or more. Plenty of time for Dayne to get a read on something fishy. The man didn't have a reputation for nothing.

Cole wanted to stay to find out more, but the risk was too high. He turned and ran, putting several miles between himself and the cottage before slowing his pace. When he got back to where he'd shifted, he dug in the earth to uncover his clothing, shook the dirt off, and changed back.

Charlee clearly cared about Jane's well-being, and Anthony didn't seem bent on her destruction either. If he let her go, she might be safe. But he knew she'd never be safe as long as she was anywhere near the vampires. Even if Anthony was willing, he couldn't constantly run interference for her. Cole could. What place could be safer than the hive?

He dressed and pulled a talisman from his pocket. It was a shiny golden stone on top of a disk with runic markings. The stone could be turned like a crude combination lock. The disk had a hole in one end where a strap of leather went through it to make a necklace.

Cole slipped it over his head and moved to a secluded spot. When he was sure he was alone, he turned the stone in the combination. A shimmery film appeared in front of him, like a small segment of the world had been wrapped in saran wrap. He stepped through the doorway, and the film dissolved behind him.

The demon dimension was always a shock when he crossed into it. Not so much because it was flaming hellfire and such—it wasn't—but because it was so normal.

It felt like stepping into the past with cobblestone paths and street fair music playing in the distance. There was a market where giant colorful tents lined the streets. The sounds and smells of sex were strong in the air, and Cole growled.

This was where the incubi and succubi lived. Male and female sex demons. They were similar to the vampires but could be corporeal or non-corporeal. Incubi often stole into women's dreams or seduced them when awake to feed their insatiable hunger. When they weren't feeding, and clearly often when they were, they hopped over to one of the demon dimensions.

Cain was the head incubus, and this was his territory. He stepped out of a nearby tent, a big goofy grin on his face.

"Cole! Buddy! You missed the action. I found the most delicious Georgia Peach."

Cole's face turned stony. "And you killed her."

Cain smirked. "My territory, my rules. I let your pack use the dimensional portals. Besides, I've told you before . . ."

"I know, I know. Nobody really dies, they just come back in a new body. But I don't see things that way. You're separating people from those they love, causing heartache, making them start over when they could break the cycle and go someplace better."

"Heaven? Oh God, don't start with that. Trust me, you don't want to go there. It's highly overrated as final destinations go."

Cole shrugged. He knew it was best not to get Cain out of a good mood, so he changed the subject. "How's Luc?"

"The house is standing empty at the moment, but as soon as there's a buyer, I've found a way to free him. I just can't tell him about it."

"Cain . . ."

"Look, it's not your business. Luc has been trapped in that house for half a century now because he fell for his food. Stupid little witch. Never trust magic users. And . . .

speaking of trust, you need to keep a better eye on your pack."

Cole arched a brow. "Oh?"

"One of them was hunting in Golatha Falls. Hunting a human."

Cole growled. "Who?"

"Now, now, that would be telling. You're smart. Figure it out yourself. I rescued the woman before any damage was done."

"Was that the Georgia Peach you just killed?"

"No, another one. I fed her to Luc. And he won't kill his dinner. Don't worry, I memory wiped her, and she's safe in her little bed."

"I don't get you."

"Not many do."

A cute blonde popped her head out of the tent giggling. "Cain, where did you go?"

"I'll be back in a minute, my love; go amuse yourself with something."

She shrugged and drifted down the street toward the marketplace, her eyes lighting as a street performer swallowed fire on a stick.

"I thought you said you killed her."

"No, you said that. This one is mildly interesting. I might keep her a few days."

"You're disgusting."

"Yes, I'm a demon. These humans all have a death wish anyway. Do you see how they live?"

"Thank you for the information about my pack. I'm sure you've got a tab running for me. I've got to go hunt."

Cain's chuckle trailed down the street behind him.

Chapter Five

Jane turned over in her sleep. Suddenly she was sixteen again with her first boyfriend. The name on his birth certificate was Richard, but everybody called him Rich. That is, until he and Jane started dating. Then everyone at school had started calling them Dick and Jane.

She was standing on the second story balcony of the frat house when she saw the monster. He looked like a demon from hell, all black and shiny with claws and fangs and glowing eyes. And he was staring right at her. A drunk and laughing frat boy stumbled into the monster then looked up at him.

"Oh, excuse me, dude." He was drunk enough to have lost his inhibitions and sense of self-preservation, but not yet drunk enough to be slurring his words.

"Not a problem," the monster said, his eyes still boring into Jane's.

A rush of memories, long buried and forgotten came back to her as the monster held her gaze. New York City. She was four and out with her parents after dark. Her mother had been anxious about having Jane out in the city at night, but her father had brushed off the concern.

As they'd crossed the street to grab a taxi, Jane had seen him. She'd been haunted by nightmares of the monster for months, her parents not knowing what to do for her. This wasn't normal, even for a child her age.

They'd taken her to a specialist in California, and after a while she forgot what she'd seen. Now it was back, and Jane was struggling to breathe. Either it was real, or she was crazy and the delusions had returned.

She watched as the demon floated up in the air and landed on the balcony beside her, graceful and silent.

"There you are, my beautiful angel. I thought I'd lost you." His voice was a rich baritone, a sound at once so pleasant to her ears and so horrible and terrifying.

She backed away until she was inside the frat house, a wall meeting her back abruptly, stopping further retreat. He closed in on her, one hand pressed flat against the wall on either side of her face. Staring at him, she could just make out the faintest image of the man the others saw. He wasn't just *a* monster. He was *the* monster. The same one she'd seen as a child.

"I've been looking for you."

Her voice came back to her then. "W-why?"

"To kill you, of course. You can see me, but I can't get into your head. My sire would love to put you in his collection. But too bad, I found you first. Do you know why you are like you are?"

She shook her head and wrapped her arms around herself. The monster dragged a finger over her cheek. He was so cold. "One of your parents has had our blood and is running free. And when I find out which one, they're dead."

"No, please."

The monster ignored her plea and continued on. "That blood now runs in your veins. You're Kindred in a weak human shell. Do you really imagine we would let such an abomination live? Tell me, child, do you dream of us? Do you get the visions you've no right to?"

She shook her head frantically. "No, I don't know what you mean."

The door flew open, and a drunk Rich stumbled in. He looked up and pointed at the monster. "You tryin' to hit on my girl?" He swaggered a bit, unsteady on his feet then pointed back at himself with bravado. "Cause, she's *my* girl. We've been going steady for . . . " He looked up at the ceiling trying to count, his facility with basic math suddenly lost to him. " . . . for awhile now." Then he turned to Jane, his eyes narrowing. "You ain't cheating on me with this pretty boy, are you baby?"

"Rich, get out of here!"

His eyes narrowed as he approached them, the situation seeming to sober him up. He jabbed a finger into the monster's chest. "You think just cause you're older and better looking than me that you can come in here and take my girl?" He turned back to her. "Seriously, Jane. What do you see in this joker?"

"Rich, go. Just go, please."

Her eyes widened in horror as the monster's clawed hands came up and gave Rich's head a firm, quick twist, and his lifeless body fell to the ground.

"That's better," the monster said. "Now you . . . "

Jane wanted to scream, but no sound would come out. Even if her exit wasn't blocked, she wasn't sure if her legs would have obeyed her desire to run. *This is a dream. It's a dream. It has to be a dream. You'll wake up. It's a dream.*

The monster looked her over. "You, my dear, I'll drink. You're not nearly as annoying as the boy. And I'm sure you taste much sweeter."

As her head was forced to the side, she squeezed her eyes shut to avoid looking at her boyfriend on the ground. The monster's fangs slid into her throat, and she was disgusted by how her body reacted to him. He chuckled against her skin. When he'd had his fill of her, he pulled away and licked the puncture marks.

"Oh yes, you undeniably have our blood running in your veins. I can't thrall you, and a normal human wouldn't have been able to withstand the pain my bite delivers. You have a high pain threshold, don't you, my dear?"

She looked out the open doorway where the sounds of the college party still going on below drifted up to her ears. *This wouldn't have happened if I'd stayed with the others.* She'd come upstairs to wait for Rich, so they'd have privacy to do what teenagers often did in strange homes away from their parents. If only she hadn't come to the party.

She shuddered as his mouth moved close to her ear. "What's more, you liked that. I can smell your reaction. Perhaps I'll keep you alive with me for awhile, and we'll see what other talents develop over time. Shall we?"

He held a clawed hand out to her, and she put her hand into his. What else could she do?

"By the way, my name is Sedrick."

The dream sped up, moving to the one destination it always ended at. The one place she could never escape. The coffin was large enough for two, maybe three people, lined in red satin, and made of solid steel. Not a drop of light could get inside.

"Don't worry," Sedrick said, "You'll probably live until nightfall. I don't use much oxygen when I sleep."

The coffin was on a timer set for sunset. He snapped a glowing wristwatch around her wrist. She'd begged him to do anything else. Tie her up in the bedroom, anything. But he said he needed her with him.

Every time the coffin locked shut she thought she'd never survive it. Almost twelve hours of darkness most days inside that box. And the last hour, so hard to breathe, counting down the seconds, watching the glowing digital numbers tick down. Running out of air, past the panic point, banging on the door. What if it didn't open in time?

Jane woke screaming, tangled on the floor in the bedsheets where she'd struggled through her dream trying to escape Sedrick. She looked wildly around. It took her a few minutes to realize where she was, to know she wasn't back in the coffin with the sadistic vampire. The cave was silent. Could the wolf have slept through that?

She turned on the light, her hand still shaking from the nightmare, and made her way out into the main room. His pillow and blanket were in a pile on the floor beside the sofa. Growing more frantic, she searched the rest of the den.

Tears stung at the corners of her eyes. "No, No, No, No." She paced back and forth in front of the sealed steel door. "No!" She couldn't get the thought out of her head that it was just another larger coffin. What if Cole never came back? What if he got hurt or killed? She could die in here.

She pressed buttons on the security keypad.

"Incorrect code."

She kept trying.

"Incorrect code."

"Incorrect code."

The recorded voice sounded so smug. She started to bang on the door.

"Let me out of here!" The room was growing smaller, shrinking until it felt no larger than the coffin, as the air got heavier. "Please! Please let me out!"

Cole's muzzle was wet from a fresh kill. He stood, running his tongue around the side of his mouth to get the last drops of life. He nosed at the bear's mauled remains, deciding he was finished. All the good parts were gone.

As he moved through the woods away from the carcass, his senses were swamped with the most heavenly smell. The most forbidden smell.

Human blood.

As a man he could have resisted, but as the wolf, the scent was too intoxicating. He salivated as he moved nearer, then whined when he reached the source. There was a small pool of blood rapidly soaking into the ground.

He dug into the dirt with his paws, pressing his nose against the scent, flicking his tongue out to get some of the precious liquid. But it was too late. He prowled around the spot, then finally growled and shifted back to his human form.

He felt momentarily ashamed by how badly he'd wanted to lap up the leftovers from a human kill. Gaining control of himself, he knelt beside the blood-soaked earth, inhaled deeply, then got to his feet again.

There was evidence of a struggle. Branches were bent. Piles of leaves were thrown about in haphazard fashion where feet had flailed and kicked. Furrows had been dug through the dirt by fingers clawing at the ground. He smelled blood on a nearby tree.

He followed the fading trail of the human and wolf. The wolf had masked his scent, wearing a human-made pheromone marketed to attract the opposite sex. It was strong and musky to his nose, but to a human would have been barely discernible. It might aid in luring a human female from a place of safety into the woods. It also made it impossible to separate the scent of the wolf's natural pheromones from the synthetic concoction.

Cole followed the trail to the edge of the forest where the mingled scents ended. There were no broken branches or disturbed leaves. Up until the spot the human had died, there had been no struggle. It wasn't a loss of control with a hapless camper. It had been premeditated.

He returned to the kill site. The killer had done this before. Many times. It was too clean. A wolf taken by the wildness of the first human kill wouldn't have had the cognitive ability to clean up the mess. He shook his head and went for his clothes. He hated when Cain was right.

He was a quarter mile away from the den when he heard the screaming and pounding. He broke into a run, panic gripping his chest.

Not Jane.

His fingers flew over the security keypad to input the code, and when the door slid open he was ready to catch her as she pitched forward into his arms. He scented the air, his eyes wild, searching for the threat.

When he realized she was alone, he carried her back inside.

She'd stopped screaming and collapsed against him, still crying, but the panic had faded. He sat her gently on the couch and took her chin in his hands, his eyes locking with hers. "I'll be right back."

She nodded.

She looked so small sitting on the couch in one of his T-shirts. He was in and out of the kitchen in less than thirty seconds with an open bottle of water.

"Drink."

She took the bottle and drank. Her face was red and flushed from crying, her eyes puffy. Her throat was no doubt raw if she'd been screaming for long. He wondered if any of the pack had woken. Well, if they had, the cat was out of the bag, and they were either going to think he was having really wild sex or torturing someone.

"I won't leave you alone here again," he said, the guilt starting to weigh on him that his behavior had been the cause of this much fear.

She nodded and lifted the bottle to her lips again. That's when the scent of her blood hit him. Her hands. She'd pounded on the door until her hands had bled. His pupils dilated but he resisted the change, glad he'd eaten a bear.

He lifted the hand she wasn't using to drink and caught her eyes. "I'm not going to hurt you. But we used the last of the ointment on your cheek. Can I?"

She looked at him confused for a second, then her eyes widened a fraction.

"I know it might seem disgusting, but it's really the best antiseptic. And I can make the bleeding stop."

She nodded.

He ran his tongue gently over her hand, and he could taste the vampire in her blood. He'd deal with that issue later. For now, what was important was to try to make her feel safe.

The guilt crushed in on him. He'd meant to help her, and instead he'd traumatized her. Well, what did he expect keeping her against her will? Had he thought she'd be A-okay with being locked up?

Her arousal hit him hard, jolting him out of his thoughts. He looked up at her, his pupils dilating this time for a new reason. She looked away, clearly mortified, knowing he'd sensed her reaction. He released her hand.

They sat silent for a few minutes. Her other hand was still bleeding and clutching tightly onto the water bottle. He didn't push the issue. Finally, after a few minutes of neither of them speaking, she shifted the bottle to her cleaned hand, and gave him her other one.

"Jane?"

"I'm bleeding."

His nostrils flared. "Yes, I'm aware of that. Are you sure you're comfortable with this?"

She nodded and looked away from him while he used his tongue to make the bleeding stop on the other hand.

When he finished, he started babbling. "I didn't mean to be gone that long. I should have known you'd panic. I should have remembered the claustrophobia. I just thought we'd dealt with that issue. But you were locked in, and I should have known how you'd react if you woke up. I shouldn't have chanced it. I should have waited until daytime, to go hunting and should have . . . "

"Had a bad dream," she croaked, interrupting the litany.

"Will you tell me about it?"

He sat in quiet horror while she recounted the dream and her history. He understood now why he could taste vampire in her blood. He'd been so close to saying something stupid, asking her why she'd fed from a vamp. Though even if she had, it likely wouldn't have been her choice. He'd been so wrong about her. She wasn't a vampire groupie; she'd been trying desperately to appease them.

"I finally worked up the nerve to stake Sedrick. He was sure he'd kept such a close eye on me, but I'd made a stake a little bit at a time when he was doing other things. I had it ready for months before I worked up the nerve to try it. I was afraid something would go wrong with the coffin and it wouldn't open. I knew if it didn't, Sedrick was strong enough to open it from the inside.

"When I staked him, I thought I would die from the smell, but the coffin opened that night, and I got out. He'd spared my parents, but I stayed away. I'd been gone three years and thought I might lead another vampire to them. So I just ran and lived in shelters for awhile. I tried to make sure I was never out after dark. But sometimes I had to go out at night, like when I had a job and had to work later than normal."

He'd stretched out on the couch and pulled her back against him, running his fingers through her hair. For a moment she tensed and he stopped, but then she relaxed again.

"I'm not them, Jane. I know you've heard bad things about the werewolves, but that's political bullshit. I don't allow my pack to hunt humans." Even as he spoke, the pool of blood from a few hours before taunted him.

"I know."

He suppressed the growls as she went on to tell him about the next vampire who caught her, and how while that one hadn't locked her in a coffin, he'd passed her around and whored her out to other vampires. Until Gregory had rescued her.

"Greg was the first vampire I met who wasn't a complete monster. After a few years I got comfortable, thought I was safe. Almost felt like a person again. Then the tournament came up, and he wouldn't turn me. He said he didn't want to curse me like that. And then he let me go because he said he couldn't be king with me."

She let out a shuddering breath. "He wanted to believe I'd be okay without a protector. But I knew I wouldn't be, so I latched onto Paul. I thought if I picked the vampire, maybe I would pick someone who wasn't that bad. Like Greg. But Paul only looked innocent.

"Almost as soon as Anthony won the tournament, he and Charlee got wrapped up in all the vampire business and politics, and Paul kept getting pushed to the fringes. He started taking it out on me, like the knife marks, and slapping me around because he'd figured out I could take more than most humans."

"They'll never touch you again."

Silence stretched between them, and Jane drifted to sleep nestled in his arms, a few of her demons purged for the night. Cole ran his fingers through her hair while she slept, quietly plotting how he'd kill Paul to make it look like a happy accident.

Chapter Six

Jane woke in Cole's bed with an arm thrown loosely across her body. She tensed. This wasn't how she remembered going to sleep. A million thoughts and feelings ran through her. Clearly her body wanted him. Then again, her fucked-up body had wanted the vampire that killed her boyfriend when he bit her, too. *Don't think about that shit. Don't even go there.*

His arm lifted and retreated back to his side of the bed. "You fell asleep, and I brought you back here where you'd be more comfortable."

She rolled over to find herself under the covers and him on top. That made her feel better at least, the thick blankets acting as a shield.

"Are you okay with this?" he asked, gesturing at the bed.

He'd been walking on eggshells since the night before when she'd told him about the dream, and then for some indefinable reason spilled her guts to him. Jane wasn't in the habit of sharing her life history with practical strangers. Especially strangers who were supposed to be the enemy. But she'd been throwing her hat in with the vampires so long out of self-preservation, she'd forgotten that one halfway decent vampire notwithstanding, vamps were the enemy, too.

At least for someone like her.

Her mother had never mentioned a history with the undead. Maybe she'd been kept as a pet and the vamp released her, or she killed him. Maybe she'd been under a thrall and didn't remember it.

Jane's skin crawled at the idea of her mother having been some vampire's pet and not remembering a second of it. She thought about the women in the back room of the club and wondered how many of them even knew what was going on. How many of them woke in the morning with a gap in their memory and no clue about their nightly activities?

The things Jane had been through had been bad. But at least she knew exactly what had and hadn't happened to her.

"Jane?"

She jumped at his voice and tried to refocus on the present. "It's fine. I'm sorry, I was thinking."

"I'm not looking for payment or a business transaction here. You don't owe me anything."

She nodded, her eyes drifting to his bare chest. Which made her want to give it to him all the more. This wasn't like Sedrick or the others. It wasn't just her body that wanted Cole. Maybe it was because she was out of her element with a werewolf, but the instincts she'd honed so well to stay alive had been flung to the wind now that she was with him.

She could feel his warmth through the blankets, and she wanted to rip away the barrier between them to feel his skin pressed against hers. But he'd made no move toward her and hadn't shown any overt interest. He knew she'd been aroused when his tongue had run over the back of her hand, and he'd ignored her reaction.

Okay, so she'd been bleeding and that had been gross, but it didn't seem like he minded. He hunted and ate raw warm meat, freshly dead. Blood was a part of that.

"Cole?"

"Yes?" His voice was tight.

She wished he'd stop treating her like she was made of glass. She'd been with Gregory at least long enough to know the signs of what she was looking for. She'd had warning bells with Paul but had thought he wouldn't be as bad as he'd become. There were no bells with Cole. Then again, maybe her evil detector only worked on vampires.

"Last night, when you cleaned up my hands, um . . . there was blood and panic, and you didn't change."

"Was there a question in there?"

She rolled her eyes. "Yes. Why?"

"The cave is bigger than the car. I'd just hunted. I was concerned for you. And your fear wasn't directed toward me. Earlier in the night, you were afraid of me. Later in the night it was something else, and my instinct shifted to protect you from the danger."

Jane turned that over a bit in her mind and then nodded, her curiosity satisfied. At least she felt safer now, knowing he was unlikely to go furry and homicidal on her.

He rolled out of bed, his hair sleep-tousled. "You can take a shower and freshen up while I make breakfast, then you get to meet the pack. I'm sending you out shopping with Rhonda."

"I don't have any money."

"I didn't ask you for any."

Jane sat against the headboard, twisting the sheets in her hands. "You've lost ten thousand dollars because of me, and now the tab is just getting higher."

"I told you that's not your fault. I have everything I need. I've got a bunch of money sitting in the bank not being spent."

"I have clothes. I can go get them," she offered.

His lips pressed into a tight line. "A) You're not going anywhere near those vampires again."

"But they'll be asleep . . . "

"And I'm sure they have guardians, do they not?"

"Yes," she said, looking down at the sheets clutched in her hands.

"B) You've been dressing according to vampiric whim for how many years now? I want you to wear what you want to wear. I mean it."

"But how will I pay you back?" She was beginning to believe he wasn't going to make her earn her keep in a pornographic way. Although, of all the people to want such a thing, this would be the first time she wasn't at least a little repulsed by the idea. He was beautiful. The first man she'd been near in a long time that didn't look like a monster to her.

"What do you do for all your money?" she asked, trying to distract herself from the inappropriate trail her mind kept going down.

"I run an Internet business."

"I'm good with numbers. I could do the bookkeeping."

"I am not turning you into an indentured servant. Paul's debt isn't yours. Believe me, I intend to take it out of his hide at the first opportunity. And the shopping is a gift, no strings. It's the least I can do after last night. Leaving you like that." A shadow fell across his face. "I owe you. All right?"

She couldn't exactly argue with that. It had been pretty heinous for him to leave her alone in a sealed cave. "Okay."

"Good. Now we need to get going. The pack meeting starts in less than an hour, and I'll have to introduce you."

Jane peeled back the cover and got out of bed, the sheet wrapped around her. "Introduce me as what?"

"A friend."

She looked doubtfully down at the wadded leather clothes she'd been wearing the night before. "Your hooker with a heart of gold friend?"

It was Cole's turn for eye rolling. "I'll go borrow something for you; just take a shower. Will you be okay if I leave you for twenty minutes?"

She crossed her arms over her chest. "Do you really think I'm that weak?"

"I never said, or meant . . . "

"I'll be fine. It was a bad dream from the stress. It's over. I want to stop talking about it."

He put his hands in the air. "Fine. I'll be back."

Forty-five minutes later, Jane was wearing jeans, her boots, and a blue sweater, which looked ridiculous with the pink hair, but at least she didn't look like a punk rock call girl.

Cole put in the security code for the steel door on the other side of the den. His hands flew so fast over the keys she couldn't have figured out the code even standing right beside him watching. Now she had to meet *the pack*, who, despite her cleaned-up appearance, was probably going to think she was a whore.

The bite marks Paul had left would likely never heal. There was one on her throat, bites on her breasts, her hips, her thighs. After her shower, while Cole was in the kitchen, she'd looked at them and the scars on her back in the mirror. He hated vampires, and she was a walking advertisement for his enemies.

"Time to face the firing squad," Cole said as the door slid open.

"Yay," Jane said dryly.

He just looked at her. What? Was she supposed to cower and whine and weep and moan 24/7 just because they'd had a few rocky hours in the beginning? Now that

the immediate danger with the wolf seemed not so immediate, she was feeling embarrassed over her weakness.
The *tough Jane* mask fell back into place like an old and
welcome friend.

The tunnel between Cole's den and the rest of the
caves was longer than Jane had expected it to be. She
wondered if his seclusion from the pack was a safety
precaution. One didn't stay pack alpha for twenty years
without being smart and probably paranoid to the point of
insanity.

They arrived at another steel door, and he punched in
a second code.

"Welcome, Cole," a computerized female voice said.

Jane stood frozen in the doorway, unable to move into
the room. There were dozens of people, no . . . wolves,
packed in together.

Most were wearing jeans and T-shirts, a decided fashion downgrade from the dramatic glitz and glamour of the
vampires. Some were playing cards. Some were rough
housing. One girl was eating a whole can of Pringles at a
rapid pace.

All the wolves were loud and rambunctious. It was a
little overwhelming, and suddenly Jane wasn't sure how
to act. Being a *vampire groupie* had taken months to get
just right.

"Go on," Cole prodded. She took a few tentative steps
into the room.

One of the wolves near them growled at Jane, his eyes
glowing golden even as he maintained his form. The other
wolves looked up, and within moments there were several
unpleasant growls being aimed her direction.

Cole moved her behind him, seemingly unconcerned,
and let out a growl that could better be classed as a roar.
It was so loud every other wolf in the room immediately
fell silent, a few whimpering.

"That's enough!" he said. "This is Jane. She'll be stay-ing with me for the foreseeable future."

One of the male wolves looked insulted. "She smells like vampire."

Jane blushed. This group was not subtle. She'd thought she'd been faced with everything, but vampires were just . . . different from this.

"Ed . . . " Cole warned.

"I call them like I see them," Ed said. The wolf looked to be about mid fifties, his hair graying at the temples. But Jane knew, given the slower rate of therian aging, he must be much older. A hundred years at least. His face was set in lines indicating perpetual grumpiness. Jane took a step back at the glare the wolf shot her.

"She isn't one of them."

"Well, she's a vampire groupie then," one of the female wolves said with obvious disdain.

Cole growled. "She's not one of those either. She is a friend of mine and therefore a friend of the pack. Is that clear?"

They all nodded, a little too quickly. Ed's nod was slower than the rest. She wondered how safe she was even with the alpha standing in front of her.

Cole looked over the group of wolves then spoke. "Rhonda."

A perky blonde stepped out from the crowd. She was dressed a little sexier than the rest, though no one seemed to notice.

"I need to speak with you."

She glided over to him. "Yes?"

"I need you to take Jane shopping. I've got to attend to the pack meeting."

Rhonda's lip curled into a sneer for a split second before she planted a placating smile on her face. "Anything for you," she purred.

"Good." He handed her a credit card and pulled something golden out of his pocket that looked like an ancient talisman attached to a long leather cord. "If you run into any trouble that you can't handle, use this. And tell Cain she's off the menu. She's mine. I want you back in four hours, no longer."

He looked from Rhonda to Jane, then led Jane down the tunnel out of hearing range. He produced a sheathed knife from his pocket. "She's the omega, the weakest wolf. She's loyal to me, but just in case."

He'd given her silver.

Chapter Seven

Cole stared off in the direction Rhonda had taken Jane, berating himself for letting her out of his sight. Rhonda had always been the weakest of the pack; he'd rescued her from bullies as a pup. She'd understand how Jane felt in all this and be someone safe.

And if he was wrong, he'd given Jane a knife to protect herself. He must be out of his mind giving silver to a human to use against one of his pack. If the others discovered he'd given her a weapon, it could get ugly.

He was losing his edge. Maybe he shouldn't continue as alpha if his concern was for Jane's safety over a member of his pack.

It was four hours. Even in some bizarre alternate reality in which Rhonda was hunting humans, she wouldn't kill this close to home, and she sure as hell wouldn't kill when she was the only possible suspect and had to know the consequences from Cole.

He turned to see Blake, the pack beta, sitting on a crate watching him. "So . . . are you fucking her?"

Every eye in the cave was on him, waiting for his reply. "No. Not that that's any of your business."

"Hey, it's my business if you bring someone in here who could turn against us. We've been trying to get you to settle down and take a mate. What's wrong with Rhonda? You know she loves you."

"We grew up together. She's like a kid sister to me."

Blake snorted. "Like a sister isn't the same as being a sister. And baby sis' is all grown up now. Have you seen the legs and rack on her? Put the poor girl out of her misery and mark her. At least then the temptation to screw the human wouldn't be there. Everyone saw how you were looking at her."

Had he been looking at Jane that way?

"Jane is not a threat to us. She despises the vampires as much as we do. She's under my protection."

"I just don't think . . . "

Cole stalked across the room to stand in front of the beta, using his considerable size as an easy intimidation tactic. "Blake, would you like to challenge me for pack alpha?"

The beta wolf's eyes grew large, and he threw his hands up in surrender. "Shit no. I'm not that stupid. I prefer life."

Cole nodded. "Good, then. The discussion about Jane is over. Any other objections to her being here?"

The room was tense. It was obvious his word wasn't good enough this time. They all thought him compromised because he hadn't taken a mate. They were probably all right about that. But he also knew he was right about Jane. She wasn't a threat to them, and he'd become invested in giving her a place of safety.

"I understand your reservations and why you have them," he began. "And if I were in your position, I would be worried as well. But just give her a chance. Get to know her before you decide she shouldn't be here. Some of you know first-hand what the vampires can be like. And believe me when I tell you, she's probably had it worse than any of those few of you who've been in that unfortunate position."

That got the desired reaction. Just a month ago one of their own had been jumped by some of the vampires and taken in for questioning. Where was the den? How did they get out of the city? Calling them terrorists. *Please.* Terrorists produced terror. The only scary thing the wolf pack was doing was avoiding assimilation into the police state Borg. Their resistance was only a threat to the vampires and others with the same agenda of control.

The wolf in question, Deric, looked down at the ground. Cole knew he'd been close to cracking when they'd reached him. "You didn't talk though. That's the important part."

Since Anthony had taken over, the vampire had been determined to get the *wolf problem* under control. The vamps had excellent PR, presenting themselves as refined and civilized, as the salvation of the preternaturals. Meanwhile, the wolves were characterized as a pack of savage beasts, intent on maiming hapless humans and everyone else who stood in their way.

Cole looked around the room, his eyes locking briefly with each member of the pack before moving on. The problem with being the alpha was that few would maintain eye contact with him for more than a second. It was too often seen as a challenge for dominance, and no one wanted to challenge him. They'd all witnessed what happened when a wolf challenged.

Was the pack afraid of him? He hadn't thought they were. He certainly wasn't the bastard the former leader had been. Rafe had been truly abusive, living up to the werewolf stereotypes. Cole had thought he'd come off differently. Perhaps not.

Wolves were faster than most of the other preternaturals, even vampires in some cases. Stronger than a lot of them too. They hunted in packs; they traveled in packs; they hung out in packs. It was rare for someone to get the drop on one. But Deric had been the exception that proved it could happen if they weren't all incredibly careful.

Since that time, the rules had become stiffer and penalties for breaking them harsher. It was what he had to do to keep them all safe.

"I'm considering moving us out of Cary Town, somewhere where we won't be a target. I'm not sure the danger is worth it anymore."

One of the wolves in the back spoke up. "But what about what they're doing? If everyone just goes along with these rules they're setting up, supposedly for everybody's safety from the humans, they'll start branching into other cities. Eventually they'll have control of everything."

Another wolf added his voice to the discussion. "Don't be such an alarmist, Mara. We'd still have access to the demon dimension."

Mara turned toward the other wolf. "There's no hunting there. No places to run. We can't live there."

Cole raised a hand, and the wolves fell silent. "I haven't said we should give up the fight. Only that with Anthony in charge, it's not as safe for us as it was under the old administration. This vampire is more ambitious than his predecessor. Even with the stronger security in place, it's only a matter of time before someone gets caught."

"I don't want to leave. This is my home," a teenage girl said. "Why do any of us even have to go into town at all?"

Cole stared at her for a moment.

"Lucy!" Her mother looked horrified by her daughter's outburst and at the same time scared for her.

Shit. The pack *was* afraid of him. He'd been protecting his status to protect them, but it clearly hadn't been interpreted that way. Jane might be the best PR he could get within the pack, assuming he could convince them she wasn't out to destroy them all.

"Why didn't I think of that?" He hadn't thought of it because it hadn't been an issue until three months ago. Deric's capture had caused massive levels of stress for everyone.

"Thought of what?" Blake said.

Cole was glad he hadn't been the only one. "No more going into town unless you have direct permission from myself or Blake. From here on out, if you aren't in the hive, you are to be outside the city limits. I'll have to get more portal charms from Cain but I think I can swing it. We can hop portals from here in the main den."

No one in the pack knew exactly how he'd struck the arrangement with Cain. Most demons didn't mingle with preternaturals that had humanity in their veins. But he'd helped Cain out of a bind once. Demons were unkillable, true immortals on this plane. Unlike vampires. But that didn't mean they didn't get into tight and unpleasant spots. Plus he thought Cain found the whole thing amusing and liked undermining the vampires. The bastard half-breeds.

Jane's muscles coiled in tension as she sat in the passenger seat of Cole's Mustang, the black wool fabric covering her eyes. How was she supposed to defend herself against a rabid werewolf if she couldn't see it?

"Sorry, but I forgot to ask Cole about that, and I've never known him to allow anyone outside the pack into the hive without it."

"No, it's fine," Jane said a little shakily, hoping she didn't sound as scared as she felt. Oh hell, Rhonda could no doubt smell it on her. And if she was the weakest of the pack, it might mean she was the least in control of the change. Jane concentrated on thinking happy thoughts.

Peter Pan thoughts. Whatever she had to do to make sure Rhonda didn't sprout fur on her.

She slipped a finger into the pocket of her jeans, felt the handle of the silver knife and relaxed a bit. If she had to, she'd use it. How hard could it be after staking a vampire?

Several minutes later Rhonda spoke, popping the bubble of girlie grunge rock music that had been pounding out of the speakers. "Okay, you can take off the blindfold."

Jane folded it and put it in the glove box, before turning and offering a weak smile to the woman. It was hard to believe she was a werewolf. Somehow, just looking at Cole, she could see it. But Rhonda looked like a slutty cheerleader.

"So where do you want to shop? Cole didn't give us a limit." She giggled.

"I don't care. Just nowhere vampire groupies would shop. And I need hair dye."

"More pink?"

Jane gave Rhonda a look like she was on acid. More pink, was she serious? "If I never see pink hair again, it'll be too soon."

Two and a half hours later, Jane had several bags of clothes and a smaller bag containing hair dye. The label on the box read "Chestnut" and looked close to her natural color, as far as she could remember her natural color. She'd gotten special instructions from the woman who owned the little boutique on how to best cover the pink without unexpected results.

She and Rhonda found an outdoor cafe for lunch. The wolf ordered steak, rare. No surprise. Jane ordered blackened chicken over a bed of romaine lettuce with ranch dressing.

"On a diet?" Rhonda said sympathetically. She patted her sleek stomach. "I'm glad I don't have to worry about that. We have very fast metabolisms."

Or maybe cattily.

Jane smiled around a mouthful of food, chewed, then swallowed and reached for the water on her table. "I'm not on a diet. This just looked good."

Rhonda didn't seem to be buying it.

During their shopping excursion she'd poked around to subtly find out the nature of Jane and Cole's relationship. Then when she was sure they weren't sleeping together, she'd started playing the *Cole and I will be mated soon* card, saying things like, "Everyone in the pack knows it's just a matter of time for us."

While Jane had been in the dressing room at the third store, Rhonda had gone into graphic detail about her and Cole's sexual interlude. Jane was glad the wolf didn't have X-ray vision or she would have seen the gagging faces being made behind the door.

Now at lunch, Rhonda had resumed her territory pissing project. "Once Cole and I are mated and he's more comfortable with you around the rest of the pack, you can stay in my little den. It's very cozy. You'll like it."

"I'm sure it's great," Jane said, forcing a smile and pushing back another impending eye roll. She didn't know why her skin felt prickly and uncomfortable about the idea. If Cole and Rhonda really were an item, more power to them. She definitely wasn't looking for a sexual relationship right now.

Her mind drifted to Cole in a towel fresh out of the shower and then his warm body pressed against hers that morning. Then her memory flashed to his tongue running over the back of her hand the night before, far more erotic than it should have been.

Jane stopped herself in time before she reached full-on arousal. If Rhonda smelled her attraction to the alpha, she might have to use the silver knife in her pocket. And how would she explain that to Cole?

She sighed and took another bite of chicken. Maybe Cole had sent her with Rhonda, hoping this conversation would happen so he wouldn't have to tell her himself. Maybe that was why he'd blatantly ignored her reaction to him the previous night. She'd thought he was being a gentleman and trying not to make her feel unsafe.

She was mortified now for ever thinking he'd want some kind of sexual payment. If he and Rhonda were together that was unlikely to be the case, and it only made her feel dirty. Rhonda went up to the front to pay the bill as Jane dug through all her bags, collecting the receipts.

She folded them neatly and put them in the pocket of her jeans. She would find a way eventually to pay Cole back. She wasn't a charity case.

On the ride back Rhonda said, "I always knew Cole and I would be together." They were back to that again? *You've made your point, really. Cole is off-limits. Gotcha.* Jane was glad for the first time the blindfold was over her eyes.

Rhonda continued with the Cole talk. "When he was nine and I was six, he said he was going to marry me. Of course, that was before he knew about mating."

"That's very nice," Jane said, trying to sound sincere. But then a smile broke out on her face.

When Cole was nine and Rhonda was six? If Cole was really so in love with her all that time, he would have mated with her by now. Jane had thought they'd just gotten together. Maybe things weren't what they appeared. He'd given her a silver knife. He wouldn't give some human woman he'd just met the means to end his future mate. *Duh, Jane.*

She tried to ignore the fact that she seemed to give a damn about Cole Riley's love life all of a sudden. Hadn't she learned by now that men were evil?

Chapter Eight

After pack business was squared away, Cole retreated to his study to catch up on emails and get an update from Mick on the Dayne situation.

He wondered if he should tell Jane how worried Charlee had been. He stared at the phone on the desk. Maybe he should give her a phone call at least. Didn't most prisoners in this country get one phone call? Then again, she'd already used up that privilege the previous night.

He was disturbed by how strongly he felt the need to care for the woman. No one in his pack had inspired such strong protective feelings in him before. If she were a wolf he'd suspect she was his mate. Werewolves didn't mate with humans . . . did they? Moments like this it was lonely being the leader. Who did Cole go to for guidance and direction? Who kept his secrets? Who listened to his fears?

That was the alpha female's job. He had no alpha female, though Rhonda had been trying her damnedest to get the position. His excuse had always been that she was like a sister. And while that was true, she was also the pack omega.

She wasn't strong enough to command respect as his mate. He *really* couldn't think of looking at Jane in that way.

His human guest had been quiet since she'd gotten back from her shopping excursion, and he couldn't get a read on her emotional state. All he knew was she'd come back with plenty of bags, which very much pleased him. That was another thing that should have him worried. Cole had always been an excellent money manager, and in less than forty-eight hours he'd lost ten grand and dropped however much Rhonda and Jane had managed to spend on clothes.

He looked up to see her standing in the doorway, and a low growl rumbled from his chest. A long lavender dress flowed off her frame. The garment had thin straps that could be ripped apart with barely any effort. Her hair was a warm honey brown now, which made her blue eyes glitter in contrast. Jane most definitely was not a vampire groupie.

He cleared his throat, searching for the ability to speak. "I . . . is this what you would wear if you'd never met me or a vampire?"

Her face flamed red. "You don't like it?"

"That's not what I asked."

"Yes. This is what I would wear."

"It's very nice. Would you like to go out to dinner?"

"The sun is down. Vampires," she mumbled.

"We'll be leaving the city."

She bit her lip, hovering in a moment of indecision, then nodded and put the rest of her things away. When she returned, he created a portal in his private den and placed the amulet around his neck.

"Shall we?"

She walked through the shimmery film with her arm in his. Cole watched her reaction as they passed through the portal together. The film felt like walking through a spider's web until it dissipated into nothing.

Thirty minutes later they were in an Italian restaurant in Georgia. Jane's expression was guarded as she took in her surroundings, trying to get her bearings. No doubt she'd been shocked going through Cain's domain. And it hadn't helped that the demon had a woman hanging off him at the time, giggling and unaware she was about to become a footnote in history.

"It's safe here," Cole said as she continued her surveillance of the room. "There are no vampires living in Golatha Falls."

"How do you know?"

"I come here a lot. It's a good area for hunting, and it's an easy entry point to get to from Cain's neighborhood."

She shivered at the mention of Cain's name and looked down at her plate. Cole smelled the fear wafting off her and could see how frustrating it must be for vampires not to be able to get into her head. It was frustrating for him, and he couldn't get inside *anyone's* head. Unsure if it was the right move, he reached across the table and took her hand in his.

"Cain and I have an alliance. It doesn't mean I approve of his behavior. But we need the portal to protect the pack."

She nodded.

He made his own visual appraisal of the room. Although there were no vampires in Golatha Falls, it didn't mean there was no danger. He let out a sigh as he noted only one person he recognized.

Quinton Worthington, CEO of *Worthington Paper Products,* was low on the danger meter. The man sat in a corner booth eating a plate of spaghetti way larger than he should and packing in the bread. Cole had heard the man had a weak heart. *He's not doing it any good being here.*

Worthington had purchased a pint of therian blood from Cole's company and found a sorcerer to work some magic over his business. Which was why his stocks had gone through the roof the past quarter. The man glanced absently in Cole's direction then went back to his dinner.

Not for the first time, Cole was glad he'd kept his identity in his company dealings a secret. The last thing he wanted was to be recognized and have to talk business while having dinner with Jane.

He'd been unable to take his hand from hers since he'd moved to reassure her. Now his thumb was running slowly over the back of her hand.

Her arousal perfumed the air, smelling better than anything else the restaurant had to offer. If she kept smelling that way, he was going to take her right here in the middle of *Mama Bella's*. Something Jane probably wouldn't be in favor of. Nor would it do anything to build trust between them after he'd said he didn't expect anything from her.

Jane's breath hitched in her throat, and her stomach tightened as Cole's thumb caressed her hand. God, what was it with her and having her hands touched all of a sudden? Couldn't she pick a normal erogenous zone? Maybe the vampires had sullied all the good ones for her. She blushed and finally jerked her hand from his.

The waitress interrupted with bread and salads.

"I'm sorry," he said when the girl had moved on to another table.

"It's okay." Jane stared at the pile of lettuce, avoiding his eyes as she ate.

"Can I ask you something?"

"All right." She was still looking at her plate, trying to eat as slowly as possible so she wouldn't have to look into his eyes.

"I don't know how to say this."

"Just say it."

This was going to be the part where he said she was a perfectly lovely girl, but his heart belonged to another. She could handle it. She barely knew him. So he was hot and didn't look like a demon. So he was warm. If she could stop mingling with the undead for five minutes, she'd find most men fit that description. She sat in her seat, her back perfectly straight as she waited for the rejection.

He sighed, a deep, put-upon sound. "I'm really trying here, Jane. I just don't understand."

"Don't understand what?" She found herself looking up at him despite her resolve not to.

He lowered his voice and leaned in closer. "I can smell your reaction to me, and I realize we've just met . . . I don't normally react to people this way, but is there a chance at some point for something between us?"

Jane blinked. "Huh? I thought you were with Rhonda." While she'd convinced herself maybe Rhonda had overplayed the whole soul-mates-since-childhood thing, it didn't mean there wasn't something between them now, a concept she'd tortured herself with earlier in the evening while she'd waited to rinse out the hair dye.

"What gave you that idea?"

"Rhonda."

Cole's nostrils flared. "Rhonda and I aren't together, and we aren't going to be together. And you and I *shouldn't* be together. It's just hard not to touch you. I know with the things you've been through, I shouldn't think in that direction."

Jane nodded. No, he really shouldn't. She should have space, time to be free. But how free was she locked away in his den? Was he ever going to let her go? She shouldn't be attracted to him or want something with him, but every time he touched her, she felt normal again.

She chanced a look into his eyes. "Just give me some time, okay?"

The conversation turned with some difficulty to the normal boring date chit chat of books and movies. He told her about his love of painting and said he'd show her his work sometime if she was interested.

By the end of the night, the pretense of two normal people out on a date fell away as they found themselves alone in the den. Jane's eyes shifted between the bedroom door and the couch, wondering what the sleeping arrangements were going to be.

Before she had the chance to awkwardly phrase her question, Cole spoke. "I'll sleep on the couch."

It was obvious he didn't want to.

"I'm smaller than you, maybe I should sleep on the couch," she said.

"I wouldn't feel right about that."

It was eleven and neither of them was tired, so they watched TV. It was so easy to snuggle against him, to feel his warm hand stroking her arm.

She'd reacted to vampires and being bitten, but no one had had this effect on her from such relatively innocent contact. Before she knew what had happened, she'd nodded off on his chest.

She woke a few hours later in bed, only Cole wasn't beside her. She had the momentary anxiety he'd gone hunting and left her locked in the den alone again. She edged out of bed and was surprised to find an easel and paints set up in the living room.

Jane moved behind Cole to see what had so transfixed him. The image coming to life on the canvas depicted a large black wolf attacking a woman tied to a chair, helpless to defend herself. The wolf tore into her, ripping her apart.

The woman was Jane.

She put her hand over her mouth to stifle the scream she feared would flow out otherwise. She backed away, bumping into the coffee table and causing him to fall out of his trance.

"Are you okay? Did you have another nightmare?"

"Yes, but I don't think I'm dreaming." She couldn't look away from the gruesome image. "Why would you paint something like that? Is that what you want to do to me?"

His eyes widened. "Of course not." He moved closer to her, and she backed up another step, her initial fear of him returning.

He wisely chose to stop his advance. "I have visions. Sometimes when I paint them, it allows me to concentrate better and see and remember more clearly what happens. I was hoping to get more information to prevent this, but it's not helping this time."

She wanted to believe him. "Who is the wolf?" There. She'd managed to say it without her voice shaking.

"I'm not sure. There are five solid black wolves in the pack."

"Are you one of them?"

He placed the brush on the easel. "Jane . . . "

She backed away, her hands out in the universal sign of *don't come any closer*. "Are you one of them?"

His shoulders slumped, and he sighed. "Yes. And there's something else I have to tell you."

She waited for whatever could be of larger import than Cole painting violent pictures of her, but he put the caps on the tubes of paint and took the brushes to the kitchen sink to clean them. She followed. Finally he turned, leaning against the counter.

"Cain told me there is a human-hunter in my pack, but he wouldn't give me a name."

"Then how do you know he's telling the truth?"

"He doesn't lie except by omission; the truth amuses him too much. And I found evidence of a fresh kill."

"How long have you known this?"

"Since last night."

"And you sent me out with Rhonda today? How did you know it wasn't her? Is that why you gave me the knife?"

"I don't believe she'd do something like that. I knew even if it was her, she wouldn't risk it. And I was right. It's not her. She's a white wolf, and the wolf in the vision was black."

Jane knew he must smell her fear. She wanted to believe he wouldn't harm her and that he could control the beast inside him, but the image of being torn to shreds by a wolf that might be Cole . . .

"You have to let me go. It's not safe for me to be with you."

"I can't."

"Cole, please."

He shook his head and pointed at the painting. "It doesn't happen here." The image looked like an old abandoned church, but that didn't put her mind at ease. "And I know it doesn't happen for awhile. I'll figure out who it is. It's not me. I wouldn't . . . "

"Why can't you just let me go?" She hadn't lately felt like a captive because he hadn't treated her like one. But the reminders of her state of imprisonment were all around her. She was locked in the den with a dangerous wolf, trapped behind steel doors with a key code she didn't know.

Cole went back to the living area and sank down on the couch, his head in his hands. When Jane came to stand in front of him, he looked up.

"I don't know what the hell is happening to me. I've never felt this way before. When a wolf finds his mate, almost always he knows immediately. It's how I knew Rhonda wasn't it. Sure, we could give the mating mark to a wolf we choose after a long courtship, or through an arranged mating. But it's not the same. It's not like having a true mate."

He stood again, growing more restless and agitated the longer he spoke. "I've never felt that, so I don't know what it feels like. But that night I was watching through the curtains, and the moment I saw Paul throw you across the room, the only thought on my mind was protecting you and getting you out of there. Wolves are very possessive. The man in me says to let you go . . . find some way to help you so you don't get sucked back in with the vampires, but I can't make myself do it."

He laid a hand against her cheek. "I'll never force you to do anything against your will, but I have to have you here with me. This isn't supposed to happen with humans. I think it might be the vampire blood in your veins."

She'd felt the pull toward him as well. She'd been afraid there was something terribly wrong with her, to react so sexually to monsters. But it still didn't make sense.

"What does vampire blood have to do with it?"

"Ever wonder why the wolves are such a big threat to the vampires?"

Jane hadn't stopped to consider it. The political alliances of the various preternaturals hadn't exactly been on her radar when she was busy trying not to die.

"Have you ever wondered why silver affects both wolves and vampires? Or why the incubus and the vampire's feeding needs are so strangely similar? For an incubus it's about sex. For a vampire it's about blood, but it's still mostly sexual. Vampires are a bastard race created originally from the joining of an incubus with a werewolf. So that vampire blood running through your veins . . . it's part wolf. Maybe it was enough, and that's why I feel this with you."

She'd seen humans turned before but had never known the origin of their species. "What does this mean?"

"It means I can't let anything happen to you, and I can't let you leave. I think you may be mine. And some day I believe you'll be happy about that."

Jane wanted to tell him she was happy about it already. She could feel her body humming over just the idea of the two of them as a couple. But it was too soon, and he didn't seem one hundred percent sure she was actually his. If she slept with him and his true mate was someone else, she'd never recover from the loss.

Chapter Nine

Cole paced inside Cain's colorful bachelor tent, jumping when the demon's hand bumped his shoulder. At the collision, a bit of brandy sloshed over the rim of the glass the incubus held out to him.

"Sit down and have a drink," Cain said.

Cole took the snifter and shot a glare at him before tossing the alcohol back and letting it burn a line straight to his stomach. He'd been in the tent for the past five hours. During that time, the demon had disappeared twice to entertain himself with women brought over from the human world.

A third woman now lay on the sofa with a drink of her own. Some fruity girlie concoction Cain seemed to be a wizard at whipping up. Quite the ladies man if you were into serial killers.

"Must be nice having takeout delivered," Cole said bitterly.

The demon chuckled. "Not the normal way of things, but I'm helping you today. Stop being so sour." He moved to the couch, raised the woman's legs to sit, and draped them over his lap. She giggled when his finger trailed up the inside of her thigh.

"How much longer is this going to take?" Cole said.

"These things take time. You can't blow in and ask for that many portal charms and expect it to be done instantly. This isn't fast food.

"Each has to be forged by demons and then incanted over and all that evil crap. You think we just pick them up at Best Buy? I said you could come back when they were ready, but you insisted on waiting." He let out a dramatic sigh.

Cole just growled. He didn't want to leave Jane twice for this. He couldn't bring himself to lock her up in his den, not with the claustrophobia, so he'd left her in the hive with the pack. He thought she'd be safe, but every minute that ticked by made him more anxious.

Finally, when Cain and the tart in his lap had forgotten Cole's presence and were on the brink of moving past foreplay, another demon entered the tent carrying a gilded box. The girl startled in Cain's lap at the sight of him. He *looked* like a demon, all muscles and horns and red-scaled skin.

"Sir, I have the portal charms."

"Put them on the table and leave us," Cain said with a flourish of his arm.

The demon obeyed the order, then silently retreated from the tent.

Cole moved toward the box, but Cain's voice stopped him. "I have every confidence you'll repay this kindness when I need your help for something."

The wolf grimaced. He'd made a quite literal devil's bargain to secure the safety of his pack. "You have my word."

"Good. Say hello to Jane for me."

A low growl rumbled in Cole's chest.

"Ha! I knew it. I knew I smelled something between you two." Cain smirked as if he'd won a betting pool on the matter.

Cole collected the box from the table and left without another word. He passed through the portal into the woods outside the hive. He'd patrolled the area before crossing into the demon dimension and thought it wise to check things out once more.

As he made his way through the forest, the sweet scent of human blood assaulted his senses. In his human form he was revolted, knowing in this area of the forest it was likely a werewolf kill. The killer was getting sloppy, taunting the alpha with how clever he was.

The wolf part of him salivated at the heady scent, and he had to fight the urge to shift into his animal form to scavenge over the remains. He took a few steadying breaths. When he was sure the beast was under control, he hid the golden box under a pile of leaves and broke into a run.

As he drew nearer he could smell the crisp scent of lilacs, possibly a shampoo or body lotion, then the copper smell of blood, and something else . . . something he knew. He fought back his mind's desire to give the thought form.

When he reached the body he doubled over, his head swamped with dizziness. No. It wasn't possible. But the scent was unmistakable . . . and the warm honey-colored hair.

Jane.

His stomach heaved, and he threw up. He crawled to her prone form, praying for a miracle to let it not be true. Entrails spilled from a gash in her stomach, and he fought back another wave of nausea. He shouldn't have left her.

When he rolled the body over, he let out a long shuddering breath.

Not Jane.

The woman in his arms had similar features and build and the same hair. But it wasn't her. He realized she smelled like Jane because she was wearing the jeans and sweater he'd borrowed on her first day in the hive.

Now that the panic was receding he could smell the woman's true scent underneath the clothing. The sweater had been ripped apart down the center, and on closer inspection, he could see that the torn fibers were embedded in her flesh. She'd been made to put the outfit on before she'd been killed.

Cole growled with disgust, rage seething beneath the surface. The clothing had been supplied by Ed's mate.

"Read 'em and weep." Jane laid down a full house.

Blake looked like she'd kicked his puppy.

"Oh man, I think he's going to," Mara said.

"You now owe me three hundred dollars," Jane said, triumphantly. She was about halfway to paying Cole back for her wardrobe.

Blake had fronted her a few chips to start her off, and she was kicking their asses. Living with vampires had given her a great poker face. After all, she'd pretended to be a vampire groupie fairly convincingly for nearly a decade, so convincingly even she had almost believed it. At least from a fashion standpoint.

She looked up to see Cole shaking his head. "Maybe *you* should have played me instead of Paul," he said. He was smiling but the smile didn't reach his eyes.

Probably so. Paul sucked at poker. Maybe he hadn't been a vampire long enough to be a good gambler. He was still a fledge and not old enough to have developed that stony stillness a vampire got to his features after a few hundred years.

Over the past couple of weeks she'd casually socialized with all the wolves. She'd been surprised by how nice most of them were. This wasn't the picture she'd expected when she'd thought of what the wolf pack did in their spare time.

Of course, Cole had reminded her she was a friend of the pack, given that role by the alpha himself. It probably made a difference in how they behaved around her. But knowing Charlee and being with Paul hadn't given her any special status with the vampires or caused them to be any nicer to her.

Cole had remained true to his word and hadn't pushed her. He'd stayed on the couch, though it was a pointless exercise. By the end of each night he always ended up in the bed with her. His presence soothed her. When he wasn't holding her, she had the dreams, waking up screaming, gasping for breath, to find herself in the den. Not the coffin.

Blake threw his cards on the table. "That's it. I'm out, chickadee. You're killin' me here."

Jane grinned at him and raked the chips toward herself. "I'd like to cash them in now."

Blake laughed. "You would. Cole, this girl is dangerous to the pack's finances."

Jane expected Cole to laugh, but all he did was stare at her with such intensity she felt compelled to look away. She pocketed the money and went to the kitchen, uncomfortable with the strange mood that had emanated from him since he'd gotten back.

"Oh. Hi," she said when she saw Rhonda with her head poked in the fridge.

After the first day shopping, the wolf had been standoffish. Jane could understand why. She'd been after Cole since before puberty, and Jane had just waltzed in and taken his attention in less than a day. She knew that feeling. She'd been there with Greg, not understanding why he didn't want something more. But it wasn't like she could give the other woman a pep talk about it, so she'd kept her distance.

"Hi," Rhonda said, her gaze still on the contents of the refrigerator.

The blonde wolf finally chose an unidentifiable bag of snack food and started to leave the kitchen. She gave Jane one slow look up and down, then took a long whiff. "Well, I don't smell him on you," she said, her voice flat of emotion.

"Excuse me?"

"He hasn't fucked you yet. The second he does, you are out of here. He'll use you just like he used me. Screwed me, then tossed me out of bed the next morning. So much for the afterglow. Cole is a confirmed bachelor. He'll never settle down, and the second you give it up to him you're out on the street, girlfriend. Back with your vampires where you belong."

Jane drew back, Rhonda's words as sharp as a slap to her face. "Whatever happened with you two isn't my fault."

"Hey, I'm just trying to help you, sweetie. You seem to have a habit of walking into the most fucked-up relation-ships you can't handle. You aren't vampire enough for the vampires and you aren't wolf enough for Cole. So get that out of your head right now."

Rhonda gave her one last sneer before turning on her heel and leaving. Jane had lost her appetite. When she returned to the main den, Cole was gone again.

"Where did Cole go?"

Blake looked up from the card table. "He had to take care of something. He'll be back soon."

"We're going to put a movie in," Mara said. "You should watch with us." The female wolf patted a spot on the couch between her and another girl named Lucy. Lucy was sixteen and just coming into her wolfiness. She had remarkable control of herself. Cole had said she was alpha female material, and some day she'd have to leave the pack to find a place more suited to her power.

It had weighed on Jane's mind considerably. Sure, Lucy was a bit young. Cole was old enough to be her father and then some. Still, the fact remained that if Cole were younger, Lucy would be a prime candidate to be his mate.

He needed someone strong, someone who was commanding and powerful. Not a human with vampire blood running through her veins. It might be different if she'd inherited some physical strength, instead of just a higher pain threshold and borderline freaky psychic senses.

She settled between the girls as they started a movie and passed the popcorn.

"The Wolf Man?" Mara said with a groan. "Jane's going to think awful things about us."

Lucy laughed hysterically and winked.

After his discovery in the woods, Cole had wanted to get Jane alone, wanted to touch her, to be sure she was real and alive. But he'd stepped back into the shadows when he'd realized she wasn't alone in the kitchen. He was livid over the way Rhonda had spoken to her.

The moment the wolf was in the hallway, he'd clamped one hand over her mouth so she couldn't scream and wrapped the other tight around her arm, jerking her through the interwoven caves and outside into the sunshine. He knew he was hurting her, and he didn't very much care.

He finally let go of her and growled. "What the hell was that back there?"

She crossed her arms over her chest and shrugged, her eyes averted from his. Whether it was an act of submission or to cover deceit, he couldn't be sure.

"You will NOT speak to her that way. She's a part of this pack now."

Rhonda's lip curled in a snarl, "She's human! You can't possibly think a human can live with wolves. She's weak."

"Says the pack omega." It was a cheap shot, but Rhonda deserved it for that display in there. He considered banishing her from the pack. Between her jealousy and Ed's murderous rampage, he needed them both gone if Jane was going to be able to run free. He couldn't keep her locked up forever.

A tear slipped down the blonde wolf's cheek. "You want to make her your mate? You can't do that. You have to think of the pack. You wouldn't take me because I'm so weak. You think you can take a human? You think they'll answer to her as the alpha female? What happened to the way you felt about me? You were going to marry me. If you hadn't taken over the pack, we could be together now."

"Rhonda, we were pups. It's true, an alpha needs a strong mate, but there are different kinds of strength. You're like a sister to me."

Her expression turned hard. "Don't give me that, *like a sister* bullshit again. You slept with me, and I was there too, Cole. There was something between us. You felt it. You had to have felt it."

It was true, he'd been incredibly turned on when he'd taken Rhonda to bed. But he also hadn't been laid in six months, he'd just lost a member of the pack, and he'd had a moment of weakness. She'd said no strings, and he hadn't realized that her *no strings* really meant *fuck me, then never let me go.*

He'd lost himself in her for a few hours, and he'd felt awful afterward. But he'd never been able to verbalize these feelings to her and thought it best not to start now. He didn't want to hurt her, but her psychological battle with Jane had to end.

"You know the circumstances that led up to that. I told you I was sorry."

Rhonda wiped the tears with the back of her hand and stalked off toward the woods.

"Leave Jane alone."

"Yeah, whatever."

Chapter Ten

The *Wolf Man* **had scared** Jane as a child because the image on the screen had reminded her of the real monster she'd encountered. The movie seemed ridiculous now, even with the flashback. The lights had been turned out, leaving the cave in darkness.

Every few seconds a tear crept down her cheek, and she wiped it away. She wondered if the wolves beside her would smell the salt of her tears and know it wasn't the popcorn. She didn't have to wonder for long. Mara leaned toward her.

"Are you okay?" She whispered.

"No," Jane whispered back.

The wolf grabbed her hand and led her out of the room back toward the kitchen, no doubt able to see perfectly well in the dark.

Jane sat at the large kitchen table while Mara fixed them ice cream sundaes.

She grimaced. "My metabolism isn't as fast as yours." Sure, she used to consider sugar a separate and necessary food group, but now she cared if she got fat.

Mara ignored her protest and set the ice cream in front of her. "Okay, so spill it. Did Cole do something? Men can be such morons."

Jane forced a weak smile. "Did he say anything to you about my past?"

"He said you hated vampires and that you'd been through a lot, but he didn't give details. The pack thought you could be dangerous because they could smell vampire on you. Cole needed to reassure everyone you're on our side."

Jane nodded. She didn't know if she'd put it that boldly. Jane was on Jane's side. It was the only way she'd known to live. Just survive, appease, hope they don't kill you.

She looked up to find Mara staring at her, curious.

"So what gives?"

Jane shrugged and took a careful bite of the sundae. "Rhonda said something that made me think Cole said something about me and the vampires. But if that's all he told you, he wouldn't tell her more, would he?"

"Oh, hell no. It's been odd between him and Rhonda for about three months now. They were real close for awhile, and then it got weird. She came into the main den one day smelling like him. Then they weren't close anymore."

Rhonda must have smelled Paul on her when she'd first come to the hive and made assumptions.

Cole stepped into the kitchen then. He moved to stand between the two girls surveying the scene, his arms crossed over his chest. "Is everything okay?" His expression was closed.

"We're fine," Mara said.

"Jane?"

"I'm fine."

He looked doubtful but let it go. "Jane, will you come with me back to my den?"

Her stomach did that thing it did every time Cole said anything that she could remotely interpret as a sexual come-on.

"Sure."

She followed him quickly from the room, hoping Mara hadn't smelled her reaction. She didn't want the entire pack to know she had the hots for Cole. Though it was probably too late for that concern. Their sense of smell and ability to read emotions was uncanny.

When they were inside the den, he led her to the couch and gestured for her to sit.

"There are some things I've wanted to say to you for awhile now."

"Oh?" Jane's tongue darted out to wet her lips. Could she even have a coherent conversation with him right now? She struggled to keep her eyes on his face and away from more interesting regions.

"I no longer have any doubts. I know you're my mate."

The blunt announcement was like a physical blow. She felt herself pulled in separate directions. In one direction she was doing back flips, floating. In the other, she was curling in on herself, waiting for another sentence to start.

She'd spent years dreaming of a nice, normal relationship with a human male and forgetting all about the world of monsters. But a human had never been in her cards. When Rich had been killed, she'd vowed to stay away from her kind to avoid endangering any more of them. Still, it was difficult to close that chapter, to know the normal, safe life that would wake her from this nightmare was nowhere in her future.

"Well, say something."

Cole was looking at her anxiously, as if he'd dropped down on one knee and proposed. In a sense maybe he had. Though she wasn't sure it was a proposal, so much as a statement. If he genuinely believed she was his, whatever did or didn't happen between them physically, she wasn't going anywhere.

He took her hands in his, and she felt the electric current pass between them. When she looked into his eyes, they were expectant.

"I know."

Normally humans lived in denial about their feelings, hiding behind masks far more effective than those of shapeshifters. But she felt it. He wondered how much vampire blood her mother drank during her pregnancy. Whatever the amount, it had been enough to link Jane to him, however remotely.

If he hadn't seen her walk in the sunlight himself, he'd think her father was a vampire. But she would have been killed at birth and wouldn't have been able to bear sunlight in any event.

He wanted to take her, mark her as his mate, and bring her fully into the pack. But that would require sex, and he was constantly aware of her history.

This moment was crucial; he could feel her hesitance, her anxiety. One misstep and he could push her away and lose her forever. "And how do you feel about that?" *Try to sound less like a therapist, Cole.*

Her face was guarded. "How do *you* feel about it? I'm not a wolf."

He growled. "Forget what Rhonda said."

"You heard?"

"Yes."

She looked down at their interlocked hands. "But I'm *not* a wolf. I can't be what a wolf could be for you. I can't share all the same experiences. I only have human strength. I'm not a leader."

"Nevertheless, you are my mate. A true mate. I could choose to mark another wolf, but I would be empty. You don't know how hard it's been to not take what my instincts say is mine." He heard her heart rate pick up, not from arousal, but from panic.

He pulled her back into his arms and stroked his fingers through her hair, conscious of his canines elongating, begging him to just mark her. Screw consent. "Talk to me. What's going through your head right now?"

"Could you turn me? Make me like you?"

"Therian breeds are born, not made."

She nodded and bit her lip, falling silent for a few moments as if weighing her next words. "What does all this mean? For me? If I didn't want to be your mate would you let me go?"

His grip tightened on her, and he had to fight to loosen it and remember that although her pain tolerance was higher, she was still fragile compared to him. He didn't want her more frightened. He kept his voice even, his words measured. "You don't want to be my mate?"

"I didn't say that. I just need to know."

"It's safe for you here with the pack."

"As long as whoever is hunting the humans doesn't eat me," she said under her breath, but not quietly enough that he didn't hear.

"I've watched them all when they're around you. I believe it's Ed, but I'll have to catch him in the act. The rest of the pack for the most part has accepted you as family." He couldn't tell her what he'd found in the woods; there was no sense panicking her. It was his burden to bear.

"Do they know?"

"It's not been stated aloud, but I think they sense the shift and the energy between you and me."

"You haven't answered my question," she said. "What would happen if I didn't want this?"

He wanted to growl at her. The wolf in him screamed to throw her down on the ground, dominate her, mark her for daring to question that her rightful place was by his side. But the man in him held the wolf in control. He refused to be just another monster in her life throwing his weight around.

It took every ounce of strength he possessed to say, "If you chose not to become my mate, you would live in one of the other dens here. You'd have your own space, and you'd be safe. Once I catch Ed and make certain you're safe with everyone else."

"But you wouldn't let me go. I'd still be a prisoner. Don't want to let go of your ten-thousand-dollar investment?"

He knew she was taunting him, pushing to see if she could make him angry. No, that wasn't right. She was pushing to find out what would happen when he *was* angry. The full moon was fast approaching, and now wasn't the time for her to be pushing buttons just to find out what they'd do. He took a few slow breaths, fighting against the primal urges that raged within him.

"You are not here because of Paul's debt, and you know that. Whether I realized it at the time or not, I took you because you belonged with me. You are not a prisoner here. This is your home. As soon as it's safe, you'll have the key codes and free run of the place like everyone else. But you're my responsibility to keep safe now.

"I can't let you walk out that door and go wherever you would go, knowing at any moment something dangerous could snag you, that you could end up back with the vampires. You can't possibly understand what it feels like to be a wolf, have found your mate, and then lose her like that. I won't force you to be intimate with me. I won't make you accept the mark. But you're asking for more than I can give here, and I think you know that."

He waited as she processed that information, as her heart started the slow trip back to normal.

"Okay."

"Okay what? Okay you'll be my mate or okay you'll live in one of the other dens when I've made sure things are safe?"

Jane looked into his eyes as his hand moved to caress the side of her throat. She felt self-conscious when his fingers trailed over the bite marks Paul had left. In all her time with vampires, she'd never been with one who'd left visible marks.

The others had always healed their bites because they didn't want her skin marred. Paul had been different. He'd wanted Jane to look like a big vamp tramp billboard. And he was the monster whose arms she'd walked right into.

Voluntarily.

Now she'd never be rid of the physical scars. She'd never be able to look in the mirror and pretend none of it had ever happened. A tear rolled down her cheek.

Cole's thumb moved to smooth it away. "Shhhh. I'm not going to do anything you don't want. Why are you crying?"

"It's not you. It's this." She pointed at the ugly scar on her throat. "How will you be able to stand being mated to me when I've been marked up by a vampire like this?"

"That isn't your fault."

"That's not what I asked. The vampires are your enemies, and you've got a visual reminder that more than one of them got there first."

Cole bent his head to her neck and kissed over the mark. His tongue darted out to gently trace the scar. He murmured against her skin, "That. Isn't. Your. Fault."

Jane wasn't finished. She didn't know where it had come from, but she couldn't stand the thought of almost having something good, only to have it ripped from her again. She pulled out of his embrace and took her shirt off, tossing it to the floor.

His nostrils flared and his pupils dilated, but that wasn't the point of the exercise. She removed the bra and shivered when she saw the feral gleam that lit his eyes

She closed the space between them, and suddenly his hands were everywhere. She whimpered softly at the contact then got control of herself, remembering her mission.

"Stop."

She could tell it was a struggle, that he thought she was teasing him. But he removed his hands and fell back onto the couch, placing them on either side of his body, digging into the leather. He didn't seem to care about the upholstery because his eyes didn't stray from her.

She stepped closer. "What about this one, and this one, and this one?" She pointed to the various bite marks Paul had left on her. "Can you really stand to be with me, when I look like this?"

Before she could say anything else, before she could even think, he'd swept her up in his arms. She blinked and they were in the bedroom. He tossed her on the bed and removed his own shirt before joining her, his eyes intense and locked with hers.

"Yes," his voice rumbled.

He proceeded to kiss each bite mark. "These are scars. They aren't a vampire claim, and they aren't a wolf's mating mark," he growled. "They are battle wounds. These are the marks that prove you're strong, that you've been through fire and walked out safe on the other side."

"They're ugly. They make me ugly."

"No, you can't think that." He flicked on the lamp. "Am I ugly?"

Jane hadn't stopped to notice before, but Cole had a few scars of his own.

"We heal fast and rarely scar, but sometimes there are things that leave a permanent mark."

She found herself riveted to the scar slashing across his stomach, a wound that would have killed him had he not been a wolf.

"What happened?"

"I was eighteen, and the pack alpha was raping my mother. I killed him and in the process got this little souvenir. He was bleeding out and dying and still sneering at me because he knew it would scar. But I didn't look at it that way. This is what I got in the process of saving my mother and becoming the leader. And those are what you got while surviving and becoming who you are."

"Scars make a man look distinguished, but on a woman . . . "

Cole quirked a brow. "Was that a joke?"

"Yeah. Lame huh?"

He just chuckled.

Jane crawled to the edge of the bed, ran her finger over the puckered mark on his stomach, and kissed it as he'd done with her. *All this could be yours, Jane.*

His hands had moved to unbutton his pants. She put her hand over his. "Wait. Don't mark me, okay?"

He looked like he was going to protest, but she interrupted him. "I want to see what this would be like with us. I can't just hand my entire life to you yet. Please promise me you won't mark me."

He sighed, but nodded, the look on his face like she'd just asked him to go vegan.

Chapter Eleven

They were really going to do this. Jane stood in her jeans and bare feet beside the bed watching as Cole peeled the jeans from his own body. She guessed this was the part where she was supposed to follow suit, but she was busily cataloging her previous sexual history, trying to convince herself this was different.

All vampires, all in one way or another to protect herself. Was this what this was too? Fucking a man to gain protection?

The idea made her feel like a whore.

No, Cole was different. She felt connected to him in a way she hadn't felt with the others. His protection wasn't conditional on her sleeping with him. He'd made that clear. He'd patiently waited weeks, not pushing her toward anything too sexual. And she wanted him.

His hand slipped up to cradle the back of her head in that deliciously possessive way she'd always wanted a man—the right man—to hold her for a kiss.

"You're thinking too much," he growled.

Before she could respond, his mouth was on hers, a soft, devouring caress that made her mind empty all its contents except for him. She could feel the hard length of his erection pressed against her stomach, and her hand automatically moved between them to stroke him.

His hand closed over hers, stilling her movements as he tore himself away from her mouth. "I've been waiting too long for this. You do that and I won't last until I'm inside you. Coming on your leg like a randy teenager wasn't exactly how I imagined this."

She blushed and moved her arms around his neck.

"Good girl. You take instruction so well."

"Cole!" She was trying to sound indignant, outraged even, but the deep gravel purr of his voice was doing wildly inappropriate things to her body. He could say nearly anything to her right about now, and she'd respond like a porn star.

He chuckled, scooped her up, and laid her on the bed. His gaze raked over her, considering. "Are you particularly attached to these jeans?"

She shrugged. "You paid for them."

"And I'll replace them."

Jane watched, enthralled, as he allowed himself to shift just enough for his hands to form fur and claws. He ripped the jeans off her, careful not to nick her skin, then shifted back to human form.

And what a form it was. Tall, broad-shouldered, well-muscled, looming over her like every girl's fantasy. The tribal tattoo was like a shiny bow on a gift wrapped just for her. Or unwrapped, as the case may be. His eyes flashed yellow at her for a moment, and her heart picked up speed.

She reached up, pulling him down on top of her, over-whelmed by the feel of flesh against flesh as his body pressed into hers. Warmth. Not the eerie coldness of a vampire's skin. He nuzzled his mouth against her throat and kissed her hungrily.

She tensed.

"Don't worry, baby. Not marking. Just kissing."

She relaxed again and bucked her hips against him. Maybe it had been her time with vampires, but a mouth on her neck immediately sent her into a tailspin.

"Please . . . "

Cole lifted himself to look into her eyes. His gaze was intense as he buried himself fully inside her. She gasped.

The emotion slammed into her, causing tears to pour down her cheeks. He was so warm. It was the first sex she'd had that hadn't in some way been a seduction to appease someone to spare her life. Even with Gregory it had been about hoping to keep his interest in her so she'd stay safe. With Cole it was because she'd wanted to know what his body would feel like inside of hers.

The intensity of his eyes changed to concern. "Did I hurt you?"

She shook her head. "No, I'm fine. Better than fine."

He feathered his fingers over her hair, his gaze scorching her.

Jane didn't think he was aware of the deep growls he was emitting as his mouth latched onto her breast. A little voice in her brain chanted in rhythm to his thrusts, *Mine. Mine. Mine. All Mine.* For a moment she thought her mind had connected with Cole's, and she was hearing his thoughts of possession toward her. But the voice in her head was her own. She wanted him to mark her.

Her body strained against his and, at the peak moment, she bit down on her lip to stop herself from begging him to bite her. Her orgasm came crashing over her, and she whimpered, part from the pleasure of her release and part from biting her lip so hard she'd drawn blood. Cole followed with a primal growl. She could see the strength of will it took for him not to bite her. Then he collapsed and rolled her over with him so they were lying together on their sides.

A part of her had feared sex with anyone would only bring back the Technicolor nightmare of her history. But the experience was so physically different she couldn't compare it. She wanted him, and despite everything she'd been taught about the wolves, she trusted him. But being mated to a wolf was serious. It wasn't something she could take lightly or rush into. Knowing he'd had the desire to mark her but held back for her benefit, made her trust him a little more.

He trailed his hand over her arm and pressed his lips against the side of her neck. She melted against him.

"Are you okay?"

She nodded, not trusting her voice as his fingers skimmed over her skin. Since joining physically with him, she felt . . . connected, like somehow he sensed what was going on inside her. Maybe he understood the crying because she'd hate to pick up the nickname, Crybaby Jane. It was as if she'd saved up years of tears to let them pour out over Cole, the one man who wouldn't use them as a weapon against her.

She rolled to face him and wrapped her arms around his neck, her lips pressing against his. He made her ache in places she didn't know she could ache, and there were no words to fill in the emotional spaces. All she could do was feel.

His arms came around her, cradling her, his fingers in her hair, his mouth consuming hers. She felt him, hard again, nudged against her, and she spread her thighs so he could slide back inside. He eased in and out of her in the most exquisite torture. His mouth moved back to her throat, and she felt his canines elongating, his struggle not to penetrate her skin and mark her seeming equal to her own struggle not to capitulate and beg him to.

A moan escaped her throat as she groaned against him, urging him to quicken his pace. He responded with a growl.

A wolf getting into his bed would have known the score, that she might end up marked and belonging to him. A human didn't understand. And with Jane's history, the last thing she needed was another situation where the choice was taken out of her hands.

All she had to do was say the word and she'd be his.

No. His mind rebelled against the future tense of that statement. She *was* his. She just didn't know it yet. It wasn't official, but she belonged to him. He felt it with more ferocity than he'd ever felt anything else in his life.

He spilled into her and felt the reverberation of her moans against his chest. His canines pressed against her throat. Just one little movement, and it would be done. The intent was sure as hell there. With great difficulty he pulled his fangs from her neck and held her, shaking from the effort it took not to mark her.

Her warm, sweet body curled into his, and he fell into a fitful sleep.

Cole was restless when he woke the next morning. Being next to his mate should soothe him, but leaving the mating uncompleted made him tense and anxious. It was the night of the full moon; he couldn't avoid the potential consequences of that.

What if he was the wolf from the painting? What if he lost control under the influence of the moon and hurt her? His logical mind told him to just avoid churches or buildings that looked like old churches. But he knew that wasn't how it worked. Any event could shift the future, and in all likelihood the course had already changed just from his knowledge of it.

He felt Jane stir and snuggle deeper against his chest. "Jane?"

"Mmm?"

"I have to leave for a few days."

"What? No!" She gripped him tighter as if her frail human strength could stop his movement.

"I can respect your wish to wait to complete the mating, but tonight is the full moon. Although I believe Ed is the wolf in the painting, I can't take the risk it's me."

"It's not you."

"I promise I'll only be gone three nights until the full moon is over."

He could hear her heart pounding through her chest and her breathing changing, becoming shallow pants like the first night when she'd learned she was locked underground. His chest tightened.

"Please, I can't stay down here by myself. I can't."

"It would just be for a few hours after sunset each night. During the day, Mara and Blake will be here with you. We know they're safe. They're also the wolves who have the most control over the change. At sunset they'll have to leave you to go hunting, but after they've hunted they'll come back to guard you."

Her nails dug into his skin. "I don't want you to leave me. Greg left."

He stroked his fingers through her hair, the guilt from causing her more distress tugging at him. "Shhhh, I'm not leaving you." Then he said it, the thought that had been tempting him since the conversation began. "If the mating was complete you'd be safe with me."

She stiffened in his arms.

Stupid, Cole. Why did you have to go there? She was starting to trust you. "I'm sorry, I shouldn't have brought it up, but it would be a simple solution."

"Cole, I can't yet. Please understand."

He nodded, the disappointment overwhelming his senses while the wolf banged against his cage intent on taking what was his. "I'm sorry."

He'd said he wouldn't leave her until sunset. He spent every second until that time, touching her, needing his skin to be pressed against hers, a shallow substitute for the completion of the mating ritual.

At five o'clock, Blake and Mara were summoned to the den.

"I'm going to give the code to your bodyguards. I'll change it when I get back." He scribbled something on a slip of paper and handed it to Blake.

Her voice cracked. "But not me."

"Jane, *please*." He felt like a monster not giving her permission to leave. What if something crazy happened and she needed to escape? But he knew she wouldn't need to escape the wolves he'd chosen to stay with her. If he gave her the code she might come looking for him.

He knew the mating call stirred within her blood as it did his. Perhaps not as strongly, but it was enough. She felt it or she wouldn't be so upset about a temporary separation. Once again he wanted to make both of their lives easier by just marking her. But he couldn't start their relationship with a betrayal of trust, even if he knew she'd forgive him once she felt the bond between them fully flare to life.

Jane clung to him as he gave her one last kiss. She looked so lost.

"Stay. It's not you. I know it's not you," she said, tears tracking down her cheeks.

He leaned in to whisper in her ear. "Even if it isn't, the full moon is the best shot I have at catching the human-hunter and removing him from the pack. A wolf that's been hunting people won't be able to resist human flesh on the full moon. I'll track him and kill him."

"But what if he kills you?"

"He won't. He's older, and I've been alpha for two decades for a reason. It'll be fine. I promise you."

Cole left her in the den, resenting every step that took him farther from his mate. He was so lost inside his head with thoughts of Jane that he bumped into Rhonda.

"What's wrong?" she asked.

He looked at her and almost snapped. He could see in her eyes the little light, the lack of true sympathy. She probably hoped something had happened between him and Jane and that she still had a shot.

He growled in frustration. "I have to leave for a few days."

"What about Jane?"

That false sympathy again.

"Jane is staying behind with Blake and Mara."

Rhonda moved to touch his shoulder. He sidestepped it. He couldn't stand her skin on his right now. He wanted to run back into the den to tell Jane he was sorry he'd been crazy. But there was the small chance without the mating mark, in an enclosed space with her on the full moon, that he wouldn't be able to control himself.

If he lost control and she expressed the slightest bit of fear toward him, it could end with bloodshed. He swallowed around the lump in his throat as he remembered the vision in detail far more vivid than the painting. He couldn't be the one to do that to Jane.

If removing himself from the equation was the only way to keep her safe, he'd do it.

He stayed far back at first so his suspect wouldn't see him, tracking him through the demon dimension and back out to the other side into Georgia. The same place Cain said he'd caught a wolf from his pack hunting a human. Golatha Falls was a small town with plenty of forests to hide in. Plenty of game to hunt. Cole quickly caught and fed off a few rabbits so he could more easily control his change.

He followed the other wolf's trail through the woods. When the smell of blood hit the air, he broke into a run. Ed looked up from his kill, crimson staining his muzzle. The deer lay dead at his feet. He reclaimed his human form.

"What's wrong?"

Cole shifted as well. "Dammit!"

"What? What is it?"

"I thought you'd been hunting humans. I was trying to catch you in the act."

Ed looked hurt. "Why me? Have I ever given you any reason to think I'd betray you? Have I ever defied an order?"

Cole quickly recounted the vision to him. "That, combined with the hostile way you've been around Jane . . . "

Ed shook his head. "I'm sorry I gave you reason to doubt me. It's not that Jane's a human. It's the vampire stuff. I thought you were being ruled by your dick and I just . . . It was inexcusable. I'm sorry. I'll help you hunt."

Cole nodded and the two black wolves returned to a shape fit for fast tracking. He felt like a clock had been attached to the night, and they were running out of time.

Chapter Twelve

Jane was doubled over, gripping the counter in the den. She felt like she had food poisoning. Mara stood beside her, holding her hand for comfort.

"You'll be fine. He'll be back."

What? This was Cole? Because Cole had left her? She looked up to see shock in Blake's eyes.

"My God. She really is his mate."

Mara's voice went up a register in a sing-song mocking tone. "I thought you said you didn't believe in that *true mate nonsense.*"

Blake stared at Jane. "I didn't. Before."

The two wolves guided her to the couch.

"Just breathe," Mara said. "If you don't panic it won't hurt."

Jane concentrated on breathing slowly in through her nose and out through her mouth, counting the breaths. "Why is this happening to me?"

"Your body wants to complete the mating. It's like a kind of limbo. You slept with him didn't you?"

She blushed and nodded. Not that they couldn't smell it on her most likely. She probably smelled more like Cole than herself right now. "If he knew this would happen, why would he leave me like this?"

"Because you're human," Blake said. "No one would think something like that would happen with a human. And Cole isn't exactly as well-versed on the intricacies of mating rituals as Mara is. She's our resident expert."

Mara punched him playfully in the arm.

Jane didn't say anything about the vampire blood. It was a good thing this didn't happen if a human slept with a werewolf. They wouldn't survive it.

Mara was talking to her again in that quiet, soothing voice. "It'll go away if you can stop panicking."

"Really?" If ever there was a time to learn to calm down, it was now.

"Yes. You're anxious, and you want your mate. But he's not quite your mate yet. It's throwing your body out of whack. If you relax, this will fade."

But Jane couldn't relax. She got up and paced the length of the den, a million thoughts swirling through her head. The primary one being: *Why did I have sex with him?* She'd wanted Cole. She felt safe with him, but now she was essentially married to him because clearly she couldn't go through life like this.

She turned sharply back to the wolves on the couch. "Will it be like this until he marks me?"

Mara shrugged. "I don't know. This almost never happens. When a wolf finds his true mate, he doesn't wait; he doesn't ask; he just marks and that's that."

Jane laughed. She had to be losing her mind to be laughing at a time like this. But Cole had, in fact, marked her. Had he not, she wouldn't feel like a whole piece of her had been cut out and was moving farther and farther away.

"Why didn't he mark you?" Mara asked.

"I wanted to wait."

It had seemed like a good idea at the time, sensible. She'd only met Cole a few weeks ago. Being a wolf's mate was a big commitment, and it seemed kind of permanent. Her entire life had been about running. Running from her fears, hiding, blending in, hoping for a protector. It had suddenly become important to her to, for once in her life, make a decision that was about what she wanted and not about side benefits like shelter and food and protection.

She hadn't wanted it to be a transaction.

But things were different with Cole, and she'd known she would let him mark her. And if she didn't, what was she going to do? Hang around the den and be a nun? Take up with another wolf in the pack? Cole would love that. And anyway, she didn't want another wolf in the pack. She wanted Cole.

"Jane, it's getting late. We have to go hunt. We'll be back as soon as we've fed enough to control the change."

Panic swept through her again, and she gripped the counter. "No! Don't lock me in here alone like this. Please."

Mara turned to Blake. "Give her the code. We'll be gone for an hour, just long enough to hunt and find Cole. Everyone else is out hunting too. She'll be fine."

Blake appeared to be debating it, weighing the pros and cons.

"Please," Jane begged.

He sighed and pulled the paper from his pocket. "Cole will kill me if you get hurt, so please don't leave the den."

Jane's hand closed over the slip of paper, and she nodded. Mara hugged her, even as the fur cropped out over her hands and legs. Then they were gone in a blur.

She waited until she knew they were out of the hive before moving to the door. Her hands shook as she punched in the first code of two written on the paper.

When the door slid open, she walked under the bright fluorescent track lighting for what seemed like forever to the main den. Then she punched in the second code.

The hive felt weird being empty and so quiet. She was used to noise and laughter and game playing in here.

She doubted she could get all the way outside. There would be a different code, but maybe not if she went back through the tunnel to Cole's den. He had a separate exit.

Jane knew she shouldn't leave. It was dangerous out there, and she didn't know how close the wolves were. She wasn't sure if some of them might have stayed in the city to hunt, despite Cole's orders. She also didn't know if she'd run into a vampire.

She'd be fine here. Cole would be back soon. The thought made her heart leap. It had been ridiculous not to let him mark her. Why did she have to be so cynical, and take such a good thing and turn it into something bad? All the suffering she'd gone through for the vampire blood in her veins, and now because of it, she was Cole's mate. She'd finally found a place where she fit, and she wouldn't have to become a vampire to be safe from them.

She wondered briefly what would have happened if she'd succeeded in getting a vamp to turn her. Would she have still been destined for Cole, or would he have seen her as the enemy?

Jane had calmed enough for the pain to subside. She laughed in the hollow room. She'd never been in physical pain from a man's absence before. *Must be love*, she thought sardonically.

She tensed and jerked her head around. She couldn't be sure, but she had the intense feeling she wasn't alone. A cramp clenched her gut. Okay, now was not the time for the incomplete mating to yell at her some more. She got it. She'd let Cole mark her at the first available opportunity.

She inched closer to the steel door that led into the tunnels, her eyes on the entrance at the other side of the room. Then the door slid open, and Rhonda appeared, standing with a big grin on her face, looking as if a canary feather might fall out of her mouth.

"Jane!" she beamed. "All alone are we?" She looked around dramatically.

"Not for long," Jane said, biting her lip against the pain that was trying to well up again. She willed herself to calm down.

"Are you all right, dear?"

Jane spun on her heel and raced for the door. She punched in the code and the door slid open. The steel panel started to shut behind her, and she let out a sigh of relief. She heard a whoosh and looked down to find Rhonda's shoe wedged in the door to stop it from closing.

Her lungs screamed at her as she ran for Cole's den, her stomach cramping from the panic overtaking her. She reached the second key pad.

As the door to the den slid open, she felt herself pulled back by her hair. "Wait for me," Rhonda said.

The blonde stood in her stockings, her shoes abandoned at the other doorway. She shoved Jane into the smaller den.

The wolf crossed her arms over her chest. "Do you know that even as the weakest wolf, I'm still about five times stronger than the average human? And faster? If my heel hadn't been wedged in the door, I would have caught you already. But it takes a lot of strength to push that steel door open with such a tiny thing stopping it from closing all the way. I thought that was pretty inventive. It comes from all those hours watching *Buffy* where she was using things in her surroundings to fight."

Jane rolled her eyes. Rhonda was a disagreeable bitch, and she wasn't about to show her fear. "I've been imprisoned with things far bigger and badder than you'll ever be," she retorted.

The comment hit its mark. Rhonda recovered quickly and laughed. "My, don't we have a death wish? But if I do the killing, I can't be with Cole."

Jane gawked at her. Rhonda was completely out of her mind if she thought she still had a chance with him.

"Cole is my mate," Jane said, feeling a bit like a possessive caveman. She *did* have the distinct urge to club the wolf over the head right then. There was nothing like a verbal cat fight to let a girl know who she wanted to be with.

Rhonda burst out laughing, bending over so her hands rested on her knees. "Oh, that's rich. Baby, you think him screwing you makes you his mate? That's so cute. Nice try, but he hasn't marked you."

She strode closer to Jane, inspecting her neck better. She ran a finger over the bite mark Paul had left the night Jane met Cole.

"But I see someone else has. Little vampire whore, thinks a wolf would want her after that? He's just playing with you. And tonight, he'll be playing with your entrails. That'll be fun. For me."

Jane's hand slipped into her pocket, fingering the silver knife Cole had given her. She'd kept it with her, always remembering that although they didn't look like monsters, they could shift into one. And if that happened, her life could be over in an instant.

In one swift movement, she pulled the knife out and slashed at the wolf. Rhonda howled and clutched her arm, smoke rising off it as if she were melting. Jane had never seen what silver did to a wolf before. She raced for the door, her fingers trembling as she punched in the numbers.

As she neared the end of the code, her leg was yanked out from under her. Rhonda's arm was still sizzling as she tugged Jane sharply toward her and punched her in the face.

The room went black.

When she came to, the wolf was crouched over her, smirking. Jane's eyes drifted to the bandage on her arm. She'd hoped the silver would kill the psycho.

Rhonda unfolded her limbs from her crouched position and stared down at Jane. "Good thing Cole keeps lots of rubbing alcohol. It hurts like a son of a bitch, but if you pour it into a cut made with a silver weapon, it stops the damage. It'll scar though, so don't think you're off the hook."

Jane slowly sat up, feeling around on the floor for the knife. Rhonda withdrew a hypodermic needle from her pocket, and Jane's eyes widened.

She took the protective cap off the needle and laughed. "Don't worry, sweetie. This isn't for you. But believe me, if it was something painful, I'd shoot you full of it." She tapped the needle to release the air and pulled an elastic band out of her other pocket to use as a tourniquet.

"I know what you're trying to do," she said conversationally, as she poked around trying to find the best spot in her vein to inject.

"What's that?" Jane asked, eyeing the crazy werewolf. The last thing she needed was for Rhonda to inject something that would make her even more unstable. Now wasn't the time for recreational drug use.

"You're trying to get me to kill you. But it won't work. Cole's going to do that. And this ensures it." Rhonda sighed as she slid the needle into her arm and pumped the drug in.

She tossed the used needle in the trashcan by the sofa and hauled Jane to her feet. She went to the bathroom, then reappeared with the silver knife. It had been cleaned of Rhonda's blood, and now it gleamed in the light.

"Turnabout is fair play."

The pain burnt down Jane's arm as the blade sliced across it, and for one crazy moment she was afraid smoke would rise off her as it had Rhonda. After all, she had enough vampire blood in her veins to see vampires, and enough to be Cole's mate. But the silver had no effect.

Rhonda smiled, satisfied with her work, "Not too deep, but we've got a nice drip going. We're going to leave a trail of bread crumbs for our hero to find."

Chapter Thirteen

Cole caught the scent of Jonathan, the last black wolf in the pack. The others had turned up clean. *It has to be Jonathan.* He couldn't accept what it would mean if it wasn't. The rich tang of blood entered his nostrils, and for the first time in his life he prayed it was a human.

The wolf looked up at him, his golden eyes confused, his muzzle wet from feasting on a bear. Cole slammed his fist into a nearby tree.

"Fuck!"

Why didn't I mark her when I had the chance, instead of acting like a human with her? Jane was his and giving her time to get used to it wouldn't change that.

He raced back to the portal entry point just inside a small natural cave. His head darted back and forth, his nostrils flaring to catch evidence of any witnesses. Before he could retrieve the talisman from his pocket, Mara and Blake came barreling through the portal. They seemed startled to see him standing there.

"That was fast. We thought we'd have to hunt for you," Blake said.

Why weren't they in their fur? They couldn't be out like this on a full moon night in human form unless they'd fed first. He looked at them suspiciously, anger creasing his brow.

Mara put her hands up defensively, "I know we aren't supposed to hunt in Cary Town, but we stayed away from everything and were quick. We needed to hunt before we came to find you."

Cole let out a breath. "What's wrong?"

"Jane. She needs you. She's in pain."

"What?"

"From leaving the mating incomplete," Mara said.

"What?!?" What was she talking about? He'd never heard of such a thing, but Mara knew mating like the back of her hand. She'd studied it and had charts and pie graphs. Now he wished he'd listened to her blabbering.

His expression grew angry as she explained the situation. "And you left her alone in the den?"

Blake shifted on his feet a little, but Cole noticed and growled. "What aren't you telling me?"

"I gave her the code," he mumbled.

"You WHAT?"

"She was in distress. She begged. You know what a softie I am if a woman's upset."

Cole didn't have time to listen to his beta's excuses.

As he ran down the street through Cain's territory, the demon poked his head out of a nearby tent. "Found the hunter yet?"

He rounded on the incubus and punched him in the nose, "NO! And if my mate dies because you wouldn't tell me the name, I will find a way to make your life hell."

He chuckled and wiped the blood off his face. "Too late. Demon, here. Good luck." He disappeared back inside the tent, and Cole wished, not for the first time, that there was a way to kill a demon.

If Jane died, he'd find a spell to pay Cain back. He should have found a magic user who could torture the hell out of him until he talked, but he'd thought he could avoid that messiness. Cain was a necessary evil at the moment if the pack wanted to retain their autonomy.

He exited the portal on the other side and raced to the den. The scent of Jane's blood hit him, and he felt a sickness sweep over him so strong he stumbled. He punched in the code, terrified of what he'd find.

He was relieved to find no body. Without the sound of her heartbeat, an empty den was the best-case scenario. The den was in disarray with end tables and books knocked over on the floor. He spotted the syringe in the trash can by the sofa and picked it up, inhaling the sickly sweet poison.

He recognized the scent immediately. It was a drug some werewolves and other therians used to resist the change. But it was dangerous. A wolf could become dependent and lose the ability to control the change, shifting without warning. It wasn't worth the risk, and Cole had warned the pack when he'd heard the drug was being sold.

Someone hadn't listened.

His eyes scanned the den, but he knew Jane wouldn't be there. She'd been moved. And she was bleeding. He shifted back into his fur.

He'd gone three miles before the trail stopped on the edge of town at an old abandoned church. The windows were cracked and broken. *Fuck. Fuck. Fuck.* He stared at the building, aware of the trap waiting inside and knowing he had no choice but to walk into it.

He pushed open the heavy rotting door with his nose and stepped just inside, working hard to change back to reclaim his human form. He had to maintain control. Whatever it took, he had to hold onto his humanity so the vision he'd painted wouldn't come true.

The church pews had been cleared out. A dome window in the center of the ceiling caused moonlight to shine brightly into the circle creating a halo of light around his mate. The scent of Jane's blood, fear, and pain almost knocked him over.

She was tied to a chair in the middle of the circle, bleeding heavily from multiple cuts criss-crossing her arms and legs. Rhonda stepped out from behind the shadows into the full moon light, smiling brightly.

"Ta da. No change." She twirled in a slutty little red dress.

Cole growled. "I found the syringe."

"You stopped to investigate the crime scene? Well, that's a shame. Our sweet little Jane could have bled to death waiting for you. She still might."

How can it be Rhonda? Cole tried to wrap his mind around the fact that the pack member he'd always kept safely protected under his wing, had taken his mate and carved her up like a Christmas turkey.

He'd believed her experience as the omega, always picked on, always the weak one, needing his protection, would have made her at least sympathetic. He hadn't realized how desperate she'd become where he was concerned, and the responsibility of his carelessness weighed down on him.

"Where's the knife?"

"Come on, Cole. She's just a human. Part of a complete and balanced breakfast."

He was keenly aware of how much blood Jane was losing. "You've been hunting humans." He was somewhat relieved there wasn't a second wolf to worry about. He watched her hand move as the silver flickered in the moonlight.

"They're very tasty. You should try one. Try Jane. I wrapped her up for you."

"Never."

"Oh admit it . . . when you found my present all laid out pretty for you in the woods, a part of you thought 'dinner.' "

Cole dove for Rhonda, but she'd been waiting for it. She tossed the knife into the center of the circle. Jane stretched her arm as far as she could, straining against her bonds. Cole could see the ropes digging into her circulation as she struggled, but she was still too far from the blade that could set her free.

Jane had felt his presence before she saw his face. The pain from the incomplete mating vanished, and a wave of calm washed over her. It didn't matter that they were in position to act out Cole's painting. She didn't believe it was true. Couldn't believe it.

Whatever he'd seen, it was wrong. Cole wouldn't hurt her. He was her mate. Or would be.

"Cole, help me!" she cried.

Rhonda moved behind him and stage-whispered in his ear loud enough for Jane to hear. "She's just a human. Kill her, and let the blood lust take you. Then join with me."

"You're sick," he said.

Rhonda's laughter rang out like a peal of bells. "Perhaps, but she doesn't have long. *Something* has to stop the bleeding. You going to stand there and watch her die?"

He backhanded the crazed wolf, sending her sailing across the floor. Rhonda struggled to her feet, wiping the blood off her face with the back of her hand.

"Foreplay, baby? You can watch her bleed out, or you can kill her yourself. Be merciful, and stop her pain. Either way, she'll die tonight. If you do it, you'll be so high from her blood, you'll mark me in the frenzy."

Cole let out a disgusted sound halfway between a snort and a growl. "You'd really want to be mated that way? You'd want me to hate you forever? You're not my true mate, Rhonda."

"I am," Jane said, "Now get in here and help me. Ignore the psycho bitch."

He turned back to Jane, a hundred emotions engaged in a battle across his features. "When the moonlight hits me, I *will* shift."

"So?"

He paced like a caged beast in the shadows, carefully skirting the pool of moonlight. "You don't understand. It's me. The vision is me. I won't be able to resist your blood."

Jane's eyes locked with his. "Cole, I am bleeding to death. Rhonda's right. You've got to take the chance. I trust you. I'm not scared of you."

"Awww. This is sweet," the psycho bitch said.

Cole took a steadying breath and stepped into the circle. The shift came on the second the moonlight touched his skin. Jane watched, mesmerized, as his shape extended and shrank, changing until everything was fur and claws and teeth. His nostrils flared to scent the air. He growled at her, more wolf than man.

But Jane couldn't call forth anxiety in her mate's presence. Her body recognized him as hers, and she knew, somewhere beneath the animal, Cole recognized her in the same way.

He was much bigger than she'd expected him to be, larger than a normal wolf. Or maybe she'd just never been so close to one before. His fur stood on end as he continued to growl at her, crouched low, ready to pounce.

"Cole," she said quietly.

He stopped growling and cocked his head to the side as if trying to determine how he knew that voice.

She crooked a finger at him. "I know you're in there. You know I'm yours."

He paced and whimpered as he scented the air. *That's good. If he's not rushing to tear me to pieces it means he's at least a little aware of who I am.*

"You have to take the risk or I'll die. Remember what you said about finding, then losing your mate? That *will* happen if you don't come over here and stop the bleeding." Her voice weakened as she spoke.

His ears perked up at her warning, and he hesitantly crossed the floor to where she sat bound to the chair. Before he reached her, Rhonda spoke.

"Kill. Feed. That's dinner, Cole."

He growled at Jane and edged closer, his attention shifting to feeding and maiming.

"You fucking bitch," Jane said. "Cole, ignore her. She's trying to kill your mate."

At the word, *mate*, he cocked his head to the side again as if he were trying hard to think things through and puzzle out what that word meant to him.

"Cole, if I die here, I won't blame you. But I don't want to leave you. So you have to pull it together."

She stretched her hand out to him, and he closed the distance between them. His tongue flicked out experimentally to taste the blood dripping over her arm as if trying to decide what to do with her. He growled low in his throat as he continued lapping at her cuts.

Jane started to run her fingers through his fur. The action seemed to soothe him, and the growling subsided.

"What are you waiting for? Rip the little bitch apart," Rhonda shouted.

The wolf's head jerked up. His eyes narrowed on the omega, and he growled.

"I think you want to shut up now," Jane said, her fingers still stroking through her mate's fur. Cole let out a short grunt and went back to the business of sealing her wounds.

When he finished, he gnawed through the ropes that bound her hands and dragged her out of the circle of moonlight into the waiting safety of the shadows. Then he shifted back. His hand cupped Jane's face, his thumb brushing a strand of hair away. Guilt shone out of his warm brown eyes.

"I'm so sorry. I should have marked you. You would never have been in danger from me if I had."

Jane nodded. "It's okay. I asked you not to."

"I could have killed you. You'll never know how close I was to ripping you apart. If I'd smelled any fear on you, I wouldn't have been able to stop." He dropped his head into his hands.

She pulled his hands away from his face and wrapped her arms around him. "You didn't though. That's the only thing that matters."

He returned the embrace, then reluctantly pulled free of her. "Let me finish this, and then I'll take care of you."

He turned to face Rhonda who hadn't had the good sense to flee when he'd been distracted. She stood at the front of the church, trembling, her hands outstretched in supplication.

"Cole . . . " She knelt, offering her throat. Submitting to her alpha. Too late for that.

"There is no forgiveness for what you've just done. You've endangered my mate."

"You hadn't marked her. I didn't know." She was shaking.

"Jane, could you hand me the knife?"

She went quietly to the center of the circle and retrieved the knife, placing it in his outstretched hand.

"You can go outside if you don't want to see this."

She nodded and made a hasty exit.

He knew she'd take the opportunity to leave the church. For all Rhonda had done to her that night, Jane still couldn't watch him kill someone shaped like a human. But it had to be done. He waited until he'd heard her footsteps recede and the door click quietly shut behind her.

He turned back to the wolf cowering before him.

"Cole, please don't do this. I'm sorry. You can't kill me. You know you can't. I'm like a sister to you, remember?"

The wolf sighed. "Rhonda, you know I've always loved you. I've thought of you as family since we were pups. I've protected you. And this is how you repay me? By trying to destroy my life?"

"I love you," she said.

"No. You love Rhonda. You knew how I felt about Jane, and you tried to make me kill her. How were you going to get me to start the mating process in all of that?"

He watched as she reached into her pocket and pulled out a bottle. He snatched it from her trembling hand and read the label. She'd pulled out all the stops. It was a love potion designed for therians to intensify the pheromones.

"You've used this on me before." He'd thought he'd just been weak and lonely. He'd been too upset to notice what had been different about her. She'd taken advantage of his mourning a lost member of the pack. "So if it didn't work that time, you thought maybe if you combined it with the frenzy of blood lust after a human kill, it would work then?"

She remained silent.

He threw the bottle across the room and it shattered, spilling the shimmering contents. She cringed.

"You don't deserve it for what you've done, but out of respect for our former relationship before you betrayed me, I'll make it quick."

"No, Cole, please." She was sobbing. Her voice rose in a shrill panic as she bargained for her life. "Have you no mercy at all? Spare me. Banish me. I'll go away. I'll never come near you or Jane again."

He felt the faintest shred of pity for her, but he couldn't be moved by it. Not when it put his mate at risk.

"I'm sorry. I just don't believe you."

He jerked Rhonda up by her hair, yanked her head back, and sliced the silver blade across her throat.

Chapter Fourteen

Jane looked to the door every few moments, her concern for Cole growing. The omega had been real chatty while she'd dragged Jane kicking and screaming to the church. The drawback of the drug Rhonda had injected was that not only could she not shift, but she didn't have access to the amount of wolf strength she normally had. She'd still been stronger than Jane, but next to Cole she was helpless as a puppy.

Still. Crazy meant unpredictable.

She'd heard the begging through the thin door. The wolf was clearly insane and had no grasp on reality, but even though Rhonda wanted her dead, Jane felt pity for the woman. She knew how badly she wanted Cole and how much in love with him she was. Jane also knew Rhonda wasn't his mate.

She was.

As she watched the first rays of sunrise peeking over the horizon, Jane prayed he would do it quickly. After several minutes, the muffled voices stopped, and the church went silent. She made the sign of the cross and waited. She didn't believe in a higher power anymore, not after all the things she'd been through. But she'd been raised religious, and old habits died hard.

When Cole joined her outside, he looked exhausted, like it had drained everything out of him to do what he'd just done.

He appeared to want to touch her, but his hands were coated in the omega wolf's blood, and Jane realized he'd cradled Rhonda in his arms while she'd bled out.

"I'm sorry," she said, feeling like somehow it was her fault he'd had to kill the other wolf.

The knife was still clenched in his hand. "We'll have to come back later. She should have a proper burial and a funeral with the pack," he said.

Jane nodded.

"Come with me."

Her stomach leaped, instinctively knowing what was about to happen, and welcoming it.

What's wrong with me? A woman had just been killed on her behalf, and the only thought running through her mind was finishing with Cole what should have been finished before. She watched the muscles in his naked body contract and expand as he strode ahead of her, her eyes drifting over his muscular back.

She stopped beside him as he bent next to a stream to wash Rhonda's blood off the knife and his hands.

"You did it fast?"

"Yes," he said, his hand trembling a little as he cleaned off the blade.

"I'm sorry," she said again. If she'd let him mark her before, surely Rhonda wouldn't have continued with her plan. Maybe it wouldn't have come to this.

"Not your fault. I should have seen it. I should have taken it seriously. I thought it was just a crush." He placed the knife on a rock beside the water and turned to face Jane. His eyes glowed visibly.

Though he held onto his human form, Jane could see the wolf peering back out at her now, and she knew what that look meant.

"I'm too tired to shift again, so if you don't want this with me, you'd better run now. I can't follow human rules of courtship. It almost got you killed once, and I won't do it again. If we'd been mated, I would have felt it the instant you'd been taken."

Jane's hands fumbled with the button of her jeans. She stripped them off and tossed them into the stream. Cole arched a brow.

"Well, I can't put them back on. They've got blood on them, and they're gross."

She supposed she could wash them, but she couldn't see herself wearing that pair of jeans again. It wasn't as if the outfit carried fond memories. *Oh yeah, and this is what I wore that time when a crazed lovesick werewolf cut me up in a wacky plot to take my mate.*

Cole nodded. He was standing in front of her, still naked from the earlier shift, his body revealing the evidence of his arousal.

All at once, he was on her, ripping her top off and flinging it aside. He made quick work of her underwear and stretched out on the soft bed of grass, pulling Jane on top of him. His hand moved between her legs stroking the warm folds of flesh. She blushed at how wet she was and the fact that he knew the extent of her need for him.

He smirked at her. "This makes it easy."

She gasped in mock horror and smacked him on the arm, surprised either of them had it in them to make a joke after all that had just happened.

His rumbling chuckle reached her ears and somehow reached into her stomach as well, searing her insides.

"Ride me, baby."

He didn't have to ask twice. She groaned at the feel of his body encased in hers. She would never get tired of how warm and alive he was. His large hands wrapped around her waist, urging her on harder. She was on top, but he controlled the rhythm as he drove into her from below.

Her hands clawed at the ground, uprooting blades of grass as waves of pleasure washed over her. A moment later, his canines elongated and his fangs were in her throat. A second orgasm came crashing over the first one, and her hands moved to his shoulders to hold onto him as tightly as he was holding her.

It was different than the vampire bites. There was no drinking, just a mark. Almost as soon as his fangs had gone into her, they were out again and he was licking the wound to make sure it healed properly.

There would always be a scar. It was the one bite mark she was proud to wear because it didn't label her a whore or meat, but the beloved mate of the pack alpha.

Jane wasn't sure which thing happened first, hearing the crunch of shoes, or Cole flipping them so he was on top of her, shielding her body. Half in defense of her safety and half in protection of her modesty.

Three pairs of shoes moved into her line of sight. Cross-trainers, hiking boots, and wedge sandals . . . Charlee?

She glanced up to see a man and woman she didn't know and Charlee armed with a bow and a silver-tipped arrow. An arrow aimed straight at Cole.

"Get off her, wolf," she said, the bow unwavering.

Alarmed, Jane tried to twist and rise, but Cole was having none of it. His body was tense, curled protectively around hers.

"Charlee, no! Put that away. He's not hurting me."

The redhead held the weapon steady. "Oh yeah, because across the way I saw him bite you. I'm sure that was just wolfy fun and games."

Jane blushed and dropped her head back to the grass. "I'm his mate."

There was a humming beat of silence before Charlee lowered the weapon and let the bow and arrow fall to the ground. "Well, crap. We thought you were in trouble. We did about fifty spells trying to locate you and work around the warding magic. Then finally you were outside the range of the shield. We were afraid you were dead."

"Sorry. He wouldn't let me use the phone," Jane said.

"That was for your protection. I couldn't let you go back to the vampires. You make me sound like a monster."

"Well? You were keeping me hostage."

Cole growled, but without menace. "Are we really going to have this argument now, Jane?"

She snorted, embarrassment over her predicament momentarily dwarfed by the humor of the moment.

Charlee sighed. "These are my friends Dayne Wickham and Greta Lawson."

Cole snarled. "You bring Dayne Wickham near my mate, and you think I'm the threat?"

Jane wasn't sure what the deal was with Dayne, but she really didn't want to be naked under a werewolf while her friend and two strangers stood and looked on. "Um, Guys? Could we maybe have this discussion a little later? When I'm not all naked?"

"Sorry," Charlee said. The others mumbled their apologies as well.

"Wait for us at the lake a few miles west of here," Cole said with the authoritative tone only an alpha wolf could manage under the circumstances.

Charlee started toward the lake but stopped. "Oh, and I almost forgot. Anthony got a confession out of Paul about the things he was doing to you. He's been locked up. The official charge is treason since he lied to his king. But Anthony wants to know if you want to be the one to stake him."

Cole growled, "I'd like to be the one to torture him slowly to death."

Charlee shook her head. "He's not going to release him to a wolf, so give up the dream." Then to Jane, "you can let me know."

When Charlee and the others had disappeared into the woods, Cole scooped Jane up in his arms and ran. He moved with such speed, she was sure to an outside observer they would be a blur. He didn't stop until he arrived at the tunnels that led to the den's private entrance. He punched in the code.

"Jane, you might want to wait outside the den."

A moment later clothes were handed out to her. She quickly slipped the jeans and T-shirt on, then stepped inside behind him.

"I guess I need to change the code."

"We were worried. We came back and smelled Jane's blood," Blake said.

"And you didn't follow it?"

"We were afraid we might be more harm than help because of the moon."

Cole nodded.

Mara let out a low whistle when Jane finally stepped out from behind him. "Wow, Cole. You marked her hard enough, didn't you?"

Jane ran her fingers over the puckered mark, a little self-conscious.

"Better to be safe," Cole said. He watched the wolves, gauging their reaction.

Mara smiled brilliantly at Jane. "Welcome to the pack."

Two days later Jane and Charlee descended the dank staircase to the cell Paul was being held in. He was stone cold and looked as if he were already a corpse, in that still, dead sleep that vampires fell into during the day. The guardians had let them pass with one imperious look from Charlee, who was taking to her role as queen like she'd been born to it.

It was hard at times to remember she was human.

A note from Anthony, sealed with a drop of his own blood, hadn't hurt anything either. Jane had brought her hand-carved wooden stake, the stake she'd used on Sedrick and had kept with her in case she got the opportunity to use it again. She hadn't been able to use it on Gregory; she'd gotten too attached to the idiot. But she was glad his political aspirations had driven them apart and enabled her to find Cole.

It would end with the last vampire much as it had with the first to try to pull her into the dark away from the sunlight she deserved.

When Anthony had first offered her the opportunity to be Paul's executioner, she'd hesitated. She didn't want to see him, to look into his eyes. She didn't have anything lame and cliché to say like: "Payback's a bitch, isn't it?" She didn't feel like torturing him for hours or making him beg, as he'd made her beg so many times.

She didn't want to become the monster. She just wanted to end it and know he was gone for good. She knew with Cole by her side the nightmares would never return. She looked down at Paul. In sleep, while the demon rested, she could only see his human form.

So peaceful and beautiful. So deceptive.

She aimed the stake over his heart, then raised it and slammed it home. The stench of death permeated the air as his flesh started to melt off his bones, slowly rotting away until there was nothing but dust.

Jane dropped the stake, and it clattered to the ground with deafening finality. She didn't need it anymore.

She ascended the narrow stairs to the surface, while Charlee stayed behind to speak to the guardian. When she opened the door, a warm hand was outstretched to her.

Cole's face relaxed when he saw her, though his voice still held a growl. "I can't believe Anthony wouldn't even allow me to go down there with you. Just because I'm a wolf . . ."

"I needed to do it by myself." She placed her hand in her mate's as he pulled her out into the sunny day.

About the Author

Zoe Winters loves talking about herself in the third person. She lives with her husband and two cats. She's proudly indie and supports indie authors gaining the same level of respect as indie filmmakers and musicians so they can exist alongside their traditionally published counterparts without stigma. Her favorite colors are rainbow and clear.

For updates on new releases, freebies, and contests, sign up for the newsletter via the contact form at: zoewinters.org.

Reading discussion groups can email:
zoewintersbooks@gmail.com
for bulk purchase discounts.

Breinigsville, PA USA
15 December 2010
251524BV00001B/6/P